The Phoenix Project

M. R. Pritchard

UTOPIA - *A society possessing highly desirable or near perfect qualities*

Phoenix

First Edition

New York

March 2013

The Phoenix Project is a work of fiction. Names, characters, places, and incidents either are the product of the author's imagination or are used fictitiously. Any resemblance to actual persons, living or dead, events or locales is entirely coincidental.

Copyright © 2013 M. R. Pritchard

ISBN-10: 1482529300
ISBN-13: 978-1482529302
ASIN: B00BN1EFCE

First Edition March 2013
M.R. Pritchard Publishing
Edited by Kristy Ellsworth
Cover illustration by Jorden Pritchard

DEDICATION

For my Zombie Apocalypse
killing partner.
I'm glad you've got my back.

PROLOGUE

I turn my attention towards Dr. Drake. He's sitting behind a large desk. His old yellowed eyes looking me up and down as I stand in front of him. I notice he's wearing the white lab coat again. It's just for show. I know this, since he hasn't laid his hands on the lab equipment in decades.

"Mrs. Somers, I suggest you think about your decision," he tells me again.

I've already thought about it. "My decision is final. I'll pack my things now," I reply, unable to look at him any longer.

"I will not offer you your job back." He taps his pen on the desk, probably expecting me to mull it over a few minutes longer.

"I don't want it back." I turn on my heel and stomp out of his office.

I'm free. I'm finally free. I never have to return to this lab again, with all its sterility and coldness.

Ian is going to be pissed. I was supposed to stick it out here for a few more months, but I can't take it anymore. I'm tired of coming home late, missing Lina's childhood. She's almost three and I feel like she spends more time at the babysitters than at home with us. To tell the truth, I was planning on leaving. I've been attending night school to become a nurse and I only have twenty-four virtual clinical hours left until I have my nursing degree.

I walk swiftly through the offices and dull hallways, headed for my workspace. I should have taken it as a sign when Dr. Drake showed me where I was going to be working. The desk is shoved between two laboratory benches in the back of the room, secluded, which is how I've spent almost every day here. I grab an empty box from

1

under the lab bench, bringing it to my desk. I pile everything inside; paper files, thumb drives, textbooks, notebooks and the few personal belongings I've brought in with me: a statue of a unicorn, a framed photo of Ian and Lina, Lina's drawings.

When I'm done, I stand there looking around, making sure I've taken everything.

I will not come back to this place. Not after what he's done to me, humiliating me in front of my peers at a national conference. I was presenting my research and I had theorized that we had the ability to create genetically enhanced organisms through selective breeding, and minor genetic alterations. I had even tried it, creating a non-aggressive, highly intelligent breed of rat. Dr. Drake's lab assistants couldn't replicate my work, so I'm sure that's what brought on his growing distaste for me. He interrupted me during my seminar, questioning my methods, arguing against my theories, claiming that he didn't see any hard evidence of my findings.

I should have been prepared for it. My college professor warned me that this could happen; the way I could answer analytical test questions with minimal work and how I had such trouble explaining my laboratory methods even though my findings always worked out perfectly. "You have something special," my molecular genetics professor told me one day. "You don't need to see the genes or experiment for years, somehow you *feel* it. I like to call it *genetic intuition*, very few can do this. It's a gift, a talent-embrace it." But whatever gift he thought I had, it wasn't getting me any respect from Dr. Drake.

I look around to make sure I have all of my belongings. I walk to the large subzero freezer and search the frozen shelves for my samples. I take out the three metal trays containing hundreds of tiny micro containers. It's all the genetic material I've worked on for the past four years. *Hydrochloric acid? No, that would make too much of a mess.* Instead, I throw them in the sink and turn on the hot water. I plug the drain with a paper towel and leave. The hot water will denature everything in those tubes, rendering it useless. Now Drake can start over from scratch. I'm done with this.

I leave the lab. I take the elevator to the main floor. I rip the badge off my blouse and throw it in a tall metal garbage can as I walk out the door. I hope I never see another genetics laboratory again.

CHAPTER ONE

There is a child in my room, giggling, hiding under the heavy covers at the foot of the bed. I have been laying here for an hour waiting for my alarm to go off so I can get ready for work. I didn't hear her sneak in though. She giggles again. I lean over the side of the bed.

"Lina?" I ask.

She sits on the floor, wearing the same princess pajamas that she has had on for two days. Her curly blonde hair is clumped into a tangle of knots at the back of her neck and the old family Bible is in her hands. She's looking at a drawing of Adam and Eve. I'm sure other parents might be appalled to see their five year old looking at a picture of mostly naked adults. But she goes to Catholic School so I'm sure she's seen this picture before.

"What are you doing?" I ask.

"I found this, Mom." She points to the apple in the drawing.

"What do you think that picture means, Lina?"

"You shouldn't eat forbidden fruit." I wait, resting my chin on the mattress and giving her a chance to continue. She runs her little finger over the image of the snake hanging over the apple, "There's always some crazy worm inside trying to turn you to the dark side." She turns the page of the Bible, moving on to the next drawing. I laugh to myself at her interpretation of the image, so naive yet so incredibly true. I get out of bed and start for the shower.

The bathroom door cracks open just as I finish, pulling the heavy mist from the hot shower out of the room. I can see one dark brown

3

eye watching me intently from the small crack between the door and the door frame. He knows I don't like to be bothered when I am getting ready for work, that I don't like talking this soon after I wake up. Finally, Ian opens the bathroom door the rest of the way.

"Your brother called."

"What does he want?" I ask.

Ian hesitates. His dark eyes turn to the floor as he runs his hand through his shaggy blonde hair. "He had a cyst removed from the back of his neck and needs someone to change the packing." He pauses for a moment, watching me. "And... you're the only nurse he trusts."

Now I know what took him so long to speak. *He knows I hate packing wounds.* I sigh and turn back to the mirror. "Let him know I'll stop by on my way to work tonight." He doesn't reply. Instead the bathroom door closes with a puff of air, knocking a pile of Lina's hair ties off the counter. I turn back to the large mirror and start drying my hair, leaning in close. I can see dark circles under my eyes, tingeing my pale skin a bluish gray and making my green eyes look darker. I search the skin around my eyes and mouth for wrinkles. I don't find any, but the disappointment is still there-the fact that I used to look at least five years younger than my actual age. Now I certainly look all of my twenty six years, and it only took four years on the night shift to age me.

I turn off the hairdryer, leaving my hair damp, and then rummage through the makeup case on the counter. I lightly apply some mascara then line my eyes with thin stripes of black eyeliner. The University Hospital dress code states that registered nurses are not allowed to wear makeup or perfume on any unit in the hospital. I don't like the idea that the hospital thinks it owns me since they were kind enough to employ me. I don't like the feeling of being controlled. I like to break the rules, but just a little bit.

Searching the laundry basket on the floor I pull out a matching black uniform and undershirt, I shake the wrinkles out of them. Dressing as a nurse is definitely much easier than dressing for the research lab I used to work in. It seemed like every day, the business attire I had to wear to the lab got ruined by caustic chemicals burning holes in them or staining them. I stare into the open closet at the row of blouses, slacks, expensive shoes, barely worn for the past few years. A few pieces still have tags hanging off them, never worn. A little piece of me misses wearing them.

I push the hanging clothes aside and reach for the shelf, selecting a well worn sweatshirt with the hospital logo. Strangely enough, the Neonatal Intensive Care Unit, of all places, is freezing at night-the unit that is filled with pre-term infants who have trouble regulating their body temperature.

Lina greets me at the bottom of the stairs, "Aw mom, you have to work tonight again." She contorts her cherub face into a sad frown.

"I will come home in the morning. Just like I always do." I pick her up and hug her tightly, kissing her cheek, breathing in the strawberry scent of her curly hair.

I turn to the couch where Ian sits. "Do you think you could give your daughter a bath tonight? Perhaps comb her hair so I don't have to cut the knots out of it again?" He glances at me then reaches for the remote, turning the volume up on the television.

He's watching another news channel. There are men talking at a desk-political babble-discussing something about the Reformation. He's been tracking the politicians, carefully honing in on who he is going to vote for in the spring elections. Come election time I'm going to wish I had watched a little bit of this, but I don't have the time right now. I can trust in Ian to make the decision for me when it's my turn to vote.

Lina giggles and runs back to the couch, sitting next to Ian, holding a book in her hand. The living room is a clutter of toys and dirty dishes. I step over them, walking towards the kitchen to start the coffee maker. Leaning my back against the cold granite counter, I stare at more dishes piled up in the sink and on top of the dishwasher, wishing Ian would do some cleaning while I'm working. The dishes will have to wait, just like the rest of the mess in this house.

"What are you making for dinner?" Ian shouts from the living room.

The disorder of the house is frustrating me and I want nothing more than to scream at him. I have exactly fifteen minutes to get on the road. There is no time for dinner tonight. "There's plenty of cereal," I shout back to him.

"Stevie," I call. Our black, shaggy Shepard mix runs to me from her dog bed in the corner of the kitchen. I pet her soft head and lead her towards the back door. Stevie runs around the backyard, inspecting its corners for intruders or anything out of place. I walk over to the garden and check for any ripe vegetables. There are a few sparse weeds sprouting out of the soil between the rows of tomatoes. I reach into the dark soil and rip them up from the roots. Nothing is ripe but I can see the small fruit starting to hang off the vines, little green tomatoes and tiny cucumber buds. Similar to the rest of the U.S., my new year's resolution was to start living a more organic lifestyle, trying to avoid eating the genetically engineered food shipped in from far away countries. So I forced Ian to build a raised garden bed. We worked for two weekends, hammering boards and shoveling dirt. At first he wasn't happy about it, but after everything was planted and now that he can see the vegetables growing, he's a little more accepting of the garden.

After Stevie is done inspecting the yard, she bounds back to where I am standing and we walk to the back door together. Once inside I look through the shelf of books in the dining room, searching for something to read if work happens to be slow. I settle on a handbook of edible plants and place it in my work bag. It's a strange book I inherited from my mother, but filled with short snippets of information-easy reading for the night shift.

"Okay, I'm leaving now," I announce, but there is no response. No one is listening. I head back to the living room carrying my bag and a travel mug of coffee. "I love you little Catalina." I bend down to kiss Lina on her nose as she reaches up and hugs me around the neck. I turn to Ian, putting my face in his line of view of the television. I kiss him hard on the lips, letting him know that even if my words aren't the nicest, I do actually love him-a lot.

"Family hug!" Lina shouts. Ian presses the pause button on the remote, finally taking his attention away from the television to notice I am leaving for work. Lina stands on the couch wrapping her little arms around us. I tell them both that I love them, that I will see them in the morning. I remind Lina to brush her teeth before bed, since I know I can't count on Ian to do it. I slip on my black rubber clogs and close the heavy wooden front door, locking it from the outside.

One day Ian asked me why I lock the doors on my way out. *So no one will get in the house and steal Lina* is what I had replied.

He laughed at me. "You don't think I can protect her?" he had responded, scoffing at me. The truth is I know he would protect her. But I don't want anything happening to either of them. They are my family, my life.

CHAPTER TWO

The highway I drive to work runs parallel to a winding river. I glance to the wavy dark water as I drive. Turning the radio on, I click through the stations but nothing catches my interest. I turn it back off and decide to drive in silence instead. When the road bends away from the river, I resort to counting things in twos as I drive, trying to keep my mind busy; taillights on cars, signs on the side of the road, window panes on the few passing houses, and the lines on the blacktop. The highway snakes past dense green forests and rolling farmlands. Clusters of sickly looking cows stand in the large fields, swiping flies off their sides with their long tails.

After a while I come to the two consecutive exit ramps on the highway, each one leading to a town with a population less than ours. Small communities formed hundreds of years ago back when our town, which sits on the shore of Lake Ontario, was a bustling port and the mouth of the dark flowing river provided a means to ship goods south. Between the port and the farms, the residents of this area enjoyed prosperous times. But those times haven't been seen in many years. Instead, a foreign enterprise erected three nuclear power plants, utilizing the bitter waters of Lake Ontario to cool the nuclear reactors and shipping the powerful current to the large cities of the northeast, providing jobs to only a few hundred of the local population. The farms have shriveled, resorting to employing immigrants only during the harvest seasons. So those of us who don't work at the power plant or the local state college must travel the forty miles south to the city for employment. Evidence of our travel lie on the shoulder of the road, which is littered with dead wildlife: deer, opossum, skunks and foxes.

Last year, the local newspaper wrote an article announcing that our county has the highest unemployment rate in the state, but this was already assumed. We have watched many of the nearby neighborhoods fall into dilapidation and most of our family and friends have moved out of state. The newly found homeless started taking up residence under the two bridges which stretch over the river, connecting the east and west sides of our town. The most disturbing events have been the number of break-ins and unforeseen deaths from drug overdoses over the past few months. Others have resorted to jumping off one of the two bridges, unable to face the bleak life ahead of them. Instead of living with dire prospects, they chose to follow the rapidly flowing dark river, turning the once vital aspect of our town into our very own local River Styx. Every few weeks the local fire department is called to collect the bodies which have surfaced at the mouth of the river. We know that eventually we will have to move closer to the city to escape the commute and the growing disparity weighing upon our small town.

--

After thirty minutes I reach evidence of civilization. There is an exit ramp ahead leading to a bustling suburb with a mall, department stores, restaurants and the large apartment complex where Sam, my brother, lives. I drive through the winding apartment complex roads and pull into an empty parking stop. I notice a small red car parked next to Sam's truck. His girlfriend is there. I think her name is Stacy or Macy, something like that. She is the second girlfriend this year and probably won't be the last.

I head inside and brace myself for the worst. *I hate packing wounds.*

The wound on the back of Sam's neck is without a doubt disgusting and I'm glad he can't see my face as I pull the gauze out of the wound, bright pea green pus strings to the gauze. I was hoping his girlfriend could make herself useful by handing me supplies, but she just stands on the other side of the room, squeaking and making "eww" sounds. I control the urge to tell her to shut it.

"Thanks for stopping on your way to work." Sam speaks as I tend to his wound.

I would like to reply but I can't open my mouth and risk puking on the back of his neck. I work as quickly as I can cleaning the wound, poking fresh, damp gauze into the gaping hole and then placing a dry bandage over it all.

"All set," I pat Sam on the shoulder.

"Thanks sis." He stands up, towering over me. He is supposed to be my little brother but my head barely reaches to his shoulders. Sometimes, it's hard to believe that we are related with such extreme differences in height. Somehow he grew tall and athletic, while I retained the body size and shape that hints on a preadolescent; short and barely shaped as a normal woman my age would be.

I give him instructions on what medications to take, how to care for the wound and sleep comfortably for the night. Of what I've found in the medical field, once you are a nurse you are everyone's nurse. And as soon as the word has been spread, be sure to welcome middle of the night phone calls and the inspection of rashes at holiday dinners.

"I'll call you tomorrow." I hug Sam and wave to the girl.

Next to Ian and Lina, Sam is all I have left. Our father died of cancer right before I graduated high school and then our mother's death from an unsuspecting heart attack a few years after that were both hard on Sam. When our mother died, he was a junior in high school and I was pregnant with Lina. He was intent on living by himself, feeling orphaned and alone. I argued with him for weeks as we cleaned out our childhood home, trying to persuade him to live with us. I didn't want him to be alone. Mostly, I didn't want to be without him-the last survivor of my immediate family. Eventually he agreed, staying in our guestroom until he finished high school a year early. Not long afterwards he came to me, telling me he was enlisting in the air force. This brought on another tidal wave of arguments. I was afraid to lose him, I was afraid that he would be sent off to war and never come back. Finally, we settled on a four year plan where he would apply to medical school; something he had talked about before our mother's death. He put his air force plans on hold, giving him plenty of time to enlist before he surpassed the age requirements if medical school didn't work out.

Now he's spending the summer working as a security guard at the local mall until the fall when he enters the University. Each time I see him I hope that he will reconsider his air force plans because I'm sure our current government would have no problem sending my baby brother into a harsh life he's never imagined, one where we have to go on without each other, splitting up the last of our family.

CHAPTER THREE

I walk through the tunnel that passes under the street, connecting the hospital to the parking garage. When I reach the hospital entrance, I nod hello to the guard sitting at the desk and lift my badge so he can see it. Just as I do, the elevator dings and I jog to the open door. I know if I don't get on now I will be waiting a long time for the next one, making me late for my shift. The elevator is packed full, a mixture of workers and visitors. Someone is carrying a tray from the cafeteria and the smell of fried fish wafts out from under the foil, making my stomach turn. I hold my breath and push the button for the twelfth floor, then squeeze myself to the back of the elevator since I will be the last to get off.

"Going all the way up, huh?" asks a man with a visitors tag on his shirt. I smile and nod at him, the heavy fish odor making it impossible for me to open my mouth and speak.

The elevator stops on almost every floor, each time a few people get off and the air around me feels a little bit lighter. The person with the fish gets off on the ninth floor. Finally, I can take a deep breath, inhaling the fishless air. There is only one other person remaining in the elevator with me and we stop on the twelfth floor. I wait for her to get off first. She turns right towards the visitor doors carrying a diaper bag and a handful of tissues. Without asking I can tell she is one of our mothers returning to the hospital to spend time with her ill infant.

I turn left towards the employee entrance and swipe my badge. The automatic doors open with a heavy click. A breeze rushes past me filled with the scent of diapers and baby shampoo and the buzz of tension in the air. There are clicks, beeps, and buzzes from monitors, IV pumps, and warming beds. It reminds me of that widespread misconception that the Eskimos have over a hundred words to describe the snow. Well, nurses have over a hundred ways to describe the beeping of alarms. Most visitors get tense as they listen to all the noise, shooting us questioning glances when we don't rush to answer an alarming monitor. Usually we continue on with our task at hand because the truth is, we know what alarm deserves a rush to the bedside.

There is a crowd of nurses waiting to search the assignment board for their name and the names of the babies they will be taking care of. While I wait to see what my assignment is, I glance up at the dry erase board which holds a listing of the nurseries in the neonatal ICU and the babies in them. We are up to fifty-five babies. It has been a busy spring, the majority of our babies have been pre-term and an abnormally large number of babies have been born with anomalies and genetic diseases. The shortage of nurses has left ample opportunities to pick up overtime, and this is an overtime night for me. The dread of a less than stellar assignment hangs over my head.

The crowd has finally filtered out, my coworkers walk off with handfuls of paper containing the lists of medications and doctors' orders for the two, three, or four babies they will be taking care of tonight. I hear a multitude of grumbles and curse words as they pass me. It seems the assignments are not good. I find my name on the sheet and the three babies I've been assigned. I collect the order sheets for my patients and head to their bedsides.

As I step into my assigned nursery I am grateful for a few things, one being the large picture window which spans the length of the nursery, facing to the north. Second, I am not assigned to the baby in the far left corner-the gastroschisis-born with his intestines spilling out of the hole in his abdomen where the umbilical cord once attached to him. He lies upon on a small elevated bed. He's ventilated with a breathing tube, has seven IV pumps running, and a central line taped to the top of his scalp. His abdominal contents are contained in a plastic bag suspended from the warming unit above him.

One of our new nurses stands at the bedside. She has been here for almost six months now and her hands quiver over her order sheets as she receives report from another nurse. She's thinking the same thing we all did when we first started. *I hope I don't kill this patient.* She will be assigned to some of the sickest patients for at least another three months, something she was never told when she agreed to work here. If she's lucky she will be assigned in the same room with senior nurses who are willing to help her, who will answer her questions without ridicule, who will check her medications and let her know when her patient is about to die. Some of the senior nurses will sit by and watch, not helping, assessing in their own minds if this new nurse has what it takes to work here.

Some nurses eat their young; they tear at their flesh with razor sharp teeth until they are a bumbling bleeding mess and want nothing more to do with being a nurse. That is a true story.

It's almost eight at night. I get a detailed report from Jan, the nurse I am replacing. She talks quickly; I'm sure so she can rush home to her four children and see them before they go to bed. She assures me that I have a "good assignment," the kiss of death, which means in a few hours something will go terribly wrong. She should know better.

I lift the quilt that's covering the isolette, which is nothing more than a Plexiglas box, and get started taking care of my first patient. Inside is a small baby girl, sleeping on her stomach. She is scrawny, all arms and legs with a large head. Her preemie sized diaper is too large, covering most of her back, all the way up to her bony shoulder blades. I open the portholes in the front of the isolette and put my arms through. The air inside is warmed to regulate her body temperature so she can retain her fat stores and gain weight. I gently grasp her head and her hips and flip her, placing her on her back. I take her temperature, her blood pressure, and listen to her with the pediatric stethoscope which hangs at her bedside. The diaphragm is the size of a quarter, covering almost half of her little chest. I watch the skin on her chest retract when she breathes, almost able to count each tiny rib. The whole time she sleeps, exhausted from being born too early, her body now responsible for doing things that the placenta normally would. She barely opens her eyes when I run my fingertip over the top of her head to feel her soft fontanel and ridges of her skull. I put a clean diaper on her and fold down the front so it doesn't look so large on her. At the bottom of her isolette is a pink blanket about half the size of a normal baby blanket. I lift her up with one hand, my thumb and ring finger under each of her bony armpits, and place the blanket under her then swaddle her in the blanket to keep her warm.

"Back to sleep baby," I whisper to her as I close the portholes to the isolette. She turns her head away from me, falling back into a deep slumber of growth.

I write in the infant's chart, listening to the chatter in the nearby nurseries as the other nurses talk amongst themselves, not bothering to talk to me. I am still under the impression that many of my co-workers mistake my silence for ignorance, since I'm not very talkative. I remember when I was done with orientation and the unit supervisor told me the other nurses thought I was too quiet. As if changing occupations wasn't hard enough; my inability to fit in here has been even harder. My response to her was that I was observing the unit. And I was watching my new co-workers; figuring out who I could trust, who I could go to for help, and who to stay away from. It doesn't help that sometimes I just feel like I don't fit in here quite yet. And if it weren't for the innocent babies, who I enjoy taking care of so much, I might look for work elsewhere.

"Andie, can you help me for a minute?" I look to my left to see Lauren standing in front of her patient, green gloves on her hands. I walk over to her. "I've never had a gastroschisis. I don't know where to start." She says flatly.

We both pause, watching its intestines hanging in the plastic tube, the fluid floating around them to keep them moist jiggles with each breath delivered by the ventilator. If this baby survives, the surgeons will slowly squeeze the intestines back into the baby's abdomen then suture it up. Hopefully he will go home in twelve to sixteen weeks, like a normal newborn, with only a small straight scar an inch long across his abdomen instead of a belly button. But right now this baby resembles something barely human. Machines are breathing for him; we are feeding him through IV lines and have suspended his vital organs in a bag outside its body.

Lauren turns to me with that look on her face. I've seen it before. It's how the new nurses look right before they run to the unit supervisor and tell her they can't work here anymore, that it's not for them, that they can't do this. Then they quit and leave, moving on to explore other units within the hospital, eventually finding a unit that they are more comfortable with.

Before she can say anything, I speak quietly so the other nurses won't hear. "You're a good nurse, Lauren. Soon you'll be doing this by yourself, no problem. Just hang in there." I rub her shoulder and she smiles a little.

I help her sedate the baby boy. We change the gauze around the plastic tube which holds the baby's intestines since the fluid seeping from the infant's abdomen keeps saturating the gauze with bloody yellow fluid. We suction the secretions out of the baby's breathing tube. And after a few hours Lauren is finally comfortable with taking care of her patient without my help. I return to the three infants I have been assigned and continue with their care.

--

At five in the morning I decide it's time for a break. My hands are shaking from hunger, my throat is dry, and I feel like my bladder is going to explode. Only then do I realize I never called home to tell Ian or Lina goodnight. A pang of guilt hits me. I know Ian probably spent most of the night telling Lina I was busy taking care of the sick babies and trying to get her to go to bed so she will be rested for Kindergarten in the morning.

I know what Lina will say when I get home; "*Mom, you never called me last night. I missed you so much.*" And then I will hug her and kiss her and let her eat some sugary cereal for breakfast to make up for it. I can only hope Ian gave her a bath like I asked.

I swipe my badge to get into the break room. Someone made coffee and it smells fresh-not good-but fresh. I pour some into a Styrofoam cup adding two packets of sugar and some milk. I know the first sip will taste terrible and bitter, the sugar and milk barely making it palatable, but I will drink it anyway because I need the caffeine to make it through the next few hours.

I take a plastic lid and walk to the nearby window while I stir the coffee. The best part of working on the twelfth floor is the view. We can see the hills, the valleys, and the soothing lights of the city at night. I watch a group of crows land on the roof of the building across the street. They look to the sky and one cocks its head to the side. I follow their gaze. The sun is starting to come up, decorating the sky in pink and orange. I take another sip of the bitter hospital coffee and write my name on the side of the cup so I don't have to worry about someone else drinking from it. I try to relax and think of my plans for the day, once I get out of work.

After I drop Lina off at school I can sleep for a few hours before she has soccer. Thankfully, I don't have to worry about cooking since there is a roast ready to go in the crock pot and fresh bread I made a few days ago. I think of the piles of dishes and toys waiting for me to clean up at home, making a mental note to add a few glasses of wine to my dinner. Ian and I struggle with dividing the household responsibilities, but we try to make it work with both of us employed full time. We're very grateful for what we've found together. Especially since over the past eight years as we've watched family and friends struggle with their marriages, their divorces, and fighting over custody of their children. Each time the children are the ones who lose the fight. We both agree that we don't ever want Lina to experience that.

Looking out the window one last time, I glance up at the sky and see a large airplane taking off from the nearby airport, the nose of the jetliner pointing up in the heavens. It looks like it's barely moving against the gray-blue morning sky. Then, I hear a high pitched whistle and a deep rumble, vibrating the double pane window glass. To the right of the jetliner six army jets race by, headed north, probably headed for the army base. My heart skips a few beats when I see how close they are to the Jetliner, but it continues its ascend while the army jets continue speeding to the north. Strange, I've seen plenty army jets flying over the city but I've never seen them risk flying so close to a commercial aircraft before.

I leave the break room and head back into the NICU. The momentary silence from the chatter of nurses, beeping of monitors and crying of babies has been relaxing. Feeling refreshed I swipe back into the unit and the doors open towards me. The noise creeps up to me, muted at first, then louder as I walk to the nursery where my patients are. I wave across the wall partition at another nurse who is watching me. She turns back to the group of nurses she is standing with, speaking in hushed tones. Another one looks at me so I keep walking and pretend I don't notice. Who knows what they are gossiping about today? I see Lauren is looking much more relaxed, the tension gone from her brow. I take small sips of the bitter coffee as I walk, holding back a grimace each time I swallow, praying that it won't actually put hair on my chest. I stop in front of the large nursery window and take in the panoramic view of the city as the sun rises.

The highways passing through the city are already starting to fill with cars. People making their morning commutes to work. My watch says it is 6:50 am, almost time to go. Jan's curse never transpired. Suddenly, a wave of dizziness hits me. I reach out to the windowsill to steady myself. Sometimes, if I close my eyes it will go away. This is nothing new; after working all night I'm usually greeted by one of two things: dizziness or nausea. I close my eyes but it doesn't stop, when I open them again I see an IV bag waving back and forth on its metal stand. This is when I realize I am not dizzy. The floor moves under my feet, the building is shaking.

CHAPTER FOUR

The trouble with hospitals; everything is on wheels.
I notice the ventilator machine rolling away from Lauren's patient. I drop my coffee in the trash can next to me and I rush forward to stop it with both hands, pushing it back into place and clicking the wheel locks with my foot. Lauren has that look again. She doesn't know what to do. I hear shrieks and chatter from the surrounding nurseries. I grab a hold of Lauren's arm, squeezing it, trying to bring her back to the present.

"Make sure all the brakes are on." I shout to her over the growing noise. I hear a few screams and babies crying from the other nurseries.

We circle around the nursery, clicking the brakes into place on everything with wheels; ventilators, isolettes, warming beds. Then, as suddenly as it began, the building stops moving. I'm sure since we are on the top level we got the worst of it. Our unit security guard has made himself present from the hallway desk. I hear him tell someone he is searching the unit for damage and injuries. The radio on his shoulder squawks to life with static, a garbled voice announces that there is a water main break in the basement.

Looking out the window I see that none of the buildings have been damaged. People have started trickling out of the buildings onto the sidewalks and streets and I can hear the faint sirens from the nearby firehouse.

For an instant my mind shifts to home. I wonder if Ian and Lina are safe, if they were awoken by this earthquake. I know that Ian is capable of taking care of Lina, that she is always his first priority. But

I can't stop the tugging deep in my chest. I have to call home; I have to check on them. *In five more minutes when the patients are stable I'll call home and check on them,* I tell myself.

But I'll never get to, because not a second later the power goes out.

--

The trouble with hospitals; everything runs on electricity.

I have never heard the unit this quiet. It's the kind of silence that echoes loud in my ears making them ring. People stop talking, babies stop crying, the hum of the ventilators and the alarms are silent. It should take less than thirty seconds for the backup generators to turn on. Thankfully, there is enough morning light from the large windows to see. Turning to Lauren's patient, I notice the duskiness starting in the baby's feet and hands. With no ventilator the baby has no way to oxygenate his body. The seconds are ticking by, and with them the grayness seeps further towards the center of the baby's small, still chest.

Why isn't the power back on? This is taking too long.

Ventilators aren't working. IV pumps aren't working. I look at the nearest isolette and see that there is no temperature reading, which can only mean there is no heat. A cold baby is not a happy baby. I turn my attention back to Lauren's baby. There is no color left in his body, he has no identifiable chest rise. This is not good.

"Get your bag, Lauren, your baby needs to be bagged. We can't wait any longer for the power." Lauren grabs the resuscitation bag hanging above the baby. Hopefully the compressed air pipes running through the hospital contain enough flow to get us through, until the power returns. Lauren turns the flow meter and the resuscitation bag comes to life, filling with air. I disconnect the breathing tube from the ventilator and attach the bag.

"One, two, three, squeeze." She whispers as she squeezes the bag. Slowly, the baby's chest rises then falls, and the gray discoloration starts to recede.

I hear Dr. Smith's voice as she's walking into the nearby nurseries asking if everything is alright. Someone must have woken her up, if the earthquake didn't. She walks up to Lauren's baby. "Is everything good here?" She looks to the baby then Lauren. "Just keep this up."

She waves her hand in a circle over Lauren's bedside as though she's casting a spell. Then turns on one heel and walks out of the room, the bottoms of her oversized wrinkled scrub pants dragging at her heels, kicking up dust as she runs into the next room.

"I need the Doctor, he's extubated," I hear someone say.

"You're doing fine, Lauren." I look into her eyes, trying to sense if she realizes the seriousness of our current situation. "I'll be right back," I tell her. I follow the doctor, standing on my toes to look over the shoulders of the five nurses standing around the bedside of a very small baby. I took care of this baby last week and his prognosis was not good. He was born 13 weeks early, still just a fetus. You could hold him in the palm of your hand and have room to spare.

I see the ventilator has drifted during the earthquake, pulling the breathing tube out of the baby's throat. Someone hands the doctor a laryngoscope to place a new breathing tube. The duskiness that was creeping up on Laurens baby has already consumed this one. Unmoving, the tiny fetus of a baby is gray all over. There is no chest rise, and he doesn't even struggle to breath. His body has already given up.

"I can't see anything. This light is not working," Doctor Smith yells. "Get me another laryngoscope!"

This is what we were trained to do, save the lives of these tiny babies. Everyone knows what needs to be done. There is a flurry of hands; cutting medical tape to secure a new breathing tube, pulling the syringes out of the IV pumps and pushing fluids by hand. Three nurses run in opposing directions, looking for the extra laryngoscopes that we keep in emergency resuscitation kits throughout the unit. One by one I hear them shout out that none of the lights are working. Someone flicks a flashlight on. Nothing.

The doctor remains quiet; she rolls her shoulders and bends down to the infant warmer. She slides the unlit laryngoscope into the lifeless baby's mouth. Someone hands her a breathing tube. She threads it down the scope, slowly. The nurse on her right attaches the resuscitation bag and starts squeezing. The baby's chest rises and falls. Everyone standing at the bedside lets out a breath of relief.

The doctor listens with the stethoscope. On this tiny baby the diaphragm covers its entire chest. She shakes her head side to side and continues to listen. We're holding our breath again.

Nervously, I tuck the loose hair behind my ears which have

sprung forward and curled up in the increasing heat. When the power went out so did the air conditioning.

"This heart rate is too low," Dr Smith says quietly. "We need to push epinephrine." For the first time she looks up, scanning our faces. "This is a full code, let's get moving people!"

The nurse next to me grabs my arm, pulling me along. We run to the nearby medication room which holds our medication dispensing robot. This tool was meant to help keep track of medications. It's a large white box with a hundred tiny drawers. A nurse or doctor would sign into the touch screen computer and select a patient name and medication and one of the drawers would pop open with the needed medication. But now, without power, the screen is black and empty.

I turn to the nurse by my side, finally recognizing her; Sheila. "What the hell?" she blurts out.

I bang my fist on the drawer labeled "epi" in red. Nothing happens. My heart is beating in my ears and I can feel the sweat beading up on the back of my neck, clinging to my hair. Someone runs up behind us and I hear Doctor Smith ask what is taking so long.

"The medication robot is locked," I yell into the hallway.

"I'll be right back," Sheila says as she runs out of the room.

I continue banging on the drawer with my fist, trying to get it to move. I shove my shoulder into the machine, but nothing happens. Less than a second later Sheila's back, carrying a rusty red toolbox. She pulls out an old flathead screwdriver and a hammer. I step back as she slides the point of the flathead into the tiny crack between the drawers of the medication robot. She lifts the hammer with her free hand and bangs it on the handle of the screwdriver. On the third hit the drawer starts to crack open. On the fourth hit she misses. The hammer hits her knuckle, I hear her groan, and bright red blood starts seeping out of her finger. On the fifth hit the drawer cracks open. Sheila reaches in and pulls out a vial then we both turn and run back to the baby.

We couldn't have been gone more than a few minutes. But when we return the whole feeling of the room has changed. Before, this room was alive and buzzing with tension, adrenaline was speeding through everyone in the room. Now that's gone, replaced with a somber heaviness and silence. I slow my pace to a walk and look towards the baby everyone was just working so hard to save. Dr. Smith looks at me and shakes her head, pushing her lips down into a pouted frown. Hanging the stethoscope on the warmer, she leaves the bedside and heads into the next room, her shoulders now slumped and heavy. There are still other babies that need her right now. I turn to the baby we were just trying to save. It's painfully apparent that we are too late. Now he looks like a tiny gray doll, limp, lifeless, a child's toy. Not something that was once alive with real parents and the hope to grow and thrive. A sharp pang starts in my nose and wells up behind my eyes. I start to walk away, breathing in deeply as one of the nurse's covers the baby with a white crisp pillowcase.

The trouble with hospitals; people, and babies, sometimes die.

--

Lauren continues to squeeze the resuscitation bag for her patient. Right now it's the only thing keeping the baby alive.

I decide I can't wait any longer. I walk swiftly to the wall and grab the black phone. I punch in the phone number to my house but there is nothing; no ringing and there's not even a dial tone. I slam the phone down and pick it up again. Still nothing. I pull my cell phone out of my pocket. The touch screen is blank and black. I hold down the power button waiting for the circular white insignia to light up in the center of the screen. But still nothing happens. I don't understand.

I try and think about what just happened. There was just an earthquake, which we don't have many of in upstate New York. I can remember four in my whole life. In the back of my mind I can see my college physics professor drawing on a chalkboard. I feel a nagging sense of urgency-this is something else, this is something bad. Suddenly all I can think about it getting in contact with Ian and Lina.

"Is anyone's cell phone working?" I call out. The four nurses near me check their pockets, each of them shaking their heads no.

I look out the window craning my neck down so I can see the street. People are milling about, talking to each other. Many have their cell phones in their hand, but no one is talking on them. I notice that none of the cars are moving. Many of them are stopped in the middle of the road, some shifted at odd angles and pointed towards the sidewalk. There is a man in a suit sitting on the hood of a car. A police officer walks down the middle of the road on the yellow lines, waving his arm yelling something. Everyone on the street just stares at him. I shift my gaze to the highway and see more of the same. The on-ramps are clogged with non-moving vehicles. There is even a city bus at a dead standstill with a cluster of people standing around the open door.

I hear the stairwell door slam open. When I turn I see people filtering out of the stairwell. There are about fifteen nurses, their faces red with exhaustion, sweat matting their bangs to their faces and the stray hairs to the back of their necks.

Dayshift is here.

Behind the dayshift crew follows the night shift supervisor. She pushes her way through the day shift swarm which is crowding around the desk. Everyone is talking. The supervisor picks up the phone. She pulls the bottom speaker close to her mouth and holds down a button trying to make an announcement. I see her lips move but I don't hear anything. She looks around while she talks then stops abruptly, frowns at the phone, and slams it down hard. The crowd at the desk hushes their chatter.

"No one is to leave the hospital!" the supervisor yells. "This is a Code Silver: Environmental Crisis. All employees are to stay on their assigned units and continue to carry out their duties. If an employee leaves this hospital, you will be charged with patient abandonment. Your nursing license will be revoked. You will face criminal charges. We will be updating you all throughout the day as we receive information as to what is going on."

The supervisor pushes her way out of the crowd huddling around the desk, and people shout questions to her but she doesn't stop. She walks quickly with determination, her heels clicking on the linoleum floor as she heads back to the stairwell doors and disappears.

The trouble with hospitals; once they hire you they think they own you.

--

People are talking. They dayshift crew has thinned out among the night shift, helping feed babies, wrapping them in extra blankets to keep them warm, and taking turns squeezing the resuscitation bags for the babies with breathing tubes. Dr. Smith continues to check on all the babies within each of the eight nurseries. I keep checking my phone, hoping it will come back to life. I feel stupid doing it, but when I look around I notice other people doing the same thing.

It's starting to get hot. Now the unit smells musty and heavy. The tinge of sweat and soiled baby diapers clings heavy in the air. Instantly I miss the cool smell of baby soap that usually greets me when walking onto the unit.

I take a hair tie out of my pocket and try to pull my shoulder length hair into a pony tail, but plenty of curly strands fall down around my face. I tuck them behind my ears and dab at my forehead with a paper towel. Not knowing what is going on at home worries me. The sun is up now and I should be dropping off Lina at school. I should be kissing Ian goodbye as he leaves for work. The ache in my chest burns deeper every time I think of them both. I don't know how I'm going to do it, but I have to get home. I can't stay here. I have worked beside these people for years, and now they are about to find out what kind of a nurse I am. What kind of a person I am. I am a coward. I am selfish. I will not abandon my family for my patients, not even if they are babies, and I am filled with horrible shame during this moment of realization.

CHAPTER FIVE

I watch out the window as a line of people collect at the door to the hospital. A row of security guards stand in front of them. The people are yelling, pointing up to the floors above them. Visitors. They must have family here on the floors below us or even babies here in the NICU. I think of the baby that died a few hours ago. His parents may be down there, waiting, not knowing that they are about to receive some of the worst news of their lives. I sit down in a rocking chair. The adrenaline which kept me running earlier during the earthquake and the full code has trickled out. Exhaustion hits me like a sharp bullet between the eyes. Trying not to think, I tilt my head up to the ceiling and stare at the white pecked tiles. I start rocking, back and forth, back and forth, and I close my eyes. Before I know it I am breaking the golden rule of the night shift, no sleeping on the clock. However, no one wakes me.

--

When I open my eyes, they are dry. I rub them with both hands. A shiver runs down my back and goose bumps prickle up on my arms. Three things happen as I sit up: I see the tiny flecks of dust quiver around the air conditioning vent above me, I hear a monitor beep, and I see someone washing their hands.

"Power's back on!" Lauren smiles at me. Her baby is reattached to the breathing machine and she rubs her sore hands.

"That's great. How long was I out?"

"About an hour," she replies.

"Do we know what time it is?"

"I'm not sure. I heard someone say they thought it was around ten."

I look out the window. The sun isn't very high in the sky so they could be right. I notice three ravens perched on the roof across the street, standing still as statues. Behind them the black tar of the roof radiates heat in dense invisible waves. It's good the air is back on because it's already evident that today will be a hot day.

"The supervisor is back. She's going to make an announcement." Lauren leaves the room and walks towards the desk.

"Attention please!" The supervisor yells. "Currently the hospital is operating under a Code Silver. You are to remain on your unit. Emergency generators are running. The phone system is still down. There are cots and blankets in the conference room for those of you who have worked all night. And the cafeteria will be delivering food to each of the units."

"What do you expect us to do, stay here?" Someone from the crowd shouts. "You can't keep us here, some of us need to go home and be with our families!" I stand on my toes to see who is talking. It's Jan, the nurse who gave me my report the night before, the one with four children.

The supervisor's brow furrows, she looks exhausted. "I understand many of you want to go home. I do too. However I have to warn you that most of the city remains without power. Transportation is out of order. There are reports of rioting downtown and some have reported hearing gunshots. Our emergency room is currently crowded with the injured and the sick. We may ask some of you to help out in triage. I suggest that each of you stay here where it is safe until, until….." I can see the gleam in her eyes, she is holding back tears. She takes a shuddered breath in, "until it is safe to leave the building."

I walk back to the window and look towards downtown. There is a sliver of smoke snaking its way towards the sky. On the highway overpass I see a cluster of men walking together, their skin is dark and contrasting against their white shirts. They all wear the same thing; black jeans and white T-shirts. They walk up to a man sitting on the hood of his car on the highway. The man jumps up and starts walking backwards, he's taking something off his wrist and out of his pockets. I see him toss them on the ground in front of him. One of the men in the white T-shirts raises his arm, he is holding something black in his hand and I realize it is a gun. Suddenly, the man walking backwards drops to the ground in a crumpled heap.

"Oh shit," I whisper to myself.

The deep rumble of propellers redirects my eyes to the sky. Overhead, dark green army helicopters are flying, but none of them stop to land in the city. They continue to the North, following the highway-the same route I drive on my way home. At the city limits I see something fall out of the last helicopter, a small white parachute erupting from it when it hits the tree line. I look back down to the highway and see the gang of men run along the main street that heads downtown. The last place I want to be stranded is in a large city without power, where rioting and looting is already taking place. All the army helicopters flying north give me a bad feeling. My stomach fills with nausea. I'm not sure if it's from fear or guilt or a combination of them both, but I have to get out of here and find my family.

I turn to Lauren. "Are the cell phones still down?"

She nods as she pulls her phone out of the bag next to her. "I've been checking mine every few minutes but nothing-it's dead," she tells me.

"I'm going to lie down in the conference room," I tell Lauren and the other nurses in the room, hoping that they don't come looking for me any time soon.

I walk out of the room and towards the hallway. Looking over my shoulder I see that no one is watching me. I take a sharp turn for the stairwell.

--

Running down twelve flights of stairs is no easy feat in rubber clogs. Since the elevators are working again, I was hoping I wouldn't run into anyone and luckily I make it to the basement before anyone else decides to use the stairs.

The door to the basement is propped open. I walk up to the glass window to my left. There is an employee sitting at a desk looking bored, tapping his pen on a notebook. Above him is a sign that says Central Receiving.

"Can I help you?" He asks without looking up.

"Yeah, we are out of baby formula in the NICU." I smile at him as he looks up with a hint of skepticism in his eyes.

"I will have someone bring some up in a few minutes," he looks back down at his papers.

"Um, could I have a package now? I have a patient that needs to eat now." He gets up and stalks through the door behind him, returning a moment later with a box of baby formula. He sets it in front of me. "Thanks so much," I tell him, doing my best to smile sweetly at him before I turn to walk away and stand in front of the elevator.

The man behind the desk puts his head back down and starts writing. I back up slowly and start walking down the long gray hallway behind me, following the signs that point towards the security offices. I walk swiftly and silently, passing the security office door, continuing a few more feet to the row of vending machines. I stand on the far side of the last one and I wait, leaning up against the cold stone wall, taking a few shallow breaths. I hear the click of the security office door as it opens and I hear talking.

"What do you suggest we tell these people, Colonel?" asks the flustered voice of a man.

"I would suggest you tell them nothing. Minimal information is the safest right now," responds a man with a deep southern accent and impeccable speech.

"You don't think we should tell them about the bomb? We have people who live in that area. Who have families, children. They are going to want to know what is going on." He's talking fast, afraid someone will interrupt him. "And what about the radiation? Are we even safe here?"

"What I would suggest is that you do not speak of this information to anyone outside of this office." It must be the Colonel speaking now. His voice is demanding and full of authority, someone who is used to giving orders. "I wouldn't worry about radiation, we are safe from that. Most of the people living up there seem to be fine. But there is another situation we are dealing with. Just keep these people calm and under control. Once the situation is contained in the northern county we will be setting up a command station here. Everything will be in place by this evening."

I hear a pair of shoes echo down the hall and the door clicks closed to the security office. I search my pocket for some change then walk around the vending machine and feed quarters into it. The security door opens again.

"Aren't you supposed to stay on your assigned unit?" I turn to see a security guard eyeing me suspiciously. The hallway light shines off the badge clipped to this right shoulder.

"We needed formula and I needed a drink." I shake the box of baby formula in front of me.

"I suggest you get back to your unit," he replies sternly. He waits for me to move.

I wait for the bottle of soda to drop and retrieve it from the bottom of the vending machine. I smile at him and turn to walk down the hall towards the elevators, his eyes burning holes in my back.

That was close. But it was worth the risk because now I know a few facts: there was a bomb, but no radiation. It was strong enough to knock out power, ruin electrical circuits and cause the earth to shake over forty miles away. I ponder these details as I walk back to the stairwell. I try to think back to my advanced physical chemistry class, to think of what kind of a bomb they could be talking about.

--

The employee locker room is empty except for me, and the guilt that hangs on my shoulders for what I am about to do. I set the formula and soda on a bench near my employee locker. I grab a towel and soap bottle from a nearby cupboard. I undress in the shower stall and take a quick shower. When I am done I wrap myself in the towel, my hands shake nervously as I twist in the combination to my lock. I pull out the spare uniform I keep in my locker. I keep it here for those unfortunate situations which occur in the NICU, like getting vomited or pooped on. The uniform is similar to the one I was already wearing. I scrub my hair with the towel, trying to squeeze as much water out of it as I can and run a comb through it. There is no time to dry it so I twist it up with a spare hair clip from the locker. I stare at the black sneakers on the floor of the locker and then at my work clogs. After a moment I decide that the sneakers will be a better choice for a forty mile walk.

Pulling my work bag out of the locker, I roll up my used uniform and tuck it in the bottom of the bag then place the small box of formula and soda in next. Before I go I look in the small rectangular mirror attached to the inside of the locker door. My face is pale with guilt and anxiety and the uneasy feeling that I am about to make one of the hardest decisions of my entire life.

--

The good thing about hospitals; there is an abundance of supplies, until they run out.

My next stop is the clean utility room where the hospital keeps all the medical supplies. There is another badge swipe. This room smells sterile and cold. It is filled floor to ceiling with cupboards. I'm not sure what I need or what I could use, so I take random supplies, a roll of sterile gauze, medical tape, a few long needles with red caps, some syringes filled with normal saline, a handful of paper towels. I place the supplies in a small plastic biohazard bag and shove it deep into my work bag. If I get injured I can use the supplies. And since I have no weapons to defend myself, the long needles might come in handy.

The door opens behind me. It is Lauren. She looks at me, her eyes wide with shock.

"I have to go," I tell her. I don't give her a chance to say anything. I just turn and walk out the door.

--

The hallway is filled with the salty smell of cured meat and the sweet smell of fruit. The door to the employee lounge is open, and inside a cafeteria worker is setting out food on the long lunch table. I walk up to her cart and take a bottle of water, two apples, a banana and a bag of pretzels. She turns and looks at me as I am placing the food into my bag.

"You should be ashamed of yourself," she scowls at me.

She doesn't need to tell me this, I am already ashamed of what I'm about to do.

I head to the stairwell, running down to the first level where I came into work over sixteen hours ago. The same security guard sits at the desk. His gray uniform is wrinkled and he looks tired. He turns to me. My hands throb, sending a tingle up each of my arms. This is adrenaline. This is fight or flight. For a moment we just stare at each other, waiting for the other to say something. We say nothing. Instead, he nods silently, crossing his arms over his chest. This must be my ticket to pass. I wonder if maybe I'm not the first person to sneak out of here. I walk past him, quickly turning my pace into a sprint. The security cameras bore holes into my back, my moment of defiance getting recorded. I am almost afraid the hospital will come to life and pull me back, that it will make me pay for all I've done in the past hour; the lies, stealing, breaking the nurse's code of conduct.

I reach the parking garage at the end of the hallway. It is dark. There are no lights here. I turn right and head towards the stairway. The tingling in my arms has reached my shoulders and has started creeping towards my neck. It feels like someone is following me, chasing me. I get the same feeling when I go into our basement at night to change over the laundry. It propels me forward and I run up the five flights of musty cement steps towards where I parked my old Jeep.

When I reach the top of the stairs, my lungs and back of my throat are burning. My chest is tingling. My leather bag feels like it weighs a hundred pounds. I push open the metal door; the heavy humid air of early afternoon envelopes me. Between the heat, the adrenaline, the fear, the guilt, I can't take it anymore. I turn to the wall of the garage and vomit.

There is a pinching in the back of my nose. I take a deep breath and sit on the curb. I have to see Ian and Lina. I have to get back to them. I know this is not a time to break down. I have to try and be strong. I take a deep breath and collect myself. I walk to the jeep and open the driver's side door with the key. I sit in the driver's seat, placing the key in the ignition. I turn it. Sadly nothing happens.

"It was worth a try." I say aloud to myself.

I look around the cabin of the jeep. I take my sunglasses. I get out and open the back door, searching the middle passenger bench. Lina's booster seat is secured behind my driver's seat with a small stuffed owl sitting in the cup holder. I take the owl and slam the door. I make my way to the cargo area and open the hatch, my eyes scanning the items that are strewn about. I grab my dark green gardening hat. It is flexible and light and will protect me from the bright sun that glares in between the levels of the garage. There is a heavy wool blanket that Stevie lays on when she rides in the car with us. I would like to take the blanket but it's too heavy. However it gives me an idea. I lift the bottom of the cargo deck. Underneath is a compartment with a snow brush, jumper cables and an emergency kit. I open the emergency kit and take out the light reflective blanket. The side of my bag is starting to bulge. I know that this is all I can bring with me. I hope it is enough to get me home.

CHAPTER SIX

I have to make it the four blocks from the parking garage to the highway on-ramp. I'm hoping since this is hospital and university property that I can get out safely, without experiencing the crime mentioned by the unit supervisor. Already I can hear the commotion of the city. I walk so fast I'm nearly running. I make it a block, then two, before I see more thick smoke rising into the sky from downtown. Hopefully all the crime will stay there, where the shops and restaurants are. I'm sure they are being looted right now. There are voices off in the distance, some laughing, some shouting. I've made it three blocks. I pick up the pace, eager to get out of here. Just as I'm nearing the highway exit I hear gunshots in the distance. It sends me into a full sprint up the on-ramp. I weave between the stalled cars until I get high above the city and onto the overpass. I stop and look behind me. The windows of the hospital glare at me. Even from this far away I can still see the line of people trying to get into the hospital, and another line has formed at the emergency room doors. I hope that no one is watching out the windows. I hope that they can't see me fleeing the city, abandoning the hospital's most helpless patients.

I follow the two lane highway as it snakes over the city, winding to the left, the right, then back again, around treetops and tall buildings. I was hoping that no one would be up here, that people would have abandoned their vehicles. Instead I see a few people sitting in their cars and on top of them. I walk by quickly trying not to make eye contact. I don't want to be delayed. I want to get home as fast as possible, before dark. I definitely don't want to be out walking in this during the night.

None of them try to stop me. They just watch me pass by, crinkling their faces up in response to the bright afternoon light.

The sun is hot on my back and I stop to remove my uniform top, leaving me with just a thin sweat soaked undershirt. I take the hat and sunglasses out of my bag and put them on then tuck the uniform top inside.

There is an exit for the airport to my right, a sign that I am almost to the suburbs. I can see ahead of me that the highway starts to slant down to the ground level. I head for the steep decline, nervous that soon I will no longer have the protection of the elevated highway. The sides of the road ahead are lined with fences and trees from the nearby housing developments and suburbs.

To my dismay, I notice a group of people on the highway ahead of me. As I get closer, I can see that it is a group of black men, all of them wearing white T-shirts. *Oh no, the gang.* They stand in a circle looking at something on the ground. Some of them yell at whatever is-I'm going to assume it's a person. I'm too far away to hear what they are saying and the stalled cars on the road are making it impossible for me to see what it is. I'm sure they are armed. I need to hide.

I walk towards the far side of the road, trying to create as much distance between us as possible. This area of the highway is open with two lanes and cement embankments on each side. I look over the side of the overpass. It's too far to jump off-if I jump from here I risk breaking a leg. I think of hiding in one of the stalled cars until they leave, but most of them have their doors open. The gang will certainly hear me or find me when they are done with what they are doing. I'm sure they will be searching the cars on their way back through. I crouch behind a small compact car, walking slowly, doing my best to be quiet while shielding myself from their view. Once I get to the back end of the car, I run as quickly and quietly as I can to an SUV parked a few feet away. I'm hoping that I'm silent enough that they won't notice me. As I reach the back end of this vehicle I wait for a moment, trying to get my timing right. I take a few silent steps towards a sedan that is parked closely behind the SUV. Now the gang is directly behind me. I squat down, my back resting against the hot metal of the sedan; I peer around the back. I have a direct view of the situation and I can see that there is a man on the ground in front of the gang, shielding his face with his arms. I can see pistols tucked into the gang members' pants, bulging out from under their shirts. One is holding a gun in his hand, pointing it at the man on the ground. I feel like I should do something to help him, but I don't want to get involved. And all I have for a weapon are the long needles in my bag which would do nothing to defend me against a gun. I just want to get home. I just want to get away from this city. So, here I am, a coward once again-twice in one day-prepped and ready to flee, to abandon someone else in need.

I look to the next car that's about four feet away, getting ready to run for it. I take a deep breath before I turn, taking one last look at the situation behind me, and then it's too late. The man on the ground sees me and one of the gang members turns, following his gaze. *Crap.* Before I know it he's walking towards me, and he's tall, taller than anyone I've ever met. Sweat marks stain the neck and underarms of his shirt. It only takes a few steps for his long legs to get to me. I stand, my heart beating in my throat, panicking. I back up until the cement embankment of the overpass hits me in the back. I should at least try to run or jump-I'd rather have a broken leg than get into this mess-but I don't. I know this large man will reach me before I could get far. That is, if he doesn't shoot me first. He grabs my shoulder, his fingers pinching into my skin as he pulls me towards the group of gang members.

"What do you think you doin' out here girl?" He asks as he pulls me beside him.

"Check her bag, maybe she got somethin' we be needin'!" Another gang member shouts, smiling, showing his row of gold teeth.

A third gang member reaches for the bag slung over my shoulder. If I make it out of this situation alive I need everything in that bag. I can't let them have it. I hold my breath, waiting for them to rip the bag off my shoulder, but his hand hovers above me. When I turn my head to look at him, I instantly know why he stopped.

"Ricardo?" I ask in disbelief. "Are you kidding me, is that actually you? What do you think you're doing?" For a moment, I'm afraid of what they might do to me for actually speaking.

I hear the man on the ground groan and roll to his side.

"What she talkin' 'bout?" one of the other gang members shouts.

We both ignore him. I'm sure it seems odd that I should know a gang member, but I have never known him like this. I never pictured him as a thug or being in a gang. I knew him as a nervous father when his girlfriend gave birth to his son five weeks early. He always dressed nicely when visiting his son. He was polite and quiet. I taught him how to change a diaper, how to dress his baby boy, how to give him a bath.

"How's Junior doing?" I ask. I wait for a response, hoping that mentioning his son might save me. He drops his arm and shrugs a little. "How old is he now, three months? I bet he's rolling over by now, isn't he?" I press on. I stand there, glaring at him. Finally he smiles, the sun bright on his white teeth, almost blinding me.

"He's great, Andie." Ricardo takes a step towards me and wraps his long arms around me. It takes a minute for me to realize that he's hugging me. He pats me so hard on the back it hurts. "I never got to thank you for all you did for us. When Junior was discharged you weren't working."

I may actually get out of this alive. "So what are you doing?" I ask him again as he pulls back from hugging me.

"After the earthquake they closed all the stores. We're out of formula for Junior." I give him a questioning look and he holds his palms in front of himself, defensively. "Hey, I'm just trying to help my family. Find food for my son."

"Well, Ricardo, this is your lucky day." I reach into my bag and pull out the box of baby formula. "I will only give you this on two conditions." Ricardo no longer looks at me, instead he is focusing intently on the box of formula. "You let me walk out of this city. I have a family to take care of too, and I need to get back to them. And, you leave that man on the ground alone."

Ricardo's features change quickly. He is no longer loose and relaxed, now he is tense with a cold look on his face, as though he's preparing himself for an argument. He turns away from me, back to his companions.

"We done here. The white girl goes." He points to the ground where the injured man lies, "Him too."

Ricardo turns to me with his hand out. I place the box of formula in it. They start walking back towards the city. One of the men stops, kicking the foot of the guy on the ground.

"Take care of that baby, Ricardo," I urge him. "He needs a father to grow up with."

Ricardo nods at me and walks away. I stand and watch them until they are so far away I can barely see them over the river of stalled cars.

The man on the ground groans. I bend down placing my hand on his shoulder and roll him onto his back. He opens one eye. The other is swollen shut and his bottom lip is cut and bleeding.

"Sit up slowly," I tell him. He groans again as I apply pressure to his shoulder, pushing him up to a sitting position. "Are you dizzy?" I ask. "Do you know where you are?" He doesn't respond.

I hold my index finger in front of his nose. "Follow my finger," I instruct him. His light blue eye follows my finger as I pass it in front of his face. I pull a paper towel from my tote and hold it to his lip. I look him over. He looks young, healthy and muscular, like he should have been able to put up a little more of a fight for himself. I don't see any more wounds or bullet holes in his shirt. Whatever the gang wanted from him they must have gotten it or I have a feeling he would be dead.

"My name is Andie. I'm... well, I was a nurse at the hospital in the city." I point back in the direction of the hospital.

"Who names their kid Andromeda," he asks me, rubbing his shoulder.

"What?"

"Your name."

"How do you know my name?" I sit back on my heels, certain he has me confused with someone else.

"You're wearing a badge."

I look down and see my hospital badge clipped to my shirt. "Oh, my parents were really into mythology." I pull the badge off and throw it in my bag, feeling like an idiot. "You look like you're going to be fine," I tell him, "but the hospital is still open if you want to get yourself checked out. Just follow this highway to the third exit."

"I'm not going back into that jungle," he tells me. It's strange, his voice doesn't waver. His tone is deep and even. Unlike that of a person who was just confronted by a gang of men with guns. And even though he was on the ground, I get the feeling he wasn't afraid of them.

"Ok then," I stand and haul my bag over my shoulder, "I have to go."

He says nothing. Just nods his head and looks down at the crusty pavement at his feet.

I walk away, leaving him in the road, and resume my walk home.

--

It is late afternoon and I've finally reached my exit to head north towards home. My thighs burn and my shirt clings to my back, saturated with sweat and the heavy humid air. I stop and lean against an empty car. My stomach is grumbling and the back of my throat is dry with thirst. I climb up onto the hood of the car and set my bag next to me. I pull out the apple and the water I took from the hospital. I twist my body, sitting at an angle, my feet dangle near the tires, so I can watch the highway extending from the city. I don't want any more surprises. It's eerily silent and I'm thankful that I haven't run into anyone else. The confrontation with the gang was enough to shake me and I'm not sure I've fully recovered from it.

I can see the back lots of a housing development from where I sit. Even though it's still bright outside, it looks like the glow from a back porch light peeks through the thin row of trees. I'm relieved at the sight of electricity. Hopefully it has been restored to the rest of the city, and that might keep people off the road.

I take a bite of the apple and open the bottle of water. I drink half of it, splashing some on my hands and rubbing my face, trying to wash the sweat off from my walk. When I look up, I see someone walking towards me. Limping actually, wincing with every other step he takes. I sit on the hood of the car and wait. There is no place for me to run out here. I watch him as he gets closer. When he's a few hundred yards away I can see that his right eye is swollen and bruised, and there is a cut on his lip. This is the man I left behind in the road.

He's looking at me as he walks straight towards me. I stay sitting on the car, holding my ground. I reach into my bag trying to find one of the long needles I took from the hospital, hoping that I don't need to defend myself from this man after I saved his life.

He stops in front of me pushing both of his hands into his pockets.

"I never thanked you for saving my life," he tells me.

"You're welcome," I respond.

There's an awkward silence because I'm sure we are doing the same thing; trying to figure the other person out, judging each other based on what we look like. He's dressed nicely enough-a pair of dark jeans, leather work boots and a dark blue T-shirt. His hair is dark brown, almost black, and I can see the dark ink of a tattoo peeking out from under his sleeve. I know what I look like, a sweaty ex-nurse, which I'm sure is not at all flattering. I continue to search my bag, trying to find one of the needles.

"My name is Adam," he pulls his hand out of his pocket and holds it out towards me. "You're Andie, right?"

"Yeah." I give up searching for the needle and shake his hand.

"Are you headed north?" He asks.

I don't have to ask him how he knows, it's obvious from the exit sign I am sitting under. "Yes," I tell him hesitantly.

"So am I. How far are you going?" He raises his hand, shielding his eyes from the bright sunlight. There is something about him that's oddly familiar, something that I can't quite place. He talks with the local dialect, pronouncing his *O's* with a harsh emphasis, like only those of us from northern New York do.

"Do I know you from somewhere?" I ask him.

"I don't think so. Where are you from?"

"Phoenix."

"So am I." He smiles showing a row of perfectly straight teeth.

I stare at him, still unsure. "I'm not sure if I believe you, Mr. Adam. Tell me what your favorite restaurant in Phoenix is?" I ask, crossing my arms over my chest.

He rocks back on his heels, still smiling, "Jacko's."

Only a townie would like that place, it's nothing more than a trailer by the river serving hot griddle meals. I continue with my quiz. "Favorite Bar?"

"Front Door Tavern."

"The name of our local homeless man?"

"Stinky."

"*Dear God*, it truly is a small world," I mumble at him, rolling my eyes.

"Would you mind if I walked with you?" He asks.

Part of me does mind. I stare at him for a moment longer, trying to judge what he might be up to. Finally, I give up pondering. What could it hurt? I started out my journey alone, but now that night is coming it might be good to have a partner to travel with.

"I guess," I reply as I hop down from the hood of the car.

I collect my things and throw the apple core across the road into the tall grass. Then we walk. Actually, he limps. For miles we don't speak much. Every so often I hear him let out a grunt when he steps down on his right foot. I let him continue for another mile or so, avoiding the fact that he is injured and slowing me down, until I can't take it any longer.

"Ok, let's take a break and I can take a look at your foot. I can't listen to your yelps of pain any longer."

He stops, exhaling deeply. I signal him to sit on the hood of an abandoned car that's low enough for me to work. I watch him as he hobbles over and sits down. I pull up his right pant leg. His ankle is deeply bruised and swollen. As I start to pull up his left pant leg he puts his hand down to stop me, grabbing my wrist.

"What?" I ask him. He doesn't say anything. Instead he reaches down and pulls it up himself. Strapped to his ankle is a gun.

I step back, my hands up. "Why are you carrying a weapon?" I ask.

"Why are you inspecting my uninjured ankle?" He stares at me sternly.

"I have to make sure *both* your ankles don't look like pounded rump roast." I glare at him. "So why are you carrying a weapon?"

"Why do you care?"He asks me, looking annoyed.

"Because I didn't agree to travel with you having a gun strapped to your body."

Adam removes the gun that's strapped around his ankle, and pulls out a Swiss army knife that was tucked down in his boot. "It's for protection."

"Then why didn't you use it against those men on the overpass?"

He laughs at me. "When it's seven to one, it doesn't matter if you have a gun."

"I didn't have a gun," I reply, standing back from him, waiting to see what he's going to do next.

"Could you just look at this, please?" He asks, setting the weapons down behind him.

I inspect each ankle and check the pulse in each of his legs. Then I palpate the swollen area, causing him to wince in pain again. "It looks like you have a sprain. I would suggest wrapping it with an ace bandage, taking some ibuprofen and staying off it for a week." I stand up straight and look around. "But it looks like we will have to improvise." I dig through my bag and pull out the scrub pants I wore last night. I toss them at Adam. "Cut these into some long strips with your weapon there." I point at the Swiss army knife.

I walk down the road, searching the glove boxes of a few nearby cars until I find what I'm looking for; an emergency First-Aid kit-which I take. On my way back to Adam, I search the tall grass and brushes off the side of the highway. It takes me about five minutes until I see what I'm looking for: a thick tall tree branch. I break the extra limbs off the branch until I have a single long stick.

Using the longest strip of my now cut up scrub pants, I wrap his foot and ankle as tightly as I can. I use another small strip to tie a knot around his ankle, holding the wrap in place, and then use another to wrap an area on the branch so Adam can hold it without getting splinters.

"Here's your new cane. Treat it well." I hold the stick out for him. "Oh, I almost forgot!" I open the emergency kit. "Jaaackpot!" I sing high and off key. Inside are a few medical supplies and a travel pack of Tylenol. I hand the medication to Adam.

"I don't know how I feel about what I just saw," he says flatly, accepting the pills from me.

"Well, most patients would be grateful they have a nurse with two brain cells to rub together. So count your lucky stars that *I* found you and not someone else." We stare at each other for a moment.

"There is something truly wrong with you." He rips open the Tylenol and throws both tablets into his mouth, swallowing them without water.

"Yeah, well, I'm bored with this playing nurse thing that's going on. And I'm kind of in a rush to get home and find my family. So if we could get this train rolling that would be great." I pick up my bag and throw the emergency kit on top. As I'm walking away I hear Adam limp up behind me. He's walking a little faster now, groaning a little less. We still don't say anything for a long time, and I'm a little angry that he didn't even thank me. I can feel him looking at me, judging me, trying to figure out if he can trust me; just as I did to him a few miles ago.

--

We have been walking for hours. Ahead of us I can see the off ramp for the mall near Sam's apartment which means we aren't far from the county line, but it's starting to get dark. I stop and look around. The area ahead of us is filled with stores and restaurants, and I know there is a hotel not far from the highway.

"I think we should stop somewhere for the night," I tell Adam. I wait for his response. "I have a brother that lives in an apartment, a few miles that way." I point off to the side, away from our final destination. He lives in the wrong direction which would put us behind, probably by another day.

"That's the wrong direction. It would put us behind. I don't know about you but I want to get home as soon as possible," Adam responds, reading my mind. I'm relieved that it's not just my decision to bypass Sam's place, but I will have to get in contact with him later. Right now, getting back to Lina and Ian is more important. "There's a hotel," he points straight ahead of us. "Looks like they have power. We can rest there for the night."

By the time we reach the front doors, the sun is gone and all that is left is the settling dusk. The air is cooler now, crisper, and a strip of fog hovers above the ground. I can hear the dense hum of a generator. Adam holds the door open and waves me in. There is a young woman at the front desk who seems shocked to see us. When I catch a glimpse of myself in a wall mirror I know why. We are disheveled, tired and dirty looking. Adam's busted face looks even worse in the overhead fluorescent lighting. His swollen eye is highlighted in purple and the split on his lip shimmers.

"Do you have any rooms for the night?" I ask the clerk.

She clicks away on her keyboard for a moment. "Do you want a king suite?" she asks raising her eyebrows at us.

"No, we actually need two rooms." I respond quickly. I see Adam, out of the corner of my eye, smirking at her question.

We pay separately and lucky for us it's half price due to the power outage. As the young woman hands us our keys she points to a dining room across the hall. "There are complimentary snacks and breakfast in the morning. That is, if we still have power."

I thank her and walk to the dining room. After working all night and walking all day, I'm hungry and exhausted. There's a buffet table with minimal food. Bread, bagels, fruit, bottles of water. I take a bagel, a banana and water and sit at one of the nearby tables. Adam follows and sits across from me. The tension from the highway is gone, and both of us are completely exhausted. Still, we find enough energy for some small talk.

He tells me he just got back from deployment in Germany for two years and he is headed home to see his parents and younger sister. I find out that we went to high school together, but never crossed paths much since he was a few years older than me. I tell him about Lina and Ian and what happened during the earthquake at the hospital. I leave out what I heard in the basement between the security guard and the Colonel. When we are done eating we part ways, our rooms in different hallways, and we agree to meet in the morning.

I close the door to my hotel room and turn the deadbolt lock. I feel a little better after hearing it click heavily into place. I have never stayed in a hotel room alone. I stare at the two beds before choosing the one by the window. I sit for a minute and stare at the phone.

When I pick up the receiver there is no dial tone waiting for me to punch in a number, there is simply no sound at all. I check my cell phone, it is still blank. The ache in my chest is back again. I think about Ian and Lina, hoping that they are safe. I tell myself that tomorrow I will see them again. I have to.

CHAPTER SEVEN

I wake up groggy, aching and still tired, the previous day's events still consuming my thoughts. It's strange; like a dream, like a nightmare. There's only lukewarm water for a shower, but it's enough to wake me up. I go out to the dining room to see if Adam is there. I am relieved to see him sitting by the window looking refreshed, even though he's wearing the same clothes as the day before. I head straight for the coffee carafe and pour some into a mug. I grab a few bagels and apples and cross the room to sit with him.

As I settle across from him I notice that I can see both of his light blue eyes and the swelling in his face has gone down. The split in his lip has even healed itself into a bright red slash.

He looks at the pile of food in front of me. "Are you starving to death or something?" He asks me.

I wasn't ready to be greeted by a bad attitude. I would like to throw one of the apples at his face but instead I wrap it in a napkin with one of the bagels and tuck it into my bag. I eat in silence and stare out the window. Outside the hotel windows I can see the morning is heavy with fog and dew. The sun is starting to rise over the suburbs and a layer of dense fog covers the ground and roads, rising slowly, in unison with the sun.

After a few minutes he speaks again. "I'm sorry. I'm not really a morning person."

I raise my eyebrows at him, "Neither am I. Usually I tell people not to talk to me before I've had my coffee. I'd say you're lucky I didn't throw something at your face."

"I thought nurses were healers not fighters."

"I thought army guys were saviors not assholes." He starts to crack a smile, but stops abruptly, wincing and pressing a napkin to the split on his lower lip. "You thought wrong, Chuckles. Now let's get moving. I want to make it past the county line today. I have to get home"

Just as we step out the front door of the hotel, a Humvee pulls up and a man in fatigues drops a stack of newspapers in front of the doors. I pick one up and read the front page.

"Seismic Activity Results in Nuclear Meltdown of Two Reactors on Lake Ontario Shores"

Adam is reading the headlines over my shoulder, his breath blowing wisps of hair in front of my face. I read halfway down the page.

"State of Emergency Instated for all of Phoenix County, No Travel Allowed."

I skim the articles. It says that the radioactive contamination has been minimal and the reason for the no travel order is so they can investigate and cleanup. Somehow, the army has already set up barricades. They are treating survivors and identifying those who didn't make it. The last article pays homage to all the residents lost in the event, which someone has estimated as up to 25,000 residents.

"That's almost half the population..." Adam whispers directly into my ear. He's standing so close and I'm not sure if it's the news or the deepness of his voice that's sending shivers down my spine.

"Let's get going." I fold the paper up and shove it in my bag.

"Are you sure you want to? The news report is pretty bleak, who knows what we will find when we get there."

I find it hard to believe that he would want to give up now after all the distance we've traveled and being so close to home.

"I don't care. I broke the law when I abandoned my patients at the hospital. I will never be able to work as a nurse again. My family is all I have. Without them there is nothing. I'm going."

"I was hoping you'd say that."

I don't look up at him to see his reaction to my confession. He is the only person I've told, but I can't let him see the sheen of tears coating my eyes. Not now, as the realization that I may have lost my entire family hits me.

We start out heading for the overpass to the northbound highway exit. I notice Adam is no longer limping and he has abandoned the cane I made him. As we get closer to the exit ramp, I can see Army Humvees and barricades blocking both exits on and off the highway and men in uniform are standing by with guns on their shoulders.

"Wait," I grab Adam's arm, "Um..." I stutter for a moment, I wasn't prepared to grab onto an arm of hard muscle. "They won't let us by, we need to go around."

We discuss our options for other roads leading north. There are a fair amount of railroads in disrepair to consider and some old back roads. Finally we decide to walk through the forest, parallel to the main highway. It is the fastest and most direct route and being late spring, the foliage is thick enough to hide us from whoever may be on the roads.

We turn around and walk behind the hotel bypassing the off ramp to the highway. At the back of the hotel there is a steep decline of tall grass which leads into the forest. More than once Adam grabs my arm to keep me from falling as I stumble through the tall brush. Just as we reach the forest line I turn around one last time and see what looks like one of the army men at the overpass pointing at us. Adam holds up a heavy tree branch for me to walk under and we enter the dense forest.

Adam leads the way, holding branches out of the way so they don't hit me in the face. It's cool in the forest and much darker than it was out in the open. Every so often I get a glimpse of the highway; there are still abandoned cars, just not as many as before. A chipmunk runs across the toe of my shoe.

It feels like hours have passed already. The back of my throat and thighs are starting to burn. Not long ago we passed a sign stating Phoenix was twenty miles away. The heavy hum of helicopters fills the sky. Adam signals for me to stop and get low. He's chewing on a stick that he pulled off of one of the bushes we passed. I see a low hanging branch nearby and crawl to it, crouching down and leaning against the trunk of the tree. We can't see the sky from the dense treetops. But we can listen, and the sound of the helicopters dissipates slowly. I reach for my bag and pull out the bottle of water that I stole from the hospital. Adam eyes me as I take a long gulp from the bottle. I realize he has nothing with him besides the stick he's chewing on. I toss him the bottle.

We continue walking for another long stretch. And now, there is the sound of thunder rumbling in the sky ahead of us.

"I want to go out to the road and get a better look at the sky." I tell Adam.

He nods and we head for the tree line. Outside of the dense foliage of the forest the sky is gray and overcast. Ahead of us thunder clouds are collecting in a large gray tower.

"There are no cars here."

"What?" I ask Adam.

"Look around us, Andie. There's not a single car."

I look behind us and in front of us, as far as we can see on the highway. He's right; there isn't a single car on the road. As I stand staring for a moment I am interrupted by a heavy low whistle. Adam and I respond the same, "trains?" This area is filled with abandoned train tracks, the whole county used to be heavy in industry and manufacturing. But now the train tracks are mostly overgrown and abandoned.

"Why are they running the trains? The paper said no travel." Adam asks. I don't respond. I'm thinking. "What about the radiation from the meltdown? They could be spreading the contamination."

Finally I tell Adam what I heard in the basement of the hospital. "There was no earthquake and there was no meltdown. That paper was misinformed."

"What do you mean?"

"I overheard some Colonel talking to a security guard in the basement of the hospital. He said that there is no radiation."

"This doesn't make sense. What is going on then? Is this a hoax or something?" Adam stares at me waiting for answers. He runs his hand through his short dark hair, then down the stubble on the side of his face.

"I don't know what's going on." I reply. "But I'd like to find out."

"Why didn't you tell me this before?" He asks.

"I'm not sure." I shrug at him. "Maybe it's the same reason you didn't tell me you were carrying a gun." I turn and start walking on the empty highway, towards home.

Eventually he follows me. Since there are no cars to amble around, we are able to walk faster, making up for the extra time it took to walk through the dense forest. I can see the stoplight for the small town of Oswego Falls ahead of us, which means we are about fifteen miles from home. What I don't expect to see is a chain-link fence cutting across the intersection of the road.

Adam and I both stop when we notice it. "Get to the forest," He tells me, pushing on my shoulder. "Run!" He pushes my shoulder harder, forcing me to run.

We sprint off the side of the highway, down the embankment, across a patch of tall grass. I can hear the loud hum of helicopters again. I want to look back and see where they are going. I slow and turn, trying to get a glance. But as I do Adam's hand reaches out grabbing my forearm and pulling me along behind him. He's practically dragging me, running. I can feel small branches stinging me as they sweep across my face. I put my free arm up to protect my eyes but it barely helps. Finally Adam stops running and lets my arm free. He's out of breath and bends over with his hands on his knees.

"What was that all about?" I ask him as I try to catch my breath, brushing the sticks and leaves out of my hair and off my shirt. I rub my hand across my forehead where one of the tree branches hit me. When I pull my hand away there's blood on it.

"There were guards or something, putting that fence up. Off to the left of the road, they had guns. You didn't see them?" He asks me between breaths.

"No." I search my bag for one of the paper towels. "But that means there are people here. And if they're working, then they aren't suffering from the effects of radiation poisoning. So that proves it, there can't be nuclear fallout."

Adam looks at me, thinking, milling the facts about in his brain. There is only one logical answer and not much time passes before he agrees. "So I guess you were right, Andie. Something else is going on here."

"Now what do we do?" I ask him, pressing a towel to the cut on my forehead.

"Let's stick to the woods and keep going. It may take us longer than expected to get home, but at least we can stay hidden."

"Okay," I agree with him.

As we start walking I notice he's limping again, it's then I realize that he's not just talking about the detour making our trip longer. He doesn't say anything to me, but he must have re-injured his ankle while he was dragging me through the woods.

We walk, weaving between the tree trunks until the sun starts to set low in the sky. There are no low branches here, just soft earth beneath our feet and branchless tree trunks. Some are thick with dense crusty bark, others as thin as my index finger, all shooting towards the sky. The sound of thunder rumbles in the distance and I can hear raindrops falling on the leaves high above us.

"I think we're going to have to stop soon," I tell Adam as my stomach grumbles loudly.

"Just a little bit further," he urges me on.

I follow him. Not because I want to keep walking but because he is my travel partner and I have to trust that he has some sort of a plan. Plus, I don't want to be left in the woods. At night. Alone.

The sun has set further and the forest is almost completely dark now. I have a hard time seeing Adam with his dark clothes. When the last bit of light dips below the tree line I can no longer see him. I begin to wonder if he really does have any type of a plan or if he's just wandering. The thought of being alone in the woods at night causes my heart to pound harder in my chest. I walk faster, stumbling until I smack into something hard, hitting the side of my head. At first I think it's a tree trunk, but then I feel hands grip around my shoulders, stopping me from falling over.

"Are you ok?" Adam asks.

"Uh, sorry," I respond, looking up. I can barely see his face above me.

"We should camp here. There's enough branches and brush to start a small fire, no one should be able to see the smoke or the light through the thick trees. We should be safe."

"No offense, but I'd rather not sleep on the ground."

"Oh, so what are you going to do?"

I look around for a moment, letting my eyes adjust to the darkness, and then I see it. Like a miracle, there is a tree house built into a huge willow tree with long, sweeping branches, and it's almost completely hidden. "I'm going to climb that tree."

Adam laughs. "Oh yeah, well, have fun with that. Do you know what it's like sleeping in a tree? I'll make sure to check your pulse in the morning when I find your body on the ground." A deep laugh erupts from his chest.

"Actually, Chuckles," I respond, "I think I see the perfect branch." I point up a few hundred feet away. Adam follows my gaze to the tree with the tree house.

"*Nice*," he responds.

We walk towards the tree house. Once we are standing underneath it I notice that the ladder is actually rough two-by-four boards hammered into the trunk. I reach for the first step, struggling with the bag on my shoulder. Adam walks up behind me.

"Let me take the bag, you climb first," he offers.

I pass it to him and continue to climb. The willow tree is large and the rungs of the rough ladder that's hammered into the trunk are spaced far apart. I struggle reaching some of the steps with my short legs. When I finally get to the base of the tree fort I haul myself up, trying to use the muscles of my arms to pull my body up. Adam follows close behind me, pushing on my feet as they dangle at the opening.

I can see that the tree house is spacious and large. It looks nothing like the tree forts we used to build as kids with uneven boards and half hammered nails. This is large and circular, wrapping around the thick trunk of the tree. This looks professional. There's a smooth floor, open areas for windows and a roof. A small bunk is built into the far wall, cupboards, a rough hewn table and chair.

"Is this where you sing 'Jackpot' again?" Adam asks.

I ignore him. I hold out my hand, waiting for my bag. He passes it to me and I sit down on the floor. I pull out the bottle of soda, the bagel and apples. I hand half of the bagel and an apple to Adam.

"You know, you could be a little more grateful. After all, I have healed you, put a roof over your head and fed you dinner." I hold my hands open, palms up, expectantly.

"Thanks, Mom," he responds laughing.

"Not funny," I tell him. "And just for that, I will not share this bottle of refreshing, warm, flat soda with you. I hope you don't choke on that bagel."

He laughs louder.

I begin to hear the heavy patter of rain on the roof and the deep grumble of thunder in the sky. I wait for leaks to break through the wooden ceiling, but like another miracle it remains dry inside.

"Well, so much for a fire up here. At least we'll be protected from the rain but I hope it doesn't get too cold tonight."

"Don't worry I have that covered too." I rummage through my bag for the reflective blanket I took from the back of my Jeep. I pull it out and shake it open. It is large, but not quite large enough for two strangers to share.

"You want to share that?" He asks.

I shrug at him. "Or you could sleep on that cold bunk."

"No, I'm saying you would sleep next to a stranger?"

"I don't think we are complete strangers anymore," I tell him, "Besides, I know you're not going to try anything."

"How can you be so sure?"

"Because my husband will hunt you down and kill you," I tell him, as seriously as I can. "I'm going to get some sleep." I push my bag under my head to use as a pillow. Reaching into the opening I pull out the little owl of Lina's and rub its soft fur. The blanket leaves about a foot of space between us. I have never slept this close to another man except for Ian. "Goodnight," I tell Adam, as I hear him trying to get comfortable on the smooth wood floor next to me.

Sleeping in a tree fort next to a man I barely know is not easy. And I was hoping the exhaustion of walking all day would push me into a deep sleep, but instead I wake up frequently. In the few moments that I do sleep, I dream of Ian and Lina. But not the pleasant dreams that one would wake refreshed from. Instead they are dark, shadowy, and I seem to be searching for something but I can never seem to find what I am looking for.

The most vivid dream of the night leaves me waking in tears: I'm running through my house searching for Lina, and when I do find her it's in the dark musty basement and she's hiding behind our old heating oil boiler. But for some reason she is older than when I left her a few days ago. Instead of a young child she resembles a tall teenager with long curly hair and dark rimmed glasses. Even though I barely recognize her in my dream, I still pull her into my arms, sobbing into her long dark hair. When I breathe in the scent of strawberries I know without a doubt that she is my daughter and I have finally found her. I am finally home.

--

When I wake up the air feels heavy and damp. There is no bright morning sunlight, just the continuous patter of rain on the roof. I wipe at my face, trying to get rid of the evidence of my bad dreams. When I finally sit up, I see Adam is leaning up against the trunk of the tree looking out into the forest. He looks relaxed with his arm resting on his bent knee, his shoulder pulling the sleeve of his T-shirt up and revealing a small Marine Corps tattoo on his upper arm.

"Look what I found." He smiles and waves his arm at the floor beside him. Lying on the floor is a leather bag, some canned food, a bag of crackers, plates, and two cups.

"Where did you find that?" He points to the cupboard on the far wall. "Are you sure you should take this stuff? It's kind of like stealing." I scan the wall and see what I couldn't in last night's darkness; it's decorated with a variety of weapons-bows, arrows, and spears–all attached to the wall. This can't belong to a child; it looks like the fanciest tree stand I've ever seen.

"I think whoever this stuff belongs to has bigger problems right now." Adam replies. My stomach growls loudly. "Sounds like you're hungry too."

"Ok," I resign, "let's eat."

Adam uses the army knife from his boot to open the cans. There's corn and peaches in the cans, and the crackers look stale. He divides up the food on the plates and I set the cups on the windowsills to catch rain water. I can see a thick layer of muddy water covering the forest floor. Since there's only one chair, we sit on the floor across from each other. The sleepless, dream filled night has left me feeling tired and miserable.

Adam watches the rain for a minute. "I think we're going to have to wait out the rain," he says between mouthfuls of food.

I was afraid of this happening today. We are so close to home. I'm sure he can see the disappointment on my face. I stand up and look out the rough wooden framed window. The forest floor remains flooded with at least an inch of water. A large frog croaks from the base of a nearby tree. My stomach sinks as I see dozens of frogs swimming and hopping along the flooded forest floor.

"I guess you're right. We can't walk in this." I walk back to where I was sitting and throw myself on the floor, disappointed.

"Have you always lived in Phoenix?" Adam asks.

I nod my head yes and give him a shortened version of my life. I tell him about Sam and how our parents died. I ask him why he became a Marine. He explains to me he wanted to protect people, keep them safe. We talk about our lives between the long stretches of silence where we turn to watch the rain and listen to the thunder. We are out of food and by evening and both of our stomachs are audibly growling.

I pull out the newspaper from the hotel and skim through it, trying to pass the time. The last page is filled with election editorials. People writing in, discussing the Reformation Party. Some think it's just what this country needs. Others are afraid that they are going to turn the country into a dictatorship. I give up on the paper, too consumed with getting home to absorb any of it. I hold it out, offering it to Adam. He takes the paper and reads it intently.

The rain has stopped, but when I look out the windows the forest floor is still flooded.

"Morning then?" Adam asks me. I know it's not really a question or a suggestion, we can't walk through all that water.

"I guess."

I stand and pace the large tree house, looking out all the windows. As I near the window on the far wall near the single bunk, I notice a herd of deer walking through the forest. Adam must notice too because I hear him walk slowly to the window next to me.

"Can you believe they are out in this weather?" I ask turning my head to look at him. "Adam, what are you doing?" I whisper harshly.

He's standing at the window with the bow and arrow from the wall, prepped and ready to shoot. "I'm hungry," he responds quietly, his body is rigid, steady, "and so are you."

"I'm not going to eat a whole deer. Stop! We will have all the food we can eat tomorrow. We're almost home." He's ignoring me, focusing, looking for the right moment to release the arrow and kill one of the deer quickly. "Adam!" I start to raise my voice. "Stop, please. You can't kill them." He continues to ignore me, the muscle in his jaw tense. I raise my voice, enough to scare the deer off. "Adam, stop!" There's the quick thud of hoof beats across the wet ground. I watch the deer run off, out of range of Adam's bow.

"Did you seriously just sabotage my kill? We could have gorged for dinner and had food for tomorrow while we travel." His voice is stern and angry as he walks back to the hooks on the wall and replaces the bow and arrow.

"We didn't need a whole deer. We'll have food in the morning."

"I hope you're happy that you got to save Bambi. I could have eaten half that animal myself." He kicks over the small chair by the wall, pouting, before he reaches down and rights the chair.

"Sorry, I didn't mean to ruin your life over one little deer." He doesn't respond. I reach into my bag, remembering the field guide I brought to work the other night. "Here, I have this guide on edible plants." I hold the book out to him.

"No thanks," he tells me as he walks to the other side of the tree trunk where I can't see him.

I decide to go to bed early. I cover myself with the blanket, and push my bag under my head. I pull out Lina's owl and hold it to my chest. I close my eyes, feigning sleep. It's not long before I hear Adam lay down next to me. And for the second night in a row, I sleep next to a man who is not my husband.

--

Morning comes early, this time with sunlight and chirping songbirds. I'm not sure if Adam was already awake, but he sits up just as I do. I walk to the window and see that the ground is mostly dry. I pack quickly, eager to leave. We barely speak, both of us eager to get home.

Just before we head down the ladder to leave I stop. "Oh, wait, I have an idea." I reach into my bag and pull out the field guide on edible plants then walk over to the empty cupboard; I leave it on the bare shelf. Now I feel a little less guilty for using the tree house stock.

We leave the tree fort behind. We have no food or water. Adam must still be mad over the deer because he makes no effort to start a conversation with me. So we walk in silence until I can hear the fast rush of the river nearby. We must be near the entrance to town.

"I'm going to check the road," Adam tells me.

I follow him to the tree line, knowing instantly where we are once the shrubbery is out of the way. We are at the point where the river runs parallel to the road and follows it into town, about a mile from the main entrance to Phoenix.

Adam creeps through the tall grass on his stomach. Right before he gets to the road he stops and looks around. I can see the furrowed wrinkle in his brow as he turns and waves me to come out to him. I try to mimic his crawl and do a wretched job at it. I'm sure I look like a fish out of water, flopping feverishly on a riverbank. When I reach him he says nothing about my pathetic stomach crawl, instead he points towards the town. I follow the direction of his hand with my gaze.

"Oh crap," I utter.

A few hundred yards in front of us there is a large wall made of stone. It's not complete but it extends past each side of the road. We can see people working near the edges of the wall. We crawl back to the cover of the forest. We decide to go around the main entrance, staying within the forest and keeping a safe distance from where the people are working. I must be making too much noise since Adam hushes me more than once as we walk.

The people on the main road are carrying supplies or pushing wheelbarrows filled with bricks. All of them seem to be wearing the same clothes: dark red tops and pants. It's strange, there's no socializing, there are no groupings of people standing around and talking. Instead they're all working methodically as if they are driven by some unknown desire to build the cement wall.

We stay within the tree line. Sprinting through open fields each time there is a break in the forest. We pass behind the county jail. Next is the local cemetery, the largest in the area. There are some large old trees that might provide us with cover, but I am afraid it's not enough and we might get caught being out in the open. I argue with Adam to take a different way in, but he's adamant about crossing through the cemetery. Once we get past the jail we wait in the tree line. Throughout this leg of the trip Adam's whole demeanor has changed; the muscles in his neck are now tight and his jaw clenched.

"What's wrong?"I whisper to him.

"There is something I have to do." He pulls a yellow piece of paper from his pocket and starts walking towards the middle of the cemetery.

"Adam!" I yell to him.

He doesn't stop or turn around or explain, he just keeps walking. I follow him, slowly at first, looking around the graveyard to make sure no one there to notice us. It's late morning now with the sun high in the sky and we're out in the open-deer in the meadow, easy targets.

He heads for the large mausoleum then stops to look at the note in his hand. I try to keep up with him but he is too tall, his stride too long for my short legs. As I get closer to him he turns to the left, walking swiftly and looking around. Finally he stops. I walk up next to him, my feet sinking slightly into the soft ground.

"Adam, what are you…" I follow his gaze.

In front of us are three gravestones. The first two are simply arched smooth gray stone, the third is larger and more elaborate with three angels perched on top. The dirt in front of them is disturbed, the grass seeds still visible. I read the names:

Jim Waters
Margaret Waters
Samantha Waters

The dates of death are from two months ago, all on the same day.

"Oh no," I start, but when I turn to Adam his head is already in his hands, and he is sinking down to the ground on his knees. This is his family. I'm not sure what to say or do. I simply lay my hand on his shoulder, squeezing lightly. "I'm so sorry," I whisper to him before I walk away to sit cross-legged under one of the large oak trees just a few feet from him.

This whole time I've been so selfish, only worrying about my family. I never thought of Adam's family. He never once indicated that they were dead. He spoke of them as though they were all still alive and well, waiting for his proud return from Germany.

I wait patiently under the oak tree, glad that no one has noticed us. In the distance I can see the people working on the wall, milling about like ants. Somehow each of them knows their task. I observe a few guards walking on the other side of the wall watching the road from the south, as though they might be expecting someone. They're wearing dark gray uniforms and carrying long guns on their shoulders. They don't look like police, or army, or any enforcement agency I've ever seen.

As I sit here, I conclude that there was definitely no nuclear meltdown or none of these people would be working so hard. They would be suffering from radiation poisoning, lying in their homes with blood pouring out of their noses and ears, vomiting, and screaming when clumps of their hair fell out on their pillows. Something else is going on here.

I shift my gaze back towards Adam. His face is no longer buried in his hands; he takes a few deep breaths before rising and wiping at his eyes. He turns and walks towards me, the knees of his pants stained dark brown from the freshly disturbed graveyard soil.

"I'm sorry, I didn't know," I start.

"I didn't tell you. I didn't want it to be true. I just had to see them one last time so I could move on I guess." He pauses for a moment before he looks into my eyes, fiercely determined. "Let's get you back to your family."

I tell him where I live and oddly enough his parents' house is a few blocks from mine. We stay off the main road, walking behind the graveyard. Now there is a large embankment that helps conceal us from the road. There's more forest and a few hundred feet of open tall grass before we scale a large hill. We look at each other when we hear the low dense whistle of a train again. When we reach the top of the hill I can see the town, the roofs of the houses, and the tree lined streets where my house is.

"Where is everyone?" Adam asks.

Slowly, we venture onto Grenadier Street. Here the oak trees are tall and old; their canopies hang over the street creating a tunnel of light green.

"There are no cars," I whisper to Adam.

We walk another block. Then I can see it. The small front porch lined with hibiscus bushes, their flower buds ready to burst with bright pinks and purples signaling the start of summer. There's the green front door and roof.

I start running, my bag smacking my back in a steady drum. I'm holding my breath with excitement. For four long days, this is what I have been waiting for; to be home, to see my family again, to hug and kiss Ian, to squeeze my little Lina in my arms and breathe in the strawberry scent of her hair. Tears start forming in the corners of my eyes, my heart thumps heavily with anticipation. I run up onto the porch and reach for the front door. Twisting the handle, I find it's unlocked. I push the door a little too hard and hear it hit the wall, cracking the drywall.

"Ian? Lina?" I shout. I look around the living room and the kitchen. I run up the stairs and search the bedrooms. Empty. It's all empty. I walk back through the living room into the kitchen; Adam walks in the front door, inspecting the damage to the wall behind it.

Standing there I notice Stevie, lying on her dog bed. She barely moves when I call her name, just opening her eyes and peering at me sadly. I walk to her, calling her name, but she doesn't get up. When I pet her I can feel her bones protruding from underneath her skin. Her muzzle, which is usually dripping with drool, is dry. I pet her and pull up her top lip noticing that her gums are pale and dry. Her food and water bowls are sitting next to her dog bed, empty.

"Oh, Stevie." I pick up her bowls and carry them to the sink. *Please work, please work...* When I turn on the cold water it sputters for a moment before the water rushes out. I fill up Stevie's water bowl then open the cupboard under the sink and get her dog food. I pour her bowl full, almost overflowing before I set both bowls next to her. Slowly she reaches over and drinks greedily from the water bowl.

"Andie, you need to see this." Adam startles me. He's standing at the island counter with a piece of paper in his hand.

"What is it?" I walk towards him as he hands me a piece of paper.

Andie,
If you are home wait for us. Don't worry. We will be there soon.
~Ian

I recognize Ian's neat handwriting and signature. But he didn't date the note. I can only hope that he wrote it recently.

"I think I'm going to get cleaned up before they get home," I say, turning to Adam.

He's watching Stevie drink from her dog bowl. "Ok. I want to go check out my parents' house." He tells me.

"I'll go with you then." I tell him, almost afraid to be here alone.

"No, stay here, It's only two blocks away. I'll be right back. I promise." I look into his light blue eyes, it seems like he is telling me the truth. I just don't want to admit that I have no desire to be alone right now.

"Fine," I respond curtly. "I'm locking the doors, though."

"Good. I'll knock three times when I get back."

Then Adam is walking out of my front door and I'm locking the deadbolt into place. The house is empty and eerie. I try to get Stevie to go upstairs with me so I don't have to be alone, but she's too weak from what appears to be days without food or water.

Finally I give up and head up the stairs. I shower, quicker than I would like to. The hot steam feels nice as it strips the dried sweat and dirt off of me. I wrap myself in a towel and head to the bedroom. All of my familiar things are here; my clothes, hairbrush, toothbrush, but it feels strange in the absence of Ian and Lina.

I brush my teeth and look in my closet. It's still quite warm so I settle on a pair of dark brown pants, a white layered top and leather sandals. When I'm done my stomach grumbles. I realize it's early afternoon and the last time I ate was yesterday morning in the tree house. As I walk down the stairs I hear three faint knocks on the heavy wooden front door. I open it slowly and see Adam looking around the side of the porch, into the back yard. I open the door wide to let him in, feeling a little safer now that he's returned.

He's changed from his muddy clothes into a fresh pair of jeans, a blue checkered button down shirt and light green jacket, with the sleeves rolled up to his elbows. He's shaved the three day stubble off and the face of a very attractive man is starting to appear from underneath the bruises. He smells like sandalwood, leather and a hint of spice. And if I didn't know better I'd say he'd stepped right out of the pages of a fashion magazine. "You clean up nice," I tell him. He smiles a little. It's obvious this revelation is not new to him.

"I was just about to make something to eat. Are you hungry?" He nods and we head to the kitchen.

I want to ask about his parents' house but the image of him crouched at the gravestones of his family is forged in my mind. I think he has experienced enough grief for one day.

I open the refrigerator, knowing that when I left a few days ago it was packed with vegetables, milk, yogurt, condiments, and leftover meals. Now as the door swings to my side and the hum of the condenser kicks on, all I see is emptiness. I close the fridge and open the cupboards, starting with the pantry, then the bread drawer, but it's all empty.

I turn to Adam.

"It's the same way at my house. All the cupboards were empty. All except for one." He points to the last cupboard which I haven't checked yet. It's where we keep the plates and glasses; there wouldn't be any food in there. I open the cupboard. Instead of shelves packed with dishes there are rows of neatly packed cans with simple white labels on them: Breakfast, Lunch and Dinner. I reach for one of the cans labeled "Lunch."

"Were these at your parents' house also?" I ask Adam, inspecting a can in my hand.

"Yes. But I didn't open them."

The can has a tab to pull up on. I pull it open. Inside is a brown gelled slab of mystery sludge. The substance is odorless. I'm not sure what it is, but I know that I can't eat it. Still, I pull a fork out of the cupboard and poke at it. Stevie whines from her dog bed. When I look up, I see she's watching us. Adam has walked closer to me to observe the canned substance. I hand the can to him. "I can't eat that. I'm starving right now. But I can't eat whatever that is." I point to the can and crinkle my nose. Then I remember the garden. I walk out the back door that's off the kitchen. The garden bed is still there and the plants are still heavy with small baby fruit.

"Are you sure this is safe to eat?" Adam asks me as I start pulling the baby cucumbers off one of the vines.

I stand up and look around. There's a gray squirrel on top of the garage and in its front paws is a cucumber. "If the animals are alive and well after eating it, I'm sure we will be fine." I reach down and pluck more cucumbers off the vine in front of me. Adam walks over to help. He's found some small ripe tomatoes, a few tiny squash, and some strawberries. We bring the harvest inside and I wash everything off with water from the tap. The cucumbers are crisp, the strawberries tart and sweet. For a moment, it's the best meal I have ever eaten.

From the corner of the room Stevie starts to whine. She anxiously looks towards the front door. Adam and I stand up simultaneously walking towards the front window. What we see is a stark contrast to what we have experienced during the past few days together.

Where the roads and town was once empty and desolate, now a steady stream of people walk down the center of the street. Adam follows me out onto the front porch. None of them seem to notice us. Every few people that pass I start to recognize. Our neighbors from a few houses down, the old man that mows his lawn every Sunday, a girl I went to high school with. I want to wave and shout "hello" but none of them look our way. They look straight ahead, turning only to enter their homes. I look up the street to see the stream of people start to thin out. Then I see him. I wait for a minute, wanting to make sure it truly is him. But his hair is shorter, and his clothes are strange. But the instant I see his deep brown eyes I know it is him, *my Ian.*

"Ian! Ian!" I shout. Then I am running off the front porch and down our driveway. He's just a few yards ahead of me and I knock into a few people on the street as I rush to greet him. "Ian!" I shout again. I'm almost to him; he is walking towards me and when he is within an arm's reach I leap into the air and throw my arms around his neck. "Oh my God Ian, I was so afraid I'd never see you again." I squeeze him so tight my arms ache.

He sputters something through my kisses. My lips pressed so hard against his mouth that I can feel the straight row of teeth behind his front lip. At last his arms cross tight behind my back, carrying me. I can feel the tears streaming out of the corners of my eyes.

"I love you, Ian," I whisper between our kisses. "I was so scared I'd never see you again," I tell him as he carries me back to our house and up the front porch steps. I hear the door open then close behind us. He sets me down in the living room. I'm bursting with energy and joy, so happy to finally be home, to finally see him. "Ian what happened here?" I don't give him a chance to answer. I'm asking him more questions and talking about our journey home on foot. I barely notice the front door opening and Adam stepping inside the living room. I keep talking and talking, more than I have ever talked before. Then it hits me, *Lina*. "Ian? Where is Lina?" I ask. In my feverish rehashing of the past day's events I barely noticed Ian was just standing there in front of me. Not talking or interjecting or asking me questions like he normally would. "Ian!" I ask him again. "Where is Lina?" He stares at me blankly. I replay what just happened in my mind. There is complete silence in the living room except for the heavy ringing in my ears. This is not right. I look behind Ian to Adam. He's just standing there watching us.

"Ian! What's wrong with you?" I ask. "Why aren't you answering me?" Then I realize I'm yelling at him, repeating myself over and over again.

"They took her," he finally answers.

"What do you mean," I can barely choke the rest of the sentence out, "they took her? Who?"

"She's not here anymore. They took her. They told me to tell you she is safe." His response is robotic, monotone and sounds nothing like Ian. This is not the Ian I left a few days ago. This is not the Ian that would do anything to protect our little girl.

"Ian!" I'm screaming at him now. "Where is she? Where is Lina?"

"They took her-" he starts to repeat again, but I interrupt him.

"No!" I yell at him. "What did you do? You let someone take her?" I fling myself across the room at Ian, and then I am hitting him, shaking him, pounding on his chest, trying to get him to wake up from whatever stupor he is in. "You are her father!" I choke out, frantic. I feel strong arms wrap around my stomach, picking me up, but I kick and scream and claw at Ian. "You were supposed to protect her! She's just a baby!" I want to beat the answers out of him. I want him to wake up from this nightmare. I want things to go back to the way they were, the three of us, happy and together. Adam is dragging me away and I can see red marks across Ian's face, on his neck. It doesn't stop me from kicking and screaming more. Adam grunts a few times and I'm sure it's because I have kicked him in my hysteria.

CHAPTER EIGHT

I can hear them talking, Adam and Ian, downstairs in the dining room. I sit at the top of the stairwell, barely able to make out what they're saying. The deepness of both of their voices is too low for me to hear from this far away. It doesn't help that I can't stop crying. I can't get over the fact that my little girl is missing. And Ian let it happen. I try to put the pieces together; the earthquake, the false reports of a nuclear meltdown, the fence and brick wall being built around the city, the strange way all the people seem to be acting, especially Ian. But I can't make sense of any of it. All I know is this person in my dining room is not my Ian.

It's not the strong man I married right out of high school. I know this. We went through college together, we've been married for six years, and we've struggled since Lina was born, but he's always promised that he would protect us. No, this is definitely not my Ian.

The one thing I know for certain is that someone took my daughter, and I'm not sure I can ever forgive Ian for not stopping them and protecting her.

Stevie is slowly walking up the stairs towards me. She must have regained enough energy to get out of her bed. She lies down next to me, nudging her muzzle under my arm. I can't stop the tears leaking out of my eyes. I lean my head against the wall and listen to their mumbling talk.

Sometime later, someone is carrying me. I don't have the strength to open my eyes and I don't much care. I feel the softness of a mattress beneath me, then the heaviness of someone lying next to me. At first I am afraid of whom it is, until I feel the rough tongue that licks my cheek, *Stevie*. A blanket is placed over us. It smells like detergent and lavender fabric softener. I know that we are in the empty guest room of the house. I keep my eyes closed, because I can't bear to look at this new reality that has taken over my life.

I dream of Lina. What she looked like as a newborn. How excited her face was every morning when she got up. Happy and brave and ready to experience more of this fascinating world I brought her into. I watch her grow to one, two, three, four, and five, bringing her to school, cooking, Christmas, Easter, remembering all of her milestones, her digging on the beach during vacation. I don't want to wake up. I want to spend every second I can with her because I know she will not be here with me when I open my eyes. I will not see her smiling face or her crooked baby toothed smile.

But I do wake up. Stevie is there to lick my cheek. I roll over and see a figure on the floor. My vision is blurry, and after a few moments I see that it is Adam sleeping on the floor near the bedroom door. I stand up and tiptoe silently out of the room heading to the bathroom. Flicking on the light I stare at myself in the mirror. I have never known what it is like to feel numbness and stabbing, gut wrenching pain at the same time. I lean in close to the mirror. The reflection is still me, but my eyes are bloodshot and red rimmed. My hair is in wild disarray around my head. There is a crusted white trail of old tears dried by my left ear.

"Clean yourself up." I whisper to myself in the mirror. I repeat the steps to myself: *Get a washcloth, run the water, wash your face, brush your teeth, wash your hands.* After a few minutes I look a little better, but the terrible feeling inside my heart still lingers. I leave yesterday's clothes on.

When I open the bathroom door, Adam and Stevie are standing in the hallway, both leaning against the wall. I say nothing to them. Instead I turn and head downstairs to the kitchen. I turn the coffee pot on, then off, remembering that there is nothing here except canned mystery sludge. I walk out the back door and sit on the back porch swing. Stevie and Adam follow me without a sound. The swing squeaks a little as I rock it. Stevie walks off the porch to check the corners of the yard. She does her doggie business and returns to my side. I stare off at the early morning clouds; I watch the birds flitting in the tall oak trees. From the corner of my eye I see that Adam is at the garden bed, picking something. The back door closes and opens again a few moments later. Adam sets a bowl of baby cucumbers and strawberries in my lap.

Eat, I tell myself.

Finally Adam breaks the silence. "I talked with Ian last night, for a long time." I don't respond. I keep watching the birds high in the trees. Adam must know I'm listening because he continues. "He's not right. Eventually he started to talk about what happened, and he said that they would find us," he pauses for a moment. "Then he ate that canned food, devoured it like it was a steak dinner. Afterwards he went back to his flat affect and minimal words act. I don't know what to think of it. But I definitely wouldn't eat whatever is in those cans. Then he just got up and went to bed. And this morning he just got ready and left like nothing happened, like we weren't even here. I've never seen anything like it before."

I'm remembering how Ian would kiss me goodbye early each morning while I slept. I'm using all the energy I have left not to burst into tears again. I stare at the songbirds, I eat my breakfast. My gaze shifts to a neighbor's garage and that's when I see two ravens standing on the roof. They're watching us, cocking their heads to the side, blinking their beady black eyes.

--

We remain on the porch until afternoon. This is the first day that we haven't heard the train whistle or helicopters in the sky. We sit, mourning the family members that we've recently lost. Stevie perks up her ears and starts whining, looking at the door. Adam and I both get up and walk inside. There is a heavy knocking on the front door, it crescendos over a few seconds, turning into a full blown pounding.

"Don't answer it," I tell Adam, reaching out to stop him, but it's too late. His hand is already on the doorknob, turning it. He stops for an instant to look at me and someone shoves the door open from the outside, hard, knocking Adam back onto the floor. He lands with a loud thud on his side, shaking the pictures on the wall. Suddenly, there are a handful of men in my living room. They're all dressed in dark gray uniforms, pistols strapped to their hips. The last to come through is a large dark man with a silver pin on his lapel in the shape of some kind of a bird. He looks straight at me.

"Andie Somers." It is not a question. He knows who I am. "You're coming with us." His voice is deep, slow and southern.

I've heard his voice before, in the basement of the hospital.

A few men head towards Adam and some start walking towards me. Panic and fear and the uncontrollable urge to run consumes me. Stevie starts barking, a vicious bark, which I have never heard her utter before.

"Control the mutt or we will put it down for you," the large man with the bird pin commands as he reaches for the pistol at his hip.

"St... Stop," I stutter out. "Stevie, go lay down." She looks at me and then back at the men, whining. She listens, leaving the room. As I watch her lay down on her dog bed I feel the grasp of hands around both of my upper arms.

I'm not sure if these men intended for me to walk, but I am mostly dragged to the waiting black SUVs in front of my house. They drag me towards the first SUV. I turn to see the other group of men leading Adam towards another SUV.

"Wait, where are you taking him? Stop!" I start to struggle against the hands wrapped around my arms, but the door to the SUV is open and they are shoving me inside. I land on my side and kick the window as they close the door. There's a caged partition separating the front seats from the back. Two of the men get in the front. I turn to see the SUV behind us where Adam is, and the large dark man with the pin is getting into the passenger side. "What are you doing with us?" I ask the men in the front. Neither of them answers.

The streets are empty once again as they drive me through town. We pass the park where I would bring Lina after school. No children play there today. But there is one man near the swings, dressed in dark red with a hat, rummaging through a toolbox. Similar to the people we saw working on the great wall at the outskirts of the city.

We are the only vehicles on the road. The first running vehicles I've seen in days. They drive us down Main Street, across the larger of the two bridges which pass over the river, dividing the city. I see more people in red uniforms, working on the bridge, taking down street signs, pulling weeds from the cracks in the sidewalks. They drive to the west side of town, to the edge, almost outside of the town limits. Then they turn onto the long road leading to the State University that sits on the lake shore. I haven't been here in years, not since I graduated. Everything looks familiar still, but there are two new buildings, and some of the older ones have been painted. The driver pulls up to the main entrance of Culkin Hall which is the main campus building and the tallest. It houses the offices of the president and vice president, the financial aid offices and admission offices of the university. I turn around and look out the large cargo area window. The SUV that Adam was in is no longer there.

The door opens and hands reach in to pull me out. I try slapping at them, but one of the men grips me hard around my upper arm and jerks me from the vehicle. A pain in my shoulder shoots upwards toward my neck, and I am afraid he will dislocate it if I keep struggling so I stop and let them drag me inside the main doors. They take me to the elevator and push the button for the ninth floor, where the presidential offices are. I try to walk fast and keep up with the men at each of my shoulders. But I have to keep skipping steps. I can feel their hands already leaving bruises on my upper arms.

There are dull gray cubicles on each side of the large office, all empty, except the last row, where two men and two women sit at computers. They are engrossed in whatever they're doing, not bothering to look up as we pass. We enter a long office at the end of the hallway where there is a small conference table and some chairs. The men deposit me in an office chair and place Velcro straps around my arms. They leave me and I am alone for only an instant before the door opens again and an old man walks in. He's carrying a metal box, which he sets on the table next to me. Clicking open the clasps on the sides, he pulls out straps and wires, then feeds lined paper into the side of the box.

I have watched enough TV to know that this must be a lie detector machine. The old man looks at me, smiling kindly; he seems out of place with these people. He wraps the straps around my arms and chest. Working diligently, without talking, he sits across from me when he is done. I hear the hum of the machine as it's turned on, the soft clicks of buttons being pushed, the faint scrape of ink being etched across rough paper.

The door opens and more people enter the room, the large dark man with the bird pin. Behind him, two more people enter the room, a short man with wild orange hair and…

Adam.

He's wearing the same gray uniform as the men who took us from my house. And he too has a pistol on his hip. I glare at him, trying to get his attention, but he won't look at me. I feel betrayed, angered beyond belief. As the guard standing outside pulls the door closed, my heart thumps loudly in the silence of the large room.

"Ah, you must be Andromeda." The short man with orange hair walks towards me, holding his hand out to greet me. When I don't move my arms he looks down and see's that they are strapped to the chair. "Well this isn't very pleasant." He bends to undo the Velcro straps from my arms, leaving the detector leads in place. His hair is so bright it looks as though it has been dyed, and when he bends in front of me I can see the tight cork screw curls which give his hair the fluffed appearance. He releases my arms and holds his hand out to greet me again. He smells sweet and musky, it makes my stomach churn.

"Who are you?" I ask. I make no attempt to raise my hand and greet him.

"My name is Burton Crane. We will be spending a lot of time together. That is, if you participate. Now, please answer my question. I'm sure you know we need to set a baseline for the detector." He smiles. I watch him, furious. His skin is pale, dotted with red freckles. He's dressed nicely in a black suit, wearing an obnoxious bright yellow tie. Finally he drops his hand. "Are you Andromeda Somers?" He repeats.

"Yes." I respond through gritted teeth. I glare at Adam, and finally he looks at me. I'm not sure why I bothered to trust him in the first place. But I did, and look where it got me. The man with the orange hair runs through a deluge of questions. Stating where I live, where I work, who my parents were, how they died-he knows entirely too much about me.

"Are you married to Ian Somers?" he asks.

"Yes." I look at the floor trying to hide the pain of yesterday.

"You have a daughter, Catalina Somers?" I glare back at him. He must know where she is, and I have a feeling he is about to use her to get whatever information he wants out of me.

"Where is she? I want to see her now!"

"She's safe. Let's continue."

But I don't want to continue. I want to know where my daughter is. I want to see her. "I want to see her now!" I demand.

"In time, Andromeda," He continues. "You hold degrees in genetics and nursing?" I glare at him, squeezing my lips together, refusing to talk. "If you choose not to participate, Andromeda, I will have to place you in a holding cell. It's unfortunate really and I'm sure neither of us wants that. Now, answer the question."

"Yes."

"That's a strange combination don't you think?" He pauses. "You were one of two people to graduate from Phoenix University. You even secured a research job before you graduated in a genetic research lab. Why did you leave?" His demeanor is starting to change; he's playing some strange good cop, bad cop game. "Andromeda?"

These are exactly the type of questions I dislike, why I usually don't bother telling anyone about my other degree. "I left because I was tired of being managed by pompous bigots who didn't think a woman belonged in the lab." I remember their snide remarks, their leering gazes, their constant arguments over my findings and reports. It still makes my blood boil.

"Did you know that they were never able to fill your position after you left?" he asks, raising his eyebrow.

I shrug my shoulders. "I don't see why they wouldn't. Anyone could have done that job."

"Do you know that the lab lost all their funding not long after you left?"

That was a surprise. I shake my head no.

"You are not as easily replaced as you may think. That lab was never able to find another person who could do what you did. You taught yourself how to manage genetic array programs created by the government, you taught yourself programming, and you had your own system that no one has been able to duplicate." He starts walking towards me, pushing a chair. "And somehow your theories, the genetic pathways you discovered and theorized about, they all happened to be correct. We've used your data for years now since you left the lab to become a nurse, of all things." He sits right in front of me, our knees almost touching. "We need your help, Andromeda." He leans forwards looking closely into my face, his own pale green eyes boring into mine.

"Why should I help you?" I ask him. "You've ruined my family. You've taken my child from me, my husband. You've done something terrible to this town."

"My Dear," he reaches forward placing his cold hands on my arms. I lean back, anticipating some sort of pain, but he just pulls the detector leads off me. "Walk with me for a moment." He holds onto the arm of the chair, spinning it around, waiting for me to stand. I notice he's short, only three or four inches taller than I am. I follow him towards the large window, spanning the width of the room and at this height; almost the whole northern county can be seen.

"Take a look, Andromeda."

My gaze follows to where his open hand points. My eyes follow the lakeshore, towards the nuclear power plants. There's no steam coming from the three cooling towers, indicating that the nuclear reactors have, in fact, been shut down. I continue to search the nearby land until I see what he is indicating. Further to the north, not far from the lake, is a large charred circle of land where a small crater lies deep in the ground. The trees are gone-disintegrated-and radiating around the blackened area are downed trees, pushing out in all directions. The forest trees lie on the ground for miles, then gradually resume their normal stature.

"What happened?" I whisper.

"That my dear, is the point of impact of the non-nuclear electromagnetic pulse. Or what the media is referring to as the epicenter of the earthquake."

I know he can see the disbelief on my face, my mouth gaping open. His face wears a smug smile. Suddenly, it all makes sense; the power outages, how none of the electrical equipment would work, the stalled vehicles on the road. The electromagnetic pulse knocked them all out.

"But the newspaper said there was a meltdown. How did you prevent that, or didn't you?" I ask him.

"Ha!" He claps his hands together, excitedly, "I knew you would be curious. These nuclear reactors have much more protection built around them, better than say, the reactors in Japan. And the blast wasn't strong enough to damage them."

I stare, trying to process the information he has just given me. "Who is responsible for this? Terrorists?"

He smiles at me. "Oh, Andromeda, this situation is a far cry from terrorism. It is indeed something greater, better even." He is much too excited talking about this, reminding me of a wound up school girl, his face overly animated.

"What are you talking about?"

"I would like to introduce you to a new society, a better society, an improved society. No longer will there be poverty, disease, depression, or indolence. Welcome to: *The Phoenix District.*" He tells me, proudly waving his arm out, spanning the window.

"What...?" I whisper.

This launches Crane into a lecture of modern society's downfall, the corrupt government, corrupt healthcare system, the lack of jobs, and downfall of a corrupt stock market. The scary part is, it's all true, every word of it, every person in the U.S. has been suffering from the worst recession since the Great Depression. "The leaders of this world are tired of watching this country spin out of control. It's embarrassing really. More people are on public assistance than those who work. The population is at unrest. It's blatantly evident; there have been uprisings, certain political groups have already started movements to overthrow the government. It's time to move on Andromeda, it's time for a better society. We can't let things stay the way they are or it's only going to get worse."

I can barely believe what he is telling me, that this could actually happen where I live. "But this is the United States of America. What about the army, the government? You will never get away with this." I argue with him.

"For someone so intelligent, you are certainly quite naïve. Your government is fully aware of this. Who do you think authorized it? Helped us sneak a bomb into the US territories? That EMP should have been blasted out of the sky thousands of miles away before it ever reached this area. Who do you think is keeping the populace away from here? Blocking travel? Feeding stories to the media? I know you've seen the papers, the barricades." He gives me a moment to collect my thoughts before he continues. "After your president saw our results from the trial in Japan, he was more than impressed and ready to get the ball rolling here in the U.S."

Japan? What happened in Japan? Then I remember. There was a tsunami that hit the shoreline of Japan, causing a meltdown to their two nuclear reactors. The last news report I saw the area was still off limits, a chain link fence equipped with barbed wire had been erected and patrolled by guards, guards in gray uniforms.

"But the people? What about all the people here? What have you done to them? To my husband? My daughter?" I'm trying to control the rising panic in my voice.

"Ah, this is where you come in, my dear. Currently, they are receiving a medication via their rations." I remember the canned food in my cupboard. "To keep them calm, subdued, happy and most of all cooperative."

"What kind of medication?"

"I really do enjoy these questions, you are so inquisitive. It's a mixture of hormones, oxytocin and testosterone inhibitors. I'm sure you know that the oxytocin works to soothe the brain, overriding the amygdala, making it much less responsive to anger and fear. It makes them cooperative, subdued, malleable." I can barely believe what I'm hearing. This man plans to take over the town and control everyone living here with these hormones. It sounds absolutely absurd. "But we need to do more," he continues. "We need a full genetic analysis of the residents, selective breeding programs need to be initiated to prevent inbreeding and bring out certain traits in people, to ensure cooperation, so we can eliminate the medications." He turns to me, eyebrows raised, making sure I'm taking all of this in.

I have to try and stop this. "You can't do this. You're talking about dissecting the human race, producing sub-breeds. We are not dogs!"

"How odd that you should bring up dogs, so you do realize that humans have been selectively breeding hundreds of species for hundreds of years. Dogs, cats, farm animals, even rats; each time getting closer to the perfect breed, the perfect species. This has been a long time coming; it's amazing it hasn't happened sooner."

"But this is eugenics. It's unethical, you would be no better than Hitler!" I try to control the panic in my voice. I look around the room, hoping for someone to speak up, to comment, but the room is silent, everyone listening to our conversation.

"Would you like to talk about ethics, Andromeda? How about the ethical treatment of patients, the ethical vow you took when you became a nurse. How about we discuss patient abandonment?" I stare at him with horror on my face. "Obviously you have no problem breaking the rules of ethics when it comes to your family."

Then, I hear from outside the door, the sound of a young child talking.

Lina!

Crane lightens his face. "Did you know that you have produced quite a gifted child?"

"What are you talking about? What did you do to her?" I can hear her talking outside the door. I start walking towards it but he reaches out, grabbing my wrist, stopping me.

"We did nothing to her, just a few tests. Did the school ever tell you her IQ results?" I shake my head no. "She scored very high. Genius level, actually. Usually, a child with her scores is also afflicted with social disorders and deficits. They're medicated for acting out, for not being able to focus, or not being able to interact with other people. But somehow, not your child. I'm not sure how you did it. But your child is very important to us, as are you."

Her school never said a thing to us about IQ testing. She has always just been a normal five year old; playing soccer, dressing up like a princess. Nothing has ever alerted us to be concerned about her development. I can hear her outside the door, chattering with someone.

"Is my mommy in there?" I hear her ask. Someone speaks to her in a low voice.

He pauses, watching me watch the door. "Do I have your cooperation?" He asks.

"I want her back!"

"Yes, I know. If you agree, we will discuss your conditions of work and her schooling and training." His orange hair looks like a glowing halo with the setting sun over the lake, and I know I am about to make a deal with the devil.

"What about Ian?"

"Sadly, Andromeda, we can't risk many people being off the medication right now. We can't risk rebellion at this tender moment in the District's organization. And it is my understanding that your reunion with Ian did not go very well." My face flushes with embarrassment. The only people that knew about my hysteria were Ian and Adam.

"What are you going to do with him?"

"Unfortunately for you, Andromeda, you do not get a choice in the matter; you get to keep your daughter. Ian is no longer of your concern." He smiles smugly at me.

"So you're taking him from me and I'm supposed to be fine with that because you're letting me have Catalina back?"

"Don't worry, he won't remember, and I'm sure in time you will move on." He pauses, giving me only a short time to think, to decide between my daughter and my husband. He gives me just a few seconds to decide who I want to save. "Would you like to see your daughter now?"

My heart starts pounding again. She is just a child. She can't take care of herself. In less than five minutes I make the hardest decision of my life. "Yes, give her to me."

"Then I need to hear that we are in agreement." He responds, smiling at me, tapping his fingertips together.

"Fine. I agree," I respond through clenched teeth.

"Excellent." He claps his hands together in excitement. "Let the child in," he waves to Adam.

I hold my breath.

CHAPTER NINE

"Mommy?" Lina asks as the door opens. "Mommy, there you are. I've been looking all over for you!" She giggles and runs to me. I scoop her up in my arms, squeezing her tight to my chest. I can barely talk through the tears as I set her down and look her over.

"Are you okay baby? Did anyone hurt you?" She's wearing her favorite pink dress and pink sandals. "Are you hungry? Did they feed you?"

"Yes mommy. They even had my favorite. Mac and cheese, it was SO yummy!"

Oh no, the food, the medication. I look to Crane who is watching us.

"Don't worry, she didn't get the medication." He answers without me asking.

I hug Lina again, burying my face in her hair, the scent of strawberries now gone. She giggles. "Mom you're squishing me."

"I'm just so happy to see you again," I tell her.

And now, for the rest of my life, I know I will forever be judged as the wife who didn't save her husband.

--

Crane provides a few details of our agreement before nightfall. I am to begin work in approximately three days while a lab is set up. We are assigned to student housing, and since I can't go back to the home I shared with Ian, guards are sent to pack up the house and bring our things: clothes, toys, pictures and books. I request our dog,

Stevie, be allowed to live with us and I am surprised when Crane agrees without argument.

A guard brings us to the local grocery store where we shop for food and supplies. After seeing the emptiness of my cupboards at home I'm amazed to find the grocery store is fully stocked. There are fresh fruits, vegetables, milk, and cereal. I stock up on our normal foods, staying away from anything canned. I grab a large bag of dog food for Stevie and new dog bowls. I decide to splurge and get two bags of coffee and filters. We see no one else at the store. It feels odd bagging up everything and walking out without paying.

As the guard drives we pass a sign pointing to the student housing. There are three rows of townhouses facing the lake, each having five units. We pull up to the middle townhouse. The guard gets out and opens the door for me. I turn to Lina and find that she has fallen asleep. I pull her into my arms and carry her towards the house. The guard retrieves the bags of groceries and proceeds to open the garage door. Stevie bounds out, running to us and licking my hand. I notice in the middle of the large garage is a pile of boxes, our belongings from home. We're led up a set of steep stairs, which brings us into an open living area. There is a large kitchen, dining space, a living room, and a deck facing the lake. All of it fully furnished. The guard sets the bags on the counter then turns to us.

"Mr. Crane requests a list of lab supplies tomorrow evening. Someone will be by to pick it up." He nods, then turns stiffly and leaves.

I lay Lina down on the couch and check all the locks on the doors and windows. I was not given a key, so I can only assume that the absence of crime is also a new objective of the Phoenix District. I search the boxes in the garage for Lina's bedspread. I find it in the second box and bring it upstairs to cover her with. She sleeps soundly. Peacefully. Like nothing in this world has ever changed. I kiss her forehead then return to the kitchen to start unpacking the groceries. I watch Stevie as she sniffs all the corners of the townhouse, inspecting. Finally she settles on the floor of the kitchen, lying down to watch me put things away. I can't figure out how this man, Crane, thinks this will work. But I have Lina back, and I will do whatever I must to keep her safe.

Stevie's ears perk up, and she walks to the front door. There are three faint knocks. I hesitate for a moment, then walk over and open it.

Standing on the front porch is Adam.

"What do you want?" I ask him. Stevie pushes past me and licks Adam's hand.

"I wanted to explain." He raises his eyebrows, hopeful.

He's no longer wearing the gray uniform. Instead he has changed into jeans and a white T-shirt. His bruises are mostly healed, leaving him looking more handsome than yesterday.

"I don't think I want to talk to you right now." I start to close the door, but he steps in, placing his foot in front of the door, stopping me.

"Andie, you don't understand. I had to-" he starts.

"You had to what Adam? Betray me? You were the only person I had left to trust here!" I speak angrily through gritted teeth, trying not to wake Lina. "It took you three minutes to jump into bed with this new Phoenix District. What did they have on you? What did they hold against you Adam? Because this entire time they've had my daughter and they took my husband."

"Andie, I have no one left. You know that." I do know that he has no one left. I saw it in the graveyard on our way into town. His family is dead, all of them. "I just need you to trust me," he pleads.

"I barely know you and whatever little bit of trust I had in you…" I shake my head. He takes his foot away from the door. "I don't know when I will be able to do that again, Adam." I think I may actually see disappointment in his eyes. But that doesn't stop me from closing the door in his face.

I lean my forehead against the door and take a deep breath. I'm sure Crane would want him as part of the security team. He's a soldier-a Marine-highly trained and skilled. I'm sure he'll move up the ranks quickly. But I can't worry about Adam right now. I have to figure out how I am going to get through this and keep Lina safe. I grab a notebook and pen and sit on the end of the couch where Lina sleeps. I start making a list of supplies for the lab. Computers, programs, backup drives, and I add some basic office supplies. I don't intend to sleep, but somewhere in my list making I drift off and dream of Ian.

It is our wedding day. I'm dressed in my wedding gown, nervous and giddy. I hear the wedding march start and head down the aisle. I can see Ian, smiling proudly. He looks so handsome in his black tuxedo. His hair is longer, but still its natural blonde. We are young-I was nineteen and he was twenty. As I get closer to him the butterflies in my stomach get stronger. Standing in front of him we listen to the pastor, then repeat our vows. I lean in to kiss Ian. But his lips never touch mine. I open my eyes and he's standing in front of me. But he's different now. His eyes are pale brown, not their usual dark brown. His smile gone, replaced with a slack face. He looks at me strangely, like he doesn't know who I am. Then without a word, he turns and walks down the aisle away from me without saying a thing. Instantly I'm crying, weeping, and my heart is broken. Our family and friends in the crowd get up and leave as I turn my back to them. The pain of him leaving me hurts so much that I fall to the ground on my knees, wrinkling the white wedding dress. I feel a hand on my shoulder. When I look up there is an old lady with red hair standing at my side. "Some things are not meant to be." She tells me in her old, crackled voice. Then she disappears, leaving smoky wisps of air where she once stood. A black feather flutters out of the smoke, brushing across my cheek, before dropping to the ground.

--

I wake up slowly. There is a heavy pain in my chest and a wet tear drops into my ear. I wipe at my face and sit up. Lina is still sleeping soundly next to me and Stevie has curled up on the floor at my feet. I miss Ian terribly and I want him back. But Crane has made his intentions known, I can only have Lina. I watch her sleep, wondering to myself how long will it take for the pain of losing Ian to go away. I know that it would devastate him if he knew Lina and I were alive and well, forced to move on without him. All I can hope now is that he won't remember any of this. It seems the medication they are giving him will probably do just that.

I work on the lab supply list and when the sun begins to rise I get up and I make a full pot of coffee, savoring the sharp scent. I put down the food and water bowl for Stevie. After she eats she goes to the sliding door in the living room and whines. I open the door and follow her out. She bounds off the back deck, inspecting the new yard.

"Mommy?" I hear Lina wake up. She walks out onto the deck and stands next to me. "Wow mom, this is amazing!" She is looking out at the lake which is a few hundred yards from the deck we are standing on.

"Yes, honey, it's very nice. Let's get you something to eat."

I call Stevie back to us and we head inside. As I'm opening the sliding glass door I see someone stepping out onto their deck, a few houses down. I don't turn my head to stare but I pause for a moment looking out of the corner of my eye, and I'm quite sure that it is Adam.

We settle on cereal for breakfast and sit down at the dining room table, which seems empty with just the two of us.

"Mommy, what happened to Daddy?" Lina asks.

I knew she would ask, but I was hoping to avoid why Ian was not with us. "Lina, Daddy is very sick and he can't be with us right now," I pause, trying to select the best words. I don't want her to know that I chose her over her father. That it's my fault it's just us now. This is a guilt she should never have to live with.

"Yeah Mommy, he was acting really weird after the earthquake." She swirls the cereal around in her bowl. "Then these people brought food to the house for us. It smelled gross, so I hid it in my napkin. But daddy ate it. And then he wouldn't listen to me anymore..." I listen to her jabber on and on.

She tells me everything, in only the way a five year old can, about how she ate Easter candy that was hidden in her room instead of the canned food. How her father left the house after the earthquake, leaving her home alone with just the dog. Later that day a lady in black came home with Ian and took Lina from the house, bringing her to the small Catholic School where we send her for Kindergarten. She tells me that the lady in black was a teacher, and some of the kids from her class were there, also waiting for their parents. They played with the toys and had a sleepover in the classroom.

"Were you scared?" I ask her during a pause. She has never slept anywhere besides our house.

Without skipping a beat she responds, "No Mommy, I knew you would find me. And the teacher said that you were on your way, they were just waiting for you to get home." I reach over and hug her.

"I love you, little Catalina, never forget that."

"I love you too, mommy."

I feel a little bit better that she was well cared for when I was gone. However, it seems strange to me that her 'teacher' would know that I was making my way home.

--

It's early afternoon. A guard has shown up on my new doorstep. "Mr. Crane has requested a face-to-face meeting instead of a list of supplies," he informs me.

I gather a few things and the guard drives us back to Culkin Hall. We take the elevator to the ninth floor again, returning to the same room as yesterday. It's much more pleasant this time, not being dragged down the hallway. Lina skips along beside me, holding my hand.

Crane is waiting with a few other people, including the man with the pin on his lapel.

"Ah, welcome, we've been anxiously awaiting your arrival." He claps his hands together then bends down to Lina. "And this little princess must be Catalina?" He holds his hand out to Lina, but instead of shaking it she cowers behind me. "It's all right, we have plenty of time to get acquainted," he tells her.

I put my hand on her arm. Lina has always been a good judge of character. So I'm not sure if it's the unfamiliar room or the sickening, sweet smell of Crane that makes her leery. I have a feeling it's probably just Crane, because I feel the same way about him.

"Let me introduce you to everyone. First we have Colonel Baillie." He points to the man with the pin and the southern accent, who's wearing a gray uniform. "Then we have Alexander," the man who performed the lie detector test. "Morris," a short Asian man whom I have never met, he takes his hat off and bows. "And finally Ms. Black." A tall, elegant woman in a black suit rises.

Lina tugs at my hand, I bend down a little and she whispers in my ear. "Mommy, that's the teacher." I squeeze her hand to let her know I heard her.

Crane continues. "I would like to welcome you all to the first official meeting of the Phoenix District Development Commission." He stands there, arms open, smiling widely. "We are about to make history. On to our first order of business, Ms. Black."

The tall woman stands up and walks towards us. "Could you come with me Catalina?" She holds her hand out to Lina.

I push Lina behind me. "She's not leaving this room. She's not leaving my side." I look around the room to see them all staring at me. "I just got her back," I whisper.

Ms. Black smiles kindly at me. Her face is soft and young, her blonde hair pulled into a loose bun. She clasps her hands in front of her waist and looks to Crane. I look to Crane also and see the man called Baillie roll his eyes and shake his head.

"That's fine," Crane starts, "this was anticipated. We can't expect Andromeda to trust everyone just yet." The door opens and guards enter carrying a small table, two chairs and piles of workbooks, crayons, and pencils. They set the supplies up in the far corner of the room. "Is this better?" Crane asks me.

"Yes, thank you."

Lina lets go of my hand and takes Ms Black's. They sit down at the table. I can see the woman open a workbook and hand Lina a pencil. She takes it excitedly and starts writing.

Crane turns to me. "Please have a seat. Let's begin. As we know, God did not build the earth and mankind in one day, and so the assemblies of The Phoenix District will not either."

I choose a seat next to Morris, the Asian man, as he looks the kindest.

We are handed legal notepads, pens, pencils, and a small metal bin with our names on them. Crane tells us that at the end of the meeting everything is to be placed in the metal bin and it will be locked in a safe until the next meeting. There are rules for being on the committee: there is absolutely no discussion of meeting topics outside this room, no materials are to be taken from the room, and there will be no discussion of topics unless everyone on the committee is present.

Crane officially starts the meeting by slamming a small rubber hammer onto a copper plate. He has an agenda already written in front of him, topics that we need to come to a decision on I'm assuming. I can see them from across the table: Social Order, Security, Guidance, Occupations, Education, Genetic Research, Propagation. The list goes on.

It makes me nauseous. I don't want this role, chosen as one of the few which will decide the fate for an entire society, a new society. It doesn't feel right to me, none of this does. But I know that I have no choice in the matter if I want to keep my daughter safe. All I can do is help make the most ethical decisions possible. I look around the table and realize that I am the only woman on this committee. Suddenly the arguments and meetings from working in the lab are fresh in my mind. This is exactly what I was trying to escape when I became a nurse.

The agenda starts with the issue of Social Order. I mostly observe, taking mental notes. There is an abundance of information you can learn about a person by just observing them, especially in a heated argument, and the men eventually argue. They go back and forth about how to identify the different classes of people. What jobs they will be doing, how they will be interacting with society. By evening it has been decided the social order will be broken up into factions, each social group living within a small radius around their given trade.

For example, the farmers will be referred to as Cultivators. They will be responsible for growing the food, harvesting it, taking care of the farm animals, producing sustenance for the District, and will be housed on many of the local farms in the new District. There will be the Orderlies, responsible for the cleanliness of the city. The Navigators are responsible for the buses, the train and road upkeep. The Currents are responsible for operating the nuclear power plants and hydroelectric plant on the river. The list goes on to include every job title needed to run a District encompassing nearly nine-hundred square miles. Alexander and Morris are assigned to head the working factions; they nod in agreement and shake hands.

Crane informs us that social order does not apply to the District Sovereign, who will include the committee members, their families, and gifted individuals selected from the residents. The Sovereign will be responsible for making decisions for the residents, for overseeing the organization and development of the District. They will carry out duties of the sciences, humanities, medicine, research, and technological development.

Security is the next topic discussed. Assigned as a District faction, the Volker-meaning people's guard-will be responsible for protecting the District. They will monitor the nearby lake, the wall, and the fence outside the wall. Crane assigns Baillie as the head of the Volker faction. I watch Baillie and see him smile arrogantly, satisfied with his new role.

Lastly, Crane assigns himself as head moderator of the District. Ms. Black will be responsible for the education and training of the gifted children chosen to lead the District in years to come, including my daughter.

I am not assigned to head any faction. So far, my sole purpose is genetic analysis and protecting Lina from these people.

Finally the committee meeting is complete. Crane passes the agenda around the table. We sign it in agreement and then place our belongings into the metal boxes. Crane collects them all then crosses the room to a tall closet door, inside is a large safe, he punches in a code, places the metal boxes inside and turns the handle. The lock clicks heavily into place. Crane turns, telling us he will send a Volker in the morning to escort us in.

The sun is low in the sky and when I look to the corner where Lina is working I see her yawn. I cross the room to collect Lina, picking her up.

Ms. Black pats her on the shoulder. "Good job today," she tells Lina quietly.

When we open the door there are guards, I suppose now we call them Volker, waiting to escort each of us home. The drive is quick and quiet. I thank the Volker when he opens the door for us. As I walk to the townhouse I notice he waits to see that we have gone inside and closed the door before he pulls away.

Stevie greets us at the door. She trails at my heels as I make a quick dinner of rice and vegetables. When we are done eating, I feed the leftovers to her.

Lina helps me carry a few more of our things upstairs, and we inspect the upper level of the townhouse. There are two rooms with an adjoining bathroom. The bedrooms have large windows overlooking the lake and they are furnished alike. There are large queen sized beds, with matching white linens, large closets, and tall dressers. I let Lina pick a room and we both bathe and get ready for bed. After tucking Lina in I stroll through the townhouse, checking all the locks on the doors and windows before I climb into bed next to her.

I try not to think about the day's events, forcing myself to breathe deeply and relax. I try not to think about Ian and Adam or the recent happenings which have turned my world upside down. I feel guilty, being chosen as a committee member. I am the last person who should be making these decisions. I find it hard to believe that Crane's goal of developing a glorious utopian society within America will succeed. Somehow I manage to sleep, but it is not long before the sun is rising.

Stevie whines to me from the foot of the bed, her signal for needing to go outside. I leave Lina to sleep soundly, kissing her temple before I leave the room to take Stevie out the back door.

The lake is calm, with seagulls and ducks floating on top of the water. Stevie bounds off the back deck, chasing a squirrel into one of the nearby trees. I follow her out into the large yard.

"Andie," I hear someone call my name.

I turn around and see Adam walking towards me. He's wearing the gray Volker uniform. I am still mad at him for betraying me, but there is nowhere to go out here in the yard to escape him. As he walks up to me I see that his dark hair is trimmed shorter, his face clean shaven. He looks more relaxed as he walks, unlike the stiff soldier I saw in the conference room two days ago after we were removed from my house.

"What do you want Adam?" I ask him.

"I just wanted to check on you. I noticed you were gone most of the day yesterday." His light blue eyes are looking directly into mine.

"Yeah, I was. I think we will be gone most of the day today, also."

"Where have they been taking you?" he asks raising his eyebrows.

"I don't think I can tell you. At least not right now. I'm not supposed to talk about it." Actually, I'm not sure what I am allowed to say. Or if I can disclose that I am actually on this committee whose sole purpose is to develop the district, to rearrange our town and its people.

"I just want to make sure you are safe. I've been assigned two units from you, if you need anything." He kicks the ground sheepishly. "Well, I have to go to training now so hopefully I'll see you soon." He smiles at me before turning and jogging back to his townhouse. I watch him, suddenly aware that he may be the closest thing I have to a friend now, wondering if it's worth it to give him a second chance with my trust.

Stevie and I head back inside. I wake up Lina and get us ready for the day. Not long after we sit down to eat breakfast there is a knock on the door. Stevie whines and pushes herself between me and the door as I open it. It's the same Volker who dropped us off last night, ready to take us back to another committee meeting. I make him wait a few minutes while Lina finishes eating and I pack my work bag with a few snacks and drinks. I find the stuffed owl that I carried with me when traveling back from the city. When I hand it to Lina she squeals with excitement.

We stop in front of Culkin Hall and the Volker opens the back door for us to get out. The first thing I notice is the sign for Culkin Hall has been removed. I wonder what it will be replaced with. The next thing I notice is that there are workers cleaning the front of the building, sweeping the sidewalks and parking lot, scrubbing the bricks and tending to the flowerbeds.

We are escorted to the conference room. The other Sovereign members are already there, waiting for us. Baillie looks impatiently at his watch as we walk through the door. Ms. Black sits at the small table in the corner. Lina releases my hand and runs over to greet her. I notice the uncomfortable office chairs have been replaced with new, thickly padded ones and unfortunately, the only seat available is the one to the right of Crane. I sit down as he proceeds to collect the metal bins from the safe and pass them out. He taps the hammer of the copper plate and the committee meeting has begun. Crane continues on with the next few subjects on his agenda: Guidance, Occupations, and Education.

We set up curfews for working days and off days. Baillie suggests we use the traffic cameras in town to monitor the District from a control room. The men discuss the possibility of adding more cameras throughout the District and along the stone wall that's being built. Although we are all in agreement that a control room would be an excellent option for ensuring the safety of the town, there is a nagging in the back of my brain reminding me that this would not only impact the privacy of the residents, but also my privacy. The County Jail at the entrance to town will be mostly used for Volker training and detaining any suspicious persons.

Crane writes nothing as all the rules and ideas are discussed. I begin to realize that we aren't the ones making many of the decisions. Crane is the one suggesting, pushing along the discussions and then making the final decisions. When we are done discussing the Guidance of the District there is a knock at the door. And when it opens, women enter the room carrying trays of food for lunch. They walk around the table and we select food from the trays they are carrying. One of the women walks over to Lina and Ms. Black, allowing them to choose from a selection of sandwiches and snacks on her tray.

As we break for a moment to eat and use the restrooms, I check on Lina.

"Look Mom," she holds up a paper and shows me proudly. In neat small handwriting Lina has finished an entire page of addition and subtraction. Something I wasn't expecting her to learn about until next year when she started first grade. I look to Ms. Black who is sitting behind Lina, smiling proudly.

"That's a very good job Lina." I hug her and kiss her before returning to the committee table just in time for Crane to signal the meeting has started again.

The agenda moves on and we discuss Occupations. Crane is prepared with a listing of the occupations assigned in Japan and the tests administered to determine a resident's assigned occupation. We listen as Crane reads off a long list.

"What about winter?" I interrupt Crane. He looks at me annoyed but doesn't say anything. I look around the table and realize I'm the only committee member who's local to this area. "We get a lot of snow here in the winters, over thirty feet. If you plan on keeping the District functioning during the winter, we're going to have to think about running plows, shoveling sidewalks and roofs."

"Alright, we will add winter preparations. I'm sure those assigned to the District Maintenance faction can handle it." Crane responds nodding. I hold in a smile, happy that I have provided a small suggestion that didn't include the mind washing of the local residents.

Crane continues on explaining how the testing of the residents will determine their occupations. First, residents will be given a paper test with over a hundred questions. The residents' choices will be tallied at the end and they will be assigned to the occupation in which they scored the highest.

Next, we move on to Education. We decide that the school year will last year round. This is necessary for preparing the future residents with acceptable skills and to keep the children off the streets and out of trouble. The children will be the only residents besides the Sovereign and Volker who will be un-medicated. Baillie tries to argue that the children should be receiving the cooperative hormone mixture just as the adults are. "To keep them in line." He says. "What are we going to do when we have a bunch of hoodlum teenagers roaming the streets?"

This was another time where I could not keep my mouth shut.

"We can't medicate the children," I argue. "The brain chemistry of children is largely unknown. And whatever hormones they are given could impact their brain development." I can feel my face flushing in anger for Baillie so casually wanting to create a society of medicated residents. "Besides, the human brain doesn't stop developing until the age of twenty-five. I'm sure there are a number of residents who are receiving these medications right now that shouldn't be."

Baillie glares at me from across the table. I look back to Crane, who turns in the direction where Ms. Black is working with Lina. She must have been listening to the argument; she nods in my direction. I feel a little better having someone in the room who agrees with me.

"So we need to decide on a compromise," Crane starts, "Residents will start receiving the hormone mixture at the age of eighteen, after their schooling and training is completed. Unless we start experiencing this hoodlum problem, then we will review this matter again."

This is not the solution I would have preferred, but I feel better knowing that the children will be able to function normally.

The meeting has lasted almost the entire day again. By the time we near the end of discussions on Education the sun is hanging low over the lake. Crane has declared the meeting over. We sign the final agreements and place our belongings into our metal bins. Crane collects them and secures them in the safe just as he did the day before.

"Andromeda," Crane signals to me as he is closing the closet door. I notice he looks tired, his shoulders sag a little, and he doesn't exude the excitement and arrogance of our first meeting. "I need your list of laboratory supplies."

I dig in my bag for the long handwritten list of supplies and hand it over to him. Crane looks over the list quickly. I know that laboratory supplies are expensive, the reagents, gel disks, nucleic acid synthesizers, micropipettes, computers, analysis programs and the microarray instrument used for analyzing the genetic material should cost over a million dollars. He says nothing about the expensive materials and computers needed to supply my lab.

"I wasn't sure what my budget was for the lab."

"There is none," he responds swiftly. I'm shocked by his response. I can only assume that some other entity is funding the District, so I decide to ask.

"Where is the funding coming from?"

"Everywhere," he responds nonchalantly.

"What do you mean everywhere?"

The corner of his mouth rises in a half smirk. Maybe it's from my questions, or maybe because he gets to explain more of his mad plan to me. I can feel the arrogance and excitement radiate off him once again. He steps closer to me, bringing the musky scent of his cologne within smelling distance, my stomach churns, pushing lunch towards the back of my throat.

"Do you remember Andromeda, when I told you this runs much deeper than you would expect? That's where the funding comes from. That is where our supplies come from. We will recycle as much as we can from this little town. And once the crops start coming in and the food processing plants are back up and running, we will become self sufficient. Until then we will rely on our Funding Entities. They were aware of the cost before they came aboard." Funding Entities? I wonder who they are-specific people, governments, countries? "I think it is time to call it a night, our precious Lina is looking tired."

Ms. Black walks up behind me carrying Lina and passes her into my arms. I don't like the way Crane says "our Lina" like she is somehow his, like he knows her or owns her. I don't like that he calls her precious, because how could he know how precious she is? She's precious to me but that's because she is my child. I raised her, watched her turn into an amusing, spunky five-year old. I am not sure what his plans are for her, but she is much too young right now to be a part of this.

I turn and leave without saying goodbye to the madman, Crane.

CHAPTER TEN

The townhouse is not our real home, and it feels like we are living in a hotel. Lina and I unpack a few more of the boxes from the garage after the Volker drives us home. She runs upstairs each time we pull out one of her stuffed animals, placing them on the bed. I find our clothes and hang them up in the closet. There's a pile of scrubs at the bottom of a box. I set them on the floor of the closet, sure that I will never wear them again. The door to the garage is open, letting in the fresh spring air. The workers who packed up our belongings included Lina's outdoor toys. As she rides her small princess bike on the cement driveway, I dig through the remaining boxes. Stevie sits by the garage door watching her. I don't want to leave her outside by herself so I set some things by the stairs for later.

It is evening, but the sun has not set yet. I'm antsy from being stuck in the office for days.

"Want to ride your bike down the road?" I ask Lina. Since there are no cars on the road, and the majority of the townhomes are empty, it seems like a good idea. I would also like a little exercise to clear my mind.

"Mommy, I'm not allowed to ride in the road. You told me so." She continues to ride around in a circle at the end of the driveway.

"I know sweetie, but there are no cars here. It's safe now. And I'll be with you."

"Ok!" she responds excitedly.

I tell Stevie to stay as I close the garage door, locking her inside. I haven't found her leash yet and I don't want to risk her running off to examine this unfamiliar area.

I follow Lina as she pedals out to the road. This road is new, the pavement smooth and easy for her to ride on. It weaves back towards the campus, splitting off a few hundred yards ahead of us with another road, towards town. The lake borders one side of the road, with dense forest on the other. Lina pedals slowly and I anticipate we won't be walking for very long.

"Mommy," she breaks the silence. "Everything is different now, isn't it?"

I can't blame her for asking questions. It's obvious that our lives have completely changed in just a few short days, and for a child it is no doubt hard to cope with. So far she hasn't displayed any negative effects of losing her father, moving, having a completely different daily routine. I'm not sure what to tell her, because I know things may change again. I'm afraid that she has lost that stability in her life we once had, the one that keeps children feeling safe and grounded, that helps them grow up feeling loved and ready for the real world in all of its ruthlessness.

"Yes, everything is very different now," I say to her. "I think we're going to see some more changes, me and you. But we will be together, always. I will keep you safe." I pat the top of her head and she looks up smiling at me. A cracking sound comes from the forest, the distinct sound of a tree branch being stepped on. It crunches loudly in the still evening air.

"I love you, Mommy," Lina responds as her little feet pedal slowly on the bike.

I feel the tiny hairs on the back of my neck start to stand up. Those hairs that tell you someone is close by or just entered an empty room.

"I love you too, Lina. Let's head home now."

I grab the front of her bike and help her make a wide curve to turn around. The evening starts to get darker but the street lights don't come on. I'm starting to feel stupid and paranoid, but then I hear another branch crack, this time closer to us. Suddenly I realize that a nice relaxing walk may not have been such a good idea. "Lina can you pedal a little faster for me?" I try not to let her hear the rising panic in my voice. I reach down and pull the front of her bike, walking faster. I scan the forest but I can't see anything through the dense shrubs and low branches. Two more branches snap sending my heart into a raging flutter. I hear something, a low breathing, or growl. I can't tell which. More branches snap, too many to count this time, the sound seems loud enough to burst my eardrums. I don't wait to see what is at the edge of the forest. I pick Lina up under her arms and start running, leaving the bike in the road.

"Mommy my bike," she shrieks, reaching behind me, struggling to get out of my arms.

"We'll come back for it, Lina. We have to get out of here, now."

For a moment I still think I am being a coward, that there is nothing in the woods tracking our movements. That is until Lina lets out a scream so loud it leaves a ringing in my eardrums. I don't turn around to see why she is screaming, I can only assume it's from whatever was in the woods snapping the tree branches.

I am not an athlete. I am not a runner, and running with a forty pound child clinging to my chest doesn't help me move any faster. There is a sound behind us, and it's something else running. It clicks on the smooth pavement, not like shoes, or sneakers. It clicks and clicks and clicks. I try to think of what it could be. Lina is still screaming in my ear, telling me to go faster. I try to run faster, using every ounce of energy in my body, and then I can place the sound. The clicks are nails, but there are too many of them for one creature. It sounds like a pack of animals running after us. I know that I am no match against an animal that has spent its life hunting and running, training for a moment just like this-the pursuit of prey. They're getting closer, whatever they are, and I can feel their hot damp breaths on the backs of my legs. We didn't walk very far but I feel like I've been running for miles already. I'm too slow and Lina is too heavy.

There is a cluster of townhomes in front of me, not far from us. I can see a few lights on and I'm hoping that someone is home. I scream for help, worrying that Lina's screams and shrieks are drowning out my calls to anyone who may be in one of the townhouses. No one opens their doors or looks out their curtains. No one is coming to help us. All that I can hear is Stevie barking fiercely from behind the garage door. I feel something scrape the back of my leg. It is just enough to trip me, knocking me down onto the pavement. I choke out a cry, pushing my hand in front of me so Lina doesn't hit the ground. Small pebbles grind into the soft skin on my hand. All I can think, is *how am I going to protect Lina?* I curl my body around her, trying to protect her from whatever is chasing us. Something scrapes the back of my leg again, this time tearing through the khaki material of my pants and sending a sharp pain up my leg. There's another swipe, this time across my back, and I can feel the nails tearing at my flesh. The tapping has stopped on the pavement and I can hear the growls and heated panting of whatever animal is at my back, moving in for the kill.

Oh no, what do I do?

At that moment, bursting through my fears and thoughts, I hear the most glorious sound, the sound of gunshots. I hear yelling and the footsteps of someone running in our direction. The animals no longer focus on us, but I stay in my curled up position, trying to protect my child.

There are more gunshots, but the animals don't move away from us. I can feel the heat radiating off their bodies, I can smell them. It's like when Stevie rolls in dead animals, but worse-stronger. They growl now, barking loudly, claiming me and my child as their own. Whoever is yelling and shooting gets closer and they let off a few more warning shots, but the beasts don't budge. I close my eyes tightly, trying to think of what to do next. Lina whimpers in the space below me. There are more gunshots. I feel a spray of dislodged pavement at my back, then there is a loud shriek from one of the animals and I feel its heavy warm body thud against my side. I know it's been shot, and it must be dead because there's no more heavy breathing or heat radiating off it. There's a yelp and more tapping on the road. It sounds like they are headed for the forest, away from us.

I stay in my position, protecting Lina, not expecting the heavy hand that clamps down on my shoulder nor the voice that accompanies it.

"Andie, are you two all right?" I look up and see Adam at my side. His eyes are large, his brow furrowed. He's wearing sweatpants and running shoes; his shirt is soaked with sweat and a gun is in his hand. I sit up on my knees, pulling Lina up and hugging her to my chest.

"Oh my God, Lina, are you okay?" I pull her up off the ground and look her over for injuries. She's crying and smudges of dirt from the pavement stain her pale cheek. "It's okay, we're safe now." I pull her towards me and hug her tightly. Looking to my side and see a large furred body next to me.

"What was that?" I ask Adam. He runs his hand through his hair, staring at the body.

"I think it was a pack of wolves; there were four or five of them. It was so strange..."

I shake my head in disbelief. Adam grabs the leg of the animal dragging it to the side of the road. My palms are burning, and when I pull them off of Lina's back I see that they are streaked with blood, leaving stains on the back of her shirt. I raise my leg up, positioning myself to stand while holding her. I adjust her weight onto my hip so I can carry her comfortably. Adam is walking towards us, wiping his hands on his pants. I step onto my right leg where the animal scratched me and pain sears up my leg, causing it to give out. I start to stumble but Adam rushes forward, catching my elbow.

"Do you want me to take her?" He asks, sounding concerned. I shake my head no. He holds my elbow, giving me support as I limp back to the townhouse carrying Lina.

When we get to the door she has stopped crying and is silent. Stevie still barks from behind the garage door and Adam opens it to let her loose. She runs to the end of the driveway and down the road to where the dead animal is, barking viciously. She stops to mark the edge of the road a few times and then runs back to us sniffing and licking our hands. Adam helps me get up the stairs to the living room, then up to the second floor.

"Can you wait downstairs?" I ask him, "I need to get Lina cleaned up."

He leaves us, heading down the stairs. I run a warm bath for Lina, checking her over as I help her get her dirty clothes off. She is unscathed, except for a scratch on her arm from the pavement. "You're safe now Lina, it's ok." I kiss her scrape and give her a quick bath. I pull a large white towel from the cupboard and wrap her in it. The scrapes on my palms have stopped bleeding, but I can feel something trickling down my back. I'm not sure if it's sweat or blood. I carry her to the bedroom, dress her, dry her hair and braid it. She reaches out and pulls the toy owl from the stack of stuffed animals on her bed, holding it close to her chest. I hold her on my lap for a long time, rocking her, kissing her on the head.

I hear a knock on the front door, then voices. I almost forgot Adam was in the house. Stevie barks a few times. I hear Adam tell her to lie down and she must, because she is quiet after that. I pull a blanket out of the closet and wrap Lina in it. She's almost asleep, but I carry her downstairs to the living room, holding tightly to the stair railing so I don't fall. The back of my leg feels like it's on fire, my back doesn't feel much better. I lay Lina down on the couch, wrapping her tightly in the blanket, as she is now sleeping. Turning, I see Adam has let Baillie into my house and what looks like a Japanese man in an EMT uniform.

"What's going on here?" I ask Adam, but I am ushered over to a dining room chair by the medic before he can answer. The medic checks my hands, pouring a cleaning solution onto them that burns. Then he cuts my pant leg off at the knee and inspects the wounds on the back of my leg. He pours more of the solution onto it, before wrapping my calf in fresh white gauze.

"I needed to report what happened," Adam replies as I am being bandaged up.

"Adam filled me in," Baillie chimes in. "We can discuss it further in tomorrow's committee meeting." Baillie looks taller and darker against the white walls of the townhouse, his hand resting on the pistol on his hip, making me very uncomfortable. I prefer that he not be in my house at all and I get the feeling Stevie feels the same way, as she growls continuously from where she lays. I don't want to talk to him, I want him to leave. I nod in agreement and he turns to leave, stopping near Adam. "I hear you're doing well in training, recruit." Adam nods at him. "Keep it up, we could use someone with your expertise and experience in the higher ranks." Finally Baillie is closing the front door, and Stevie stops her growling.

"Now, I need to see your back," the EMT instructs me.

I stand up and pull my arm out of my shirt, exposing most of my back and bra. Usually I'm modest but I can tell by the pain that my back needs to be taken care of. I can feel the heat rise in my cheeks when I notice Adam watching the EMT closely.

"This needs to be stitched. I need to see more of your back." The EMT goes back to his bag, pulling out a vial and syringes. I can see from the label that it reads: *Lidocaine*. "I need you to lie down," he tells me as he draws the medication into the syringes.

The only places for me to lie down are the floor or the table. I choose the table.

Although I have assisted many times at work, I have never actually been the receiver of stitches, and the thought of the sutures pulling through my skin makes me feel sick. I don't want Adam to see me in just my bra, but the pain makes me not care much anymore.

Adam must sense my unease. "It's ok, I've had stitches plenty of times," he tells me. "You won't feel a thing."

I pull the rest of my shirt off and lay down on the table on my stomach. I watch the EMT finish pulling up the medication. He threads the needle and gloves up all in a sterile manner that I know is not familiar to an EMT. This man is a doctor. I turn my head away from the doctor and squeeze my eyes shut. The needles pinch as he numbs the area where the deep scratches are. He waits a moment for the numbness to kick in before he cleans the area with the antiseptic, and then I feel the tugging of the sutures. Bile piles up in the back of my throat. I take deep breaths, trying to stop myself from vomiting. When I feel someone squeeze my hand I open my eyes, and Adam is standing next to me. He smiles a little before his gaze shifts to the doctor as he works.

No one has ever seen me like this before. Vulnerable, barely dressed. Only Ian. No one has ever seen the tattoo that slides down my left side, over my ribs; a single raven in flight. Trailing behind are the words: *be brave*. I want to laugh at the thought of the tattoo, especially after tonight, but I'm too afraid I'll puke if I move. I wonder if Adam sees it, if he is staring at my back. Suddenly, I am very self conscious. I squeeze my eyes closed and try and focus on the heat coming from Adams palm that is lying over my hand. After a long time I hear the doctor open packages of gauze and tape to cover his stitches.

"I'm sure I don't need to tell you to keep your wounds clean," the doctor instructs me in perfect English. "Your leg wounds are just on the surface, but your back wounds are very deep." He hands me an envelope of medication. "Antibiotics twice a day and take pain medications as you need them. The stitches can come out in about a week."

I thank him as he collects his things and leaves.

"How did you report what happened?" I ask Adam as I stand up slowly and pull the bloody ragged shirt back on.

"Your phone," he tells me, pointing to the white phone on the wall. "Didn't you check it? Because it works, you just press any number and it directs the call to a switchboard."

I never thought to check the phone. I just assumed they were all out of service.

"What did Baillie mean by needing someone with your experience?"

He crosses his arms and leans against the wall. "I'm not sure I can tell you. At least not right now. We aren't supposed to talk about it," he responds mimicking my comment from this morning. I'm not sure whether to laugh or cry after the events of this evening and I can't deal with the tension between us anymore. Maybe I could try to get over being mad at him for betraying me because really, I have no one else here.

"Thank you, for saving us," I tell him. "I don't know what would have happened if you didn't show up." I can feel the pressure of tears welling up behind my eyes. Breathing in deep, I swallow them down.

"I think you should stay away from the woods and don't go walking alone in the evening. After all that's happened, you never know what's hiding out there." He runs his hands through is hair and sits down across from me. "Make sure you keep your dog around, she seems to be pretty good at trying to protect you two."

I look back at Stevie who is now sleeping on the floor next to where Lina lays on the couch. When I turn Adam is staring at me. The furrow between his eyebrows is back. "What?" I ask.

"Did you look at those wolves?" I shake my head no. "They were just skin and bones, like they hadn't eaten in days."

"That's strange. There's been plenty of wildlife around here, squirrels and deer."

"I went back out to check the woods, near where you left the bicycle, while you were upstairs. There were crates, four of them, back in the trees."

"What? But that doesn't make sense. Who would crate wolves in the forest?"

"Andie, I think someone crated them there on purpose."

"What do you mean? Like they were waiting for us?"

"Yes." Adam looks into my eyes. He's right. I know it.

And now it hits me, harder than before, that now I must be unyielding in my efforts to keep my daughter safe, because someone is planning to harm us.

CHAPTER ELEVEN

There has been a steady stream of Volker assigned to watch us around the clock. I see them parked outside my house at night and during the evenings when we're dropped off. Crane has forbidden me from going anywhere without a Volker, including trips to the grocery store or while playing outside. It's starting to make me feel more like a prisoner.

Because of the details of the wolf attack Crane changed the guidelines to the Volker duties. They are now required to monitor and protect all Sovereign committee members as though they are our personal body guards. Like now, as a Volker drives us across campus to another meeting. I look out the window and see a stream of people filing into a large building-adults and children. The children will be assigned to educational training, attending school during most of the day and returning to their parents in the evening. That is, if their parents are deemed fit.

Yesterday, Crane made the decision that all those residents with criminal histories will be sterilized and assigned menial labor jobs without testing, jobs such as building the stone wall. I thought of arguing with him and the rest of the committee, but deep down, I knew it was what I wanted. As much as I didn't want to make these decisions, sometimes I feel like Crane was right when he pointed out why he chose me. So far, with minimal effort, I have helped decide the course of a few thousand people's lives.

After the residents are assigned occupations then they will undergo health exams. DNA samples will be taken and placed in a deep freezer until a lab is ready. The adolescent residents showing excellent health and athletic ability will be assigned to Volker training and weaned off the medication. Children showing similar abilities will be assigned training in their last few years of schooling. My heart breaks for those gifted children showing exceptional learning abilities. Those children with high IQ marks-they would be taken from their families and assigned to a program to train them to take over running the District. They will receive more schooling than the other children, the training required to become the next generation of Sovereign. I guess I'm lucky that I get to keep my daughter with me during her training.

Crane informed us that one hundred helpers from the Japan District would be arriving soon, to help with the organization and documentation of these changes. It seems strange to me that in a few short days all this will be taking place. The medications they are feeding the people of this town have prevented any uprisings. People walk calmly, smiling, some even chat quietly as they wait. It's hard to believe that over the past few days, during the committee meetings, this was all determined and today I see it taking place before me.

We stop in front of Culkin Hall. The sign has been replaced. It now reads *"Phoenix District Headquarters."* The last committee meeting was cancelled the day after the wolf attack so Baillie could do a full investigation. I'm not sure what he investigated, because I never spoke to him.

I get the feeling that Baillie doesn't care much about our safety here, just as much as I can tell he doesn't care about my suggestions during the committee meetings.

The Volker that drove us also escorts us to the Committee room.

Ms. Black is there to work with Lina again. Alexander and Morris both stand and greet me with smiles. Morris is closest to me and pulls out a chair for me to sit in. I notice more changes, the table is now large, round and made of dark wood. The floor looks different also. The only seat left is opposite Baillie. I'm not happy that I have to go through the entire meeting with this pain in my back and watching him stare me down. Crane starts the meeting. The only things on today's agenda are Genetic Research and Breeding.

"Andromeda, are you sure you are ready?" Crane asks. He's staring at me, trying his best to look concerned. I gaze around the table. Alexander and Morris have their eyes on me as well as Baillie.

Ms. Black is even watching me from the corner where she works with Lina.

Somehow, I know that one of these people tried to kill me and Lina. And I need to find out who it was.

"I'm fine," I say as I try and straighten my back, without pulling the stitches.

"Then let's begin. We will discuss the details of the genetic research program. The lab for Andromeda should be completed soon, as well as the samples from all of the residents. Here are some examples of Andromeda's work for you all to look over."

I watch in dismay as Crane passes thick packets to Alexander, Baillie, Morris, even Ms. Black. I lean over and watch Morris shift through the papers inside. Crane has compiled a collection of every research paper I've ever published: articles, abstracts, presentations, everything.

"Why are you handing those out?" I can feel the humiliation of long ago, from all those research meetings I attended in which I was ridiculed, told my work was worthless, no good. I want to try and stop Crane. "These are old papers. They don't apply to what you are trying to do here."

"Andromeda, the Committee needs to see what you are capable of."

I watch the committee members glance through the stack of papers, hoping that I can remember how to analyze the data, hoping that I can remember how to do what I did before. It's been four years since I analyzed anything. I know that I have to remember if I want to keep us safe. It is the only thing keeping Crane from sending us to a fate similar to that of the other residents. Medicating me into oblivion and splitting us up.

I sit and wait for a long time as they review the papers. They take notes, make lists. Eventually, Crane interrupts them. "Let's move onto the details of the Genetic Research of the District. What we would like to see is the organization of residents who are related. We want to create the greatest genetic diversity possible. This will help decrease genetic diseases, mental instabilities, etc., etc. I'm sure you all understand the benefits. Also, a major goal of ours is to locate the genetic link to pro-social behavior and less dominant personalities. Once this is complete we can decrease the amount of medication the working factions are receiving, and ensure cooperation with all residents."

Deep down, I feel like this is an unattainable goal. This is going to take an insurmountable amount of digging into the human genome to find these traits and even more to try and develop a method for humans to continually express these traits as a dominant. Years ago, I attempted something similar in rats. I was even successful, but these are not rats we are talking about. These are human beings.

Crane continues. "This brings us onto the next topic, which is breeding. As you know, there are only about 10,000 residents left after the blast. There are some children here but not enough to support the Phoenix District into the future. Once Andromeda has determined the residents' genetic backgrounds then *she* will be responsible for pairing them. Creating couples with the ability to produce genetically sound children, ensuring the growth of the district." Suddenly all of them are staring at me, aware of the task that has just been placed upon my shoulders. I control the urge to run out of the room, collecting my daughter along the way. "You will all be notified of when the next Committee meeting will take place, we are finished for the day." Crane slams his hammer down, ending the meeting. As he collects our trays he stops next to me. "We need to talk when we are finished here."

I wait in the hallway with Lina after the rest of the committee members leave. Crane locks the door and walks towards us, smiling. "I have something very exciting to show you, Andromeda. Come, follow me." He reminds me of an excited puppy the way he bounces as he walks, smiling more than I've ever seen him smile. The last time I saw him this excited was when he showed me the blast radius. I'm afraid of what he plans on revealing to me now. We walk out of the building to a waiting SUV and the thought of being stuck in there with him sends my stomach churning. I sit in the back with Lina and roll the windows down. We drive down a few winding campus roads, heading to the science buildings. They're hard to forget; large, wide buildings with shimmering glass fronts facing the campus center and the lake. The SUV stops in front of the Chemistry Hall. Crane gets out and holds the door open for me. I notice there are Volker guards standing at the main entrance and a group of recruits runs by us in a cluster, humming a harmony to keep the pace with each other.

"Come, this is very exciting," Crane beckons me.

I take Lina's hand as we walk into the Chemistry Hall. There's a large atrium as we enter the building. Each of the four floors is visible all the way to the glass roof.

"Wow," Lina whispers as she looks all the way up. Her eyes large, taking in the massive windows.

"I would like to welcome you, Andromeda, to your new laboratory," Crane exclaims. "Come, follow me." We walk through a set of glass doors. "The entire first floor has been set aside as work space for you. I think you'll find it quite accommodating." I take a moment to look around. There are lab benches, all of the equipment on my list, even the expensive microarray instrument, computers, freezers-it's a fully stocked lab. This is unheard of, especially acquiring all this in such a short period of time. "The best part is over here." Crane reaches for my hand, but I force a cough and cover my mouth. I follow him to the middle of the room where there is a large wooden desk and rows of low filing cabinets. The best part is the computer. Three large computer screens line the wall behind the desk.

I always complained in the last lab that my computer was never fast enough to handle all the data, the screen never big enough, but there was never money in the budget to replace anything at my workstation. This is unbelievable.

Crane must have seen my mouth hanging open. "You like it, don't you? I knew you would." He clasps his hands in front of him.

"Crane, this is too much. This lab, it must have cost a fortune."

"As I told you, Andromeda, we have a lot of funding and we want you to succeed with your work."

I walk away from him, running my hand over the smooth desk surface. Lina jumps into the office chair, spinning herself and giggling. "What about Lina? Where will she be while I work?" I ask Crane, concerned. I don't want her far from me. I don't trust these people.

"Yes, I knew you would be concerned with her location. A classroom will be set up in the atrium right outside your doors. And for your safety, living quarters are being constructed on the fourth level."

"What do you mean living quarters?"

"Due to the recent events I think it would be best to house you somewhere safer. Here you will have Volker security and you will be able to work whenever you want."

"I'm not sure I like this, Crane. It feels like you are trying to keep me captive."

"No, Andromeda, I'm just trying to keep you and Lina safe. You are both very important to me and to the District."

--

Crane has informed me that lab assistants will be arriving from the already established Japanese District, with the other helpers. They are expected to arrive in a few days. Until then, I am free to do whatever I want. Except go anywhere by myself.

Lina and I sleep in, she plays with her toys, we play board games, and throw sticks for Stevie to fetch. One day, Lina tells me she wants to read to me. She pulls out one of her books and proceeds to read the entire thing out loud. She never pauses to sound out a word, or asks me to pronounce something for her. I tell her I am very proud of her, and that she did such a good job. But deep down I am sad at the fact she is growing up and learning so much, so fast, without her father here to see it.

After she reads to me I have one of the Volker bring us to the large park by the docks. There are a few children playing. The Volker stands off to the side, watching us. Mothers stand off to the other side, watching the children, talking quietly amongst themselves. Usually there is at least one inappropriate mother yelling loudly at her children, smoking near the garbage cans or hollering into a cell phone, but not today. They all act eerily controlled. I notice them watching me. I let Lina play with the children for an hour or so as I stand there alone, feeling strange and uncomfortable.

When we get back to the townhouse, Adam is getting out of a black SUV parked in his driveway. He's in full Volker uniform with a badge on his chest and a gun on his hip. I haven't spoken to him since the wolves attacked us almost a week ago and I haven't even seen him in almost three days. Whatever Baillie is doing with him, it's keeping him very busy.

Lina is helping me cook dinner when there is a knock at the door. I open it to find Adam standing there, his hands in his pockets.

"Hi," I greet him, holding back a smile.

"Hi Adam!" Lina shouts from behind me. "We are cooking dinner. Do you want to eat?"

Adam looks to me smiling. "I'm not sure, that's up to your mom."

"Mom! Mom! Can he stay?" Lina asks, bouncing on her chair.

"I guess," I respond, watching Adam, trying to figure out what he's up to. "Besides we made *your favorite*, vegetables and rice. So it would be rude not to invite you in," I tease him while opening the door wide so he can enter the kitchen.

"At least it smells good," Adam laughs.

Lina and I set the table for dinner. It's the first time there have been three people at the table since we lost Ian. I listen to Lina tell Adam all about our day, how she got to play at the park with some other kids. Then she tells him about the lab we toured a few days ago, and that we are moving there soon. Adam stops, lowering his fork to his plate he looks at me, concerned. I nod yes at him to indicate that she is, in fact, telling a true story. After dinner Lina drags Adam to a stack of playing cards in the living room and they play go-fish while I clean up. Lina beats him each time and finally, after the fourth game, Adam gives up. I suggest we go throw rocks by the lake while the sun sets.

"Are you sure moving into that building is a good idea?" Adam asks me when we get to the rocky lakeshore. Stevie follows us, jumping into the shallow lake waves and biting at them.

"I'm not sure what you want me to do," I tell him. "I don't like the idea of it. But we aren't safe here. I'm not sure we are safe anywhere."

Adam turns to me, staring into my eyes. I hear Lina tossing rocks behind us.

"I can protect you, Andie." Adam reaches for my hand. His feels warm and strong. I want him to protect us, but I relied on Ian to protect us and look where that got me. I can't make that mistake again, I have to be able to rely on myself to keep Lina safe.

"I got promoted today," Adam changes the subject, "to the head of the University Unit. I will be responsible for patrolling this area, assigning guard duties and training." This is not what I was expecting to hear from him, that he's moving up in the ranks, quickly becoming one of them. If he is the head of a unit that means he works directly under Baillie. He will be taking orders from Baillie. Just as I was starting to think I might be able to trust him again. I try and pull my hand away, but he squeezes it. "I was hoping you would be happy for me Andie." Then he pulls my hand, forcing me to move towards him. I don't recognize the look on his face. He reaches out with his free hand and pulls me towards him as though he is hugging me. He smells like the Adam before everything changed, when he was in my house, and I was waiting for my family to come home. I stop trying to pull away. I can hear Lina still throwing rocks behind me. At first it feels nice, to have his arms around me, to have contact with another adult. "Andie," Adam whispers in my ear, "I need you to listen, I need you to listen because they are watching and listening at all times. Your townhouse is bugged, so is mine. Crane is looking for rebels who might be trying to destroy the district he is working so hard at creating. He is looking for anyone who might not cooperate. I want you to know that I'm with you. I have to get close to them, so I can find a way out for us. I *need you* to trust me." He pushes me back so I can see the seriousness in his eyes. I search his face. I have that gut feeling that this is the truth, and even if it may be the first truth he is telling me, right now he is our only hope of getting out of here and back to the real world.

"Did I ever tell you what I was doing in Germany?" He asks, raising his eyebrow. "Intelligence officer, for the Marines. I was their best, top of the class."

"That is the most excellent thing I've heard in days," I whisper between our close faces. It is all I can say, all that I can think of. I'm overjoyed with the possibility of getting out of here, of running away from this new District that Crane is creating and keeping us captive in. As I reach out to hug him I feel a pair of soaking wet paws collide with my back. I cry out as I fall into Adam, Stevie scraping her claws down my recently stitched wounds.

"Down Stevie!" Adam commands our dog. She stops and sits, cocking her head to the side, unsure of what she did wrong. Adam is holding me under my elbow as Lina runs over to us.

"Mom, are you ok?" she asks, her eyes searching my face for what is wrong.

"Yes, Lina, Stevie hit the stitches on my back." I choke back a few tears. "It's ok. It's time for them to come out soon anyway." I take a few deep breaths and wait for the pain in my back to subside. I move to a large flat rock and sit, keeping my back perfectly straight as I watch Lina resume throwing rocks and Stevie chase the waves.

"I can take them out," Adam says as he sits down beside me. "The stitches, I can do that for you."

"Ok, after I get Lina to bed," I tell him, "I don't want her to see the scars."

We sit and watch the sun until it is almost gone before we walk back to the townhouse.

I get Lina to bed and bring down the small scissors from the first aid kit in the bathroom. Adam is standing by the sliding doors, looking out at the moonlight over the lake. He looks relaxed, calm. It's hard to admit but I feel a little safer having him here. Stevie is curled up at his feet, looking guilty for hurting me. I walk over and rub her head.

"It's ok Stevie. I know you didn't mean it." Her tail sways back and forth then she lays her head down again.

Adam looks to the scissors in my hand. "I guess I shouldn't be surprised that you would be hoarding medical supplies here." He laughs lightly at me. The skin around his eyes wrinkle slightly as he smiles.

"How do you want to do this?" I ask nervously. I think back to him watching the doctor stitch me up as I lay nearly topless on the dining room table.

"Let's go over to the table where the light is better."

I walk over to the table. Adam sits in one of the chairs, and I lift the back of my T-shirt, exposing the scars from the wolf scratches.

"Thanks for doing this," I tell him. "I have no idea where that doctor came from and I don't have anyone else to ask." I hear the small snips from the scissors as Adam clips at the stitches, removing them from the almost healed wounds. I stand still, barely breathing as he snips away. He rests his warm hand on my hip, to steady the scissors. The skin underneath tingles, sending small ripples up my side. Finally I hear the *ting* of the scissors on the table, he is done. Adam stays sitting, staring.

"What's wrong?" He doesn't answer. "Does it look that bad?" I try and crane my head around, to see what he is looking at on my back. "Is it not healed?"

"You never told me you had a tattoo," he finally replies, a clever smirk pulling at his lip.

"Nobody knows about it." I let my shirt fall back into place and walk away to wash the scissors in the sink. "What does it matter anyway, no one will notice the tattoo after they see my wolf scars."

"I'm not so sure about that. The tattoo suits you. I like it. The wolf scars are pretty cool too. Who else can say they've survived a wolf attack?"

"Yeah well, there's definitely nothing brave about me. Sometimes I think the tattoo was a mistake."

"You got your daughter back." He stops, abruptly, as though he was going to say more. Then it occurs to me Adam knows the townhouse is bugged, whatever he was going to say, he doesn't want anyone else to know.

"OK, it's late, and I'm sure you have to work in the morning, so thank you for taking out my stitches and eating my food and letting my kid beat you at cards." I try and pull him out of the chair from under his arm. But my hand is much smaller than his bicep and I can barely get a grasp on him. He looks at my hand and laughs quietly.

"I think you're right." He gets up and walks towards the back door. "Andie, try and stay out of trouble." He says, as he walks out the door and through the back yard to his townhouse.

--

There is a loud noise from the kitchen. The shattering of glass, a loud thud, it wakes me instantly. At first I'm not sure where I am. But I remember when I see the pale walls of the bedroom. Reaching over I check to make sure Lina is safe. She's still sleeping soundly next to me. Stevie is at the bedroom door pacing, pawing at the wood. I walk over and crack the door. She bounds down the stairs to inspect what happened. I close the door quietly behind me.

The stairway smells strange, sour and damp. Stevie growls from the kitchen. As I walk down the stairs the smell gets stronger, the sourness turning into something much more putrid. There's a warm breeze blowing through the open living area, I look to the kitchen and see it's coming from a broken kitchen window in the front of the town house. Stevie continues to growl at something on the floor in the dining room. I walk closer to it, slowly, pulling my shirt up over my nose. There's a lumpy mass, it's brown and white, leaves and twigs stick to it. As I look around I see there are dark marks on the floor where it must've rolled across the room. I can't move much closer to it, the smell is so strong, so putrid it seeps through the loose weave of my nightshirt, and I cough a few times, trying to get the thick smell of rot out of my nose and mouth. I walk around the mound, noticing that the white areas are moving slowly; they are piles of maggots crawling and squirming. When I get to the other side I see what looks like a triangular ear, and a snout. It's the decapitated, half decayed face of a wolf staring at me, one dark dead eye sagging open.

I stifle a scream with my hand. I can't have Lina waking up and seeing this in the dining room. I tiptoe across the kitchen floor, trying to miss the glass shards from the broken window, but I fail to spot one and it stabs sharply into my heel. I balance on one foot and pull the glass from my foot. I notice the blood specks on the floor from my bleeding wound. I grab a garbage bag from under the sink and open it. I throw the open end over the decaying wolf head and pull one side under it, so I can get it in the bag without touching it. There is a damp spot on the carpet that will have to be scrubbed clean before the stain sets. Stevie continues to growl at the bag as I tie it up, holding my breath so as to stop myself from vomiting. I head for the front door, turning as soon as I hear the tap of Stevie's nails on the floor.

"Stevie, stay," I tell her, "stay with Lina." I point up the stairs where Lina is sleeping. "I'll be right back." I close the front door behind me and look around the cluster of townhouses. I wish I had a flashlight. There are no lights, only the moonlight. My plan was to toss this in the ditch by the road, but I don't want to venture far out in the dark. Whoever threw this through my front window could still be out there, but I'm sure they're trying to get away from here; they wouldn't be stupid enough to stick around with all the Volker watching us.

I remember the sound of the wolves chasing us down the road. A chill runs up my back and my heart starts thumping in my chest. The thought of Lina waking up to find this mess scares me more. She has already been through enough, and I've tried so hard to keep her safe after the wolf attack. She barely slept for days, waking in the night, screaming. If she sees this I have no doubt it will start all over again. I take a deep breath and run down the front steps in my bare feet. I feel the cement of the sidewalk, the smooth pavement; a few small rocks jab into my soles. There's just enough light from the moon for me to see where I'm going. I can make out the flat landscape, the grass, small sidewalk, more grass. I can see the road, the ditch on the other side where I plan to throw the bag containing the wolf head.

The smell of rot is seeping through the thin plastic garbage bag, getting stronger and somehow more putrid. I try not to gag as I run across the sidewalk, then the grass, and finally making it to the road. I look behind me to make sure the door is still closed. Stevie's wet nose is on the glass next to the door. The rotting smell is still getting stronger, but I'm almost close enough to where I can swing the bag and throw it. The road is dark; shadows from the tall forest trees block the bright moonlight. I can barely see in front of me. The smell keeps getting stronger. Just a few more steps, I step down and feel something slimy and crunchy under my foot. It trips me and I fall on the pavement, my knees landing in whatever is in the road. I drop the bag, freeing my hands to hit the rough pavement and stop my fall. The bag must have ripped because the rotting, putrid smell is stronger than ever. I roll over and look down to see what I tripped over, giving myself a moment for my eyes to adjust to the darkness. There's a dark mound in front of me. I can make out four legs, a high hip bone, and a tail. That's all it takes for me to realize, I'm looking at the decaying body of a wolf, the body that belongs to the wolf head that was thrown through my window.

"Not good," I whisper into the darkness.

I scramble to get up and run back to my front door, realizing that this was a big mistake. I'll just leave the mess where it is, someone else can deal with it in the morning. I'm almost to my feet when I feel someone grab the hair on the back of my head. They also grab my upper arm and drag me across the pavement, down the street into the darkness. I start screaming and slapping with my free hand. I can see the cluster of townhouses, and hear Stevie barking from behind our front door. It's as I'm screaming that I notice there is no Volker vehicle parked in front of my townhouse, like there has been for days.

"Adam!" I scream as loud as I can, "Help!" I scream it over and over.

Whoever is dragging me lets go of my hair and clamps their hand over my mouth. I can't scream anymore, I can't even get air out of my mouth. Suddenly I am filled with the same fear I've felt too many times in the past few weeks, during the earthquake and the wolf attack. *Lina.*

Whoever is dragging me lets go of my mouth I am able to get out a few more screams and shouts, hoping someone will hear them. My captor responds with a sharp slap to my face, when that doesn't shut me up he progresses to a punch to the other side of my face. This is enough to almost knock me out. There's a pillowcase placed over my head, my hands are tied behind my back. Then I'm roughly tossed into the cargo area of a truck. The truck starts, and I kick the sides of the cargo area, then the top, trying to find a way to get out. The driver speeds over potholes and bumps in the road, tossing me around. There's the metallic taste of blood in my mouth. Ringing in my ears. I can't see where we are going but the truck stops just a few minutes after it started. I hear heavy footsteps and the back of the truck opening. Someone drags me by my foot, dropping me on the ground outside of the cargo area. There isn't enough time to get my feet under me and my balance is off with my hands tied behind my back, I land hard on my hip. There is a loud rushing noise from underneath me and a cool breeze blows by my legs and hands that are on the ground. It takes only a few seconds before I realize we are on one of the bridges that pass over the large rushing river which separates the town.

The person grabs the pillowcase and the back of my hair, pulling me to my feet. I stumble as I'm pulled across the bridge and slammed up against the metal barrier of the sidewalk guard. The pillowcase is finally pulled off my head and thrown in the air. I watch the wind carry it like a ghost, over the barrier and down towards the rushing water.

"What do you want?" I can barely get the words out, my jaw and hip hurt so badly.

There is a deep grumbling laughter from in front of me. My captor walks towards me, into the moonlight, so I can see him. I look around quickly. There is no one on the street to help me. Ever since the curfew was enacted the streets are bare at sundown. I struggle against the ties around my wrists, trying to get my arms free.

"What do I want?" The voice in front of me repeats. It's deep and southern, and I know instantly who it is. *Baillie.* He steps in front of me. His skin is so dark I can barely see his face in the night. He's tall, much taller than I am. "What do *I* want?" he repeats, mockingly.

"I don't know," I whisper.

"What I want is your useless excuse for a human being out of the Phoenix District Committee meetings." I have never been spoken to so coldly before. But there is no mistake in the seriousness of his voice. He does not want me being any part of the committee or this place. "I tried to take care of that with the wolves but they obviously didn't get the job done because here you are, as weak and annoying as ever."

"I've never done anything to you," I tell him. "Why are you doing this to me?"

I can feel the pressure behind my eyes from impending tears. Baillie must sense this. He starts laughing his deep, thunderous laugh.

"See, I've barely even done anything and here you are cowering like a fool. There is nothing special about you. You are worthless, never giving any decent contributions to committee meetings. I don't know why Crane keeps you around. Making you Sovereign was a waste." He reaches for my waist, picking me up, resting my hips on the top of the metal barrier, my upper body hanging over the dark rushing water. "But we are going to fix that, right now."

"Stop, please," I try and plead with him. "I have a child, I'll do anything."

"I don't care about you, or your child. You are both a waste of space. I can't believe they let you past the fence. We were told you were something great, you would bring so much to the committee, the District. But you just sit there, barely speaking, and when you finally decide to speak your disagreeing with my every word. You may think you're smarter than me but if I didn't know any better, I'd think you were a moron." His words cut deeper than any knife could. This is not the first time my intellect has been questioned because I have been quiet and observant. It's something I've struggled with my whole life.

"Please, stop." The wind from the river whips my hair across my face. "I never wanted any of this."

"Maybe with you out of the way Crane can focus and get some real work done." Baillie lets go of my waist, grabbing my neck and squeezing. I thought he was just going to throw me over the bridge and let the river have its way with me. But it seems as though he may want to finish the job himself. Either way, by the time they find my mangled body it won't matter how I died or who did it. Thoughts of Lina start running through my mind as Baillie squeezes my neck harder, cutting off the blood flow to my brain from the carotid artery. I know what's going to happen. Soon, permanent damage will be done. My brain will be starved of oxygen rich blood cells and my brain cells will start dying. Darkness starts to creep in around my eyes. My last words are the only person I can think about.

"*Catalina.*"

I hear something; a faint rumble, a loud squeal, the smell of burnt rubber. I wonder if this is it, death. But men are yelling. I just can't make out what they're saying. I think Baillie's grip loosens around my neck, and I feel myself falling. I wait to feel the river envelope me in its cold darkness. A few moments pass before I realize I am sliding down the metal barrier towards the hard sidewalk and not floating towards the river as the pillowcase did.

"Colonel Baillie, stop. We are required to protect all District Sovereign, even if it's from you. We will shoot."

Baillie lets loose his deep rumbling laughter. There is the metallic heavy click of a bullet falling into the chamber of a gun next to my head. I open my eyes in time to see Baillie pointing a gun at my face. This is followed by multiple gunshots from multiple guns. Baillie's body twitches; his shoulders, arms. Then he is falling backwards, away from me, falling to the ground. A dark pool of blood seeps from under his body.

"Andie," a familiar voice is at my side. It's Adam. "You're safe now." He picks me up like I weigh nothing. "Get the doctor to her house," he tells one of the nearby Volker guards.

"Where is Lina?" The ringing in my ears has returned and I can barely hear his response.

"She's safe. Stevie is with her, and Ms. Black. We're going back now."

He carries me to the back of an SUV, sliding in with me on his lap. I make no attempt to move. The pain in my hip and jaw are intense. I let my head rest on Adams chest, listening to his heart thud, his slow breaths. Each bump in the road brings a sharp intake of breath and pain shoots down my left hip. We arrive at the townhouse in just a few minutes. The road is lined with dark SUV's. People are outside near the lumps of decaying wolf carcass. Adam slides out of the SUV carrying me towards the townhouse. Someone is replacing the kitchen window. Ms. Black steps out, holding the door open for Adam. The kitchen smells like cleaning solution.

"Careful," I tell Adam, "broken glass."

"That's all cleaned up." Ms. Black eyes me, concerned.

"Where do you want her Doc?" Adam asks the Doctor who

stitched up my back.

"The table would be best." He points to the dining room table. "I'm sure you remember me, I'm Dr. Akiyama." He stands next to Adam so I can see his face.

"Wait. Where's Lina? Where is she?" I look around the room. I am surprised when I see Crane standing in the corner of the living room, watching me, his face pale.

"She's sleeping upstairs. She hasn't woken up." Ms Black is now standing next to me, speaking in a soft soothing tone. "Your dog would barely let me in her room."

I try and smile, stopping when the sharp pain from Baillie's punch spreads over my jaw. Adam sets me on the table and the Doctor starts cutting at my night shirt. My face flushes with embarrassment, the last thing I want is everyone to see me like this, stripped down.

"No people," I tell the Doctor, waving at the room, he nods understanding.

"I need everyone out, except you," he points to Adam. "I need your help. Go get some ice for her face"

Ms. Black and Crane leave without saying a word. I can still hear the commotion of people outside, but at least there is no one in here while the Doctor does his work except for Adam, and I'm sure he is about to get quite the show. The Doctor cuts off my top and shorts, leaving me in just my underwear. I close my eyes, and try not to think about Adam seeing me like this. My injuries are cleaned, bruises inspected. When they roll me onto my stomach, so the Doctor can check my back, he lets out a low whistle.

"You should have waited a few more days on those stitches, you're wound is ripped open, I'm going to have to stitch it again." I let out a deep groan. "There's too much scar tissue. I'm going to give you a little morphine for the pain." He gives me an injection of the anesthetic. It takes the pain away almost immediately, leaving my mind in a hazy fog. He stitches my back, applies medical glue to my lip and my foot, then packs up his bag. "We need to stop meeting like this, Andie." He squeezes my hand and gives Adam a list of instructions on how to care for me.

As he leaves Adam follows him, speaking to someone outside the door for a moment before closing it. I make no effort to move, and when he walks back to the dining room table I'm still lying on it in nothing but my underwear, unable to move. I can't remember when I shaved my legs last or if I'm wearing my good underwear, but the morphine helps me not care much.

Adam stands over the table, watching me for a moment and sighing, "Well, we can't just leave you here like this." He goes upstairs and opens the bedroom door. Stevie bounds down the stairs and stand up next to me, her front paws on the table. She licks the side of my head.

"Good girl, Stevie," I tell her.

Adam returns with some clothes and helps me put them on. He holds my elbow, helping me slide off the table. But when my feet hit the floor, both of my knees give out. Adam sweeps me up in his arms before I drop to the floor.

"The morphine," I hear myself mumble to him.

He carries me upstairs to the room where Lina is, so I can see her sleeping peacefully. He takes me to the other bedroom and sets me on top of the comforter. I make no effort to cover myself. I don't want to sleep but the morphine is too strong, the Doctor must have given me too much. I am out instantly.

--

I wish I could say the morphine helped me rest, but my dreams are filled with terror and I never stop running. There are wolves, shadows, darkness. I hear screams from Lina, see Baillie's bloodied corpse rise from the puddle of blood on the bridge. He chases me, and the only place I can think of to run to is my old house. It's night in my dream, but the lights in the house are on, the door unlocked. I run in and turn the deadbolt into place. Baillie's corpse pounds and claws at the door, eventually it gives up and walks to the street where there is a waiting hearse. The corpse climbs in the back and lies down, then the hearse drives away.

"Where have you been?" A familiar voice asks. I turn around to see Ian standing in the living room with me. I'm afraid to tell him what has happened. I'm afraid of his response when I tell him that I abandoned him and that I chose to save our daughter over him. How I made no effort to save him or to beg that he come with us. Somehow I get it out. I tell him everything; that our town has changed into something new-the Phoenix District-and we are being held captive. That I had no choice, Crane had Lina and I had to get her back. She's just a baby, she's my baby.

"Ian, I miss you so much," I choke through the tears running down my cheeks. The guilt of trying to move on so quickly is catching up with me. Ian makes no attempt to hug me, or kiss me, or welcome me home. He listens to my story, a stern look on his face, and when I am done there is nothing but silence.

"You think I don't know about your little friend? What's his name, Adam?" Ian spits out. "I've seen you with him. You didn't even let my corpse get cold before sneaking off with your new boyfriend."

"Ian, it's not like that. He helped me get home. He helped me get to Lina. With you gone, Adam is the only one I can trust. I have to keep her safe. I have to get her out of here."

"Did you ever think to keep me safe?" Ian tugs at his finger and pulls off his wedding band. "I knew I couldn't trust you with my heart." He reaches back and throws the wedding band through the living room window, shattering the glass. And that is all it takes for my heart to truly break. Warm tears flow down my cheeks. Somehow, I know this is all a dream, but it's so vivid, it feels so real.

"Ian, I love you. I want you to come back to me…" I reach out for him while walking across the living room. But now there is a glass in his hand, filled with ice water.

He waits until I'm almost next to him, "Enjoy your new life, *District Sovereign*, be careful of whom you trust." He swirls the ice in the glass for a moment. "You know what they say, if it talks like a pirate and it smells like a pirate then it's a pirate." He throws the ice water in my face and then he is gone.

--

When I wake up there is something cold on my face and it makes me wonder if I wasn't dreaming. But when I reach up with my hand I feel a frozen pack of ice. The morphine must have worn off because my joints are aching and stiff. I pull the blanket off myself and attempt to sit up. Another heavy bag of ice falls off my hip and onto the floor. When I reach down to pick it up I have to stop halfway, the new stitches in my back giving a sharp tug. The bag will have to stay there.

Lina bursts into the room. "Mom, you're awake." She throws her arms around my neck. "How do you feel?"

I can only assume she is staring at the bruises on my face. "Who is downstairs with you Lina?"

"Oh, Ms Black is here, and Adam and someone named Bugtown Pane, I think..." She taps her little finger on her chin, trying to remember.

"Did you just say Bugtown?" I laugh lightly. Lina giggles back. "Did you mean Burton Crane?" I ask her, enunciating each syllable.

"Oh, yeah, that must be it. Mommy, Adam made the best pancakes, with apples in them, you have to try some."

"Okay, Honey, I just want to get cleaned up first."

Lina kisses my cheek and then I hear her run down the stairs announcing to everyone that I am awake.

The walk to the bathroom is painful. For the first time in my life I wish I had a cane. When I get to the vanity I inspect my face in the mirror. I had braced myself for the worst, but the ice packs must have helped. There is a cut on my bottom lip that still has the gleam from the dried medical glue. A bluish-green bruise covers my jaw. A collection of dried tears collected near both of my ears. I look down further to see the faint imprint of Baillie's fingers across my neck. I try to think of what other damage was done to my body last night. I pull the band of my shorts away and stare at the large bruise covering my hip. I would like nothing more than to soak for an hour in a hot bath. But unfortunately the bathtub here is shallow, and short. So instead I take a long, hot shower.

The hot water rinses the dried blood from my body and it collects in a puddle by the drain. The scratches on my palms and knees burn under the soap. There's a sharp ache in my chest. At first I try and remember if I injured myself, then I remember the dream, losing Ian. I realize the ache is not physical, but emotional. Thankfully the shower is loud enough to muffle my sobs.

I do my best to choose clothes that cover the wounds, even though the heat of summer is starting. I don't want everyone seeing what happened to me last night, especially Lina. She has seen enough already. I pull on a pair of brown linen slacks, a loose black blouse, and sandals. I open my makeup case and try to cover the bruises on my face and neck. When I am done I stare at myself in the mirror. I hope I look presentable enough to go downstairs. Still, I don't want to face Crane.

My descent down the stairs is slow and painful. Stevie waits at the bottom, wagging her tail. Adam shows up when I am close to the bottom and holds his hand out to me. But all I can think of is my dream, when Ian yelled at me. I don't look at Adam or take his hand. Instead I hobble over to one of the plush living room chairs and ease myself down into its cushioned seat.

There's a stack of books on the coffee table and sheets of paper with Lina's handwriting on them. Ms Black is outside with Lina on the porch. They each hold magnifying glasses, looking at something on the railing. Crane eyes me from the couch. He looks pale and troubled, similar to last night when Adam carried in my busted body.

"How are you feeling?" Crane asks.

"I've felt better."

I'm not in the mood for talking. And I'm sure whatever Crane wants to talk about will be serious, requiring me to use my foggy, aching brain.

"I'm sure you're not up to talking right now, but there's no time to waste." He pauses, giving me a chance to speak up but I say nothing. "As you know Baillie has been dealt with. I tried to choose Committee members who wouldn't hold such simple grudges, who had a higher level of thinking and compassion for others. Obviously he was the wrong man for what we are trying to do here. We will search for his replacement on the Committee. Until then, I think we should have Adam sit in on the Committee meetings. His background is superb; he may be just the person we need to take Baillie's seat." Crane pauses again and we both look to Adam. He's still standing near the stairs, where I brushed him off. "We will be working around the clock on your new living quarters. Until then, you are not to leave this house without a Volker at your side."

"Stop trying to keep me captive, Crane."

"I've told you before, I'm trying to keep you safe. You obviously have no desire to keep yourself safe, which is apparent after you ventured out by yourself at night."

"There was more to it. I couldn't have Lina see what had been thrown through the window."

"Yes. I figured. Either way, pack your things. Construction should be completed in a few days. Now that Mr. Baillie has departed us I'm sure I don't have to worry about any more threats to your life. But, one can never be too careful." With that Crane stands, bows to both

116

of us and leaves.

I stare at the wall, fuming. I'm so tired of Crane telling me what to do. Controlling my life. Controlling my daughter's life. I miss our old life. I miss Ian.

Adam sets a plate of pancakes in my lap, and a steaming cup of coffee on the table next to me. Ian rarely cooked. I was always the one cooking at home. I stare at them for a long time, trying not to cry again, thinking.

Lina bursts into the room. "Mommy, you have to try them. Oh, and look what we found." She is holding what looks like a large black bug between her fingers. "It's a cicada skin. Isn't it cool?" She giggles then bounds back out the door.

"You have a remarkable daughter, Andie." Adam finally speaks from the couch where Crane was just sitting.

"Yes. I know. Everyone keeps telling me this."

"I know last night was really bad, but you're safe now. I want you to know I won't let anything happen to you or Lina."

"I know. You are required by District regulations to protect all Sovereign."

"This is more than regulations, Andie." A slight crease is starting to form in Adams forehead. I've seen it a few other times when he is concerned or slightly angered.

"I'm sorry. It's just, everything is starting to sink in, and I just want my old life back…" I cover my face with my hands and take deep breaths, trying not to cry. Trying not to show Adam that I am much weaker than he probably already thinks I am.

Finally, when I recover, I eat the breakfast Adam made. Lina was right, the pancakes are delicious and so is the coffee. Adam sits for a while, watching me. I'm too embarrassed by my crying to look at him. When I'm done eating he takes my dishes to the kitchen and cleans them. I walk out onto the sunlit porch with Stevie and watch Lina inspect the yard with Ms. Black. They get along well together and Lina has already learned so much. Something at the edge of the yard catches my eye, a person in dark clothes. I lean forward to get a better look. It's a Volker guard. I scan the yard and see more of them watching and patrolling near the trees and the lakeshore and the townhouses next to mine.

It's not long before the pain in my hip and jaw start to ache. I turn around to go inside and the sight of Adam standing silently behind me startles me. "I think I need to go lay down," I tell him flatly.

"That would be a good idea. You should get your rest after last night."

He opens the sliding glass door for me and follows me inside. I scale the stairs slowly and lie down in my room. Adam shows up not long after I pull the covers over myself. He carries a bag of ice in each hand. He places one on my jaw, and then lifts the blanket, placing the other on my sore hip.

"I'm sorry," I tell him.

"I know."

"No you don't. I had a dream about Ian. It wasn't good. It was actually pretty terrible." I try to control the trembling of my chin.

"I know." Adam pulls the blanket up to my shoulders.

"How do you know?" I ask.

"You talk in your sleep."

He brushes a piece of hair off my forehead, tucking it behind my ear, just like Ian used to do, then he leaves the room. I wonder how much of the conversation he heard. Did he hear me pleading with Ian? Could he hear the guilt in my voice for leaving my husband behind?

I hear Lina giggling in the back yard. I focus on the sound of her voice and before long I am asleep. This time there are no morphine dreams.

CHAPTER TWELVE

Lina wakes me. She's tapping on my forehead, her eyes an inch away from my face, at least twice their normal size. They are so big I can see the tiny dark flecks in her green irises. I notice she's examining me with the magnifying glass.

"Hi, mom," she greets me, distracted with whatever she is looking at magnified on my face. "Adam says dinner is ready." She speaks through the glass, magnifying the size of her lips and baby teeth. I reach my arms out and hug her.

"I love you, little Catalina," I whisper in her ear.

"I love you too mom. Let's go."

She pulls my hand trying to tug me out of bed. Getting up is much easier this time and so is walking down the stairs. I smell the sweet and tangy scent of spaghetti sauce and the pungent aroma of garlic. The table is set for three and I can see Adam's back as he works at the stove.

"Where is Ms. Black?" I ask Lina.

"She went home. She said she would come back tomorrow and we can learn more fun things."

Adam turns around. "Good, you're up. Dinner's done."

Adam collects the plates from the table and takes them back to the kitchen. He returns a moment later, each plate piled high with spaghetti and garlic bread. Lina fills me in on her day as we eat. She talks nonstop, even with food in her mouth. Any other day, I would remind her that it's not ladylike to talk with food in her mouth. But after all she's been through, I decide it is ok for her to be a poor mannered child for the moment.

I still can't bring myself to look Adam in the face. Even after all he has done for us. We clear the table together. Then I leave Adam in the kitchen while I get Lina ready for bed. She plays in the bathtub for a while and after she reads me a book. By the time I get her tucked into bed the sun is almost done setting over the lake.

I return to the living room to find Adam sitting on the couch. I hold back the urge to throw myself on the couch next to him and sit on the opposite end of it instead. I try to think about what I can say to thank him for all he's done, to apologize for being rude to him earlier. I know it's wrong that I want him to wrap his arms around me like he did last night when he carried me home after Baillie's attack.

"I know you're upset about Ian. Don't you think he would have done the same thing if he were in your position right now?" Adam asks. He's leaning back on the couch, arms resting on the side and back of the couch, pulling the fabric of his T-shirt tight against his bicep.

"I don't know. I would hope that he would do whatever he could to protect Lina." I stare at his arm, his chest; finally I look in his eyes, the now familiar pale blue.

"I think you are doing exactly what he would have done." I know he's just trying to make me feel better but the guilt of losing Ian still lingers in the back of my mind. "I know what it's like to lose a member of your family."

I remember he lost his entire family. I saw the fresh graves myself, when we were walking into town. "I don't want to talk about it anymore." I shake my head and cover my eyes with my hand.

"How are your bruises?" Adam changes the subject.

"Fine, I guess. The only thing that hurts right now is my hip."

Suddenly he is scooting himself closer to me, so he's sitting mostly on my cushion of the couch. He reaches out, holding my chin gently with his fingers. I watch him nervously from between the fingers of the hand that is still across my eyes.

"The ice must have helped. The bruise on your jaw is barely visible." He rubs his thumb across my bottom lip. "This looks good too." He smiles a little. I think he's looking at the cut on my lip. I hold my breath, afraid that he is so close to me, inspecting me. I tell myself it's nothing, twice now he has seen me barely dressed, getting stitched together on the dining room table. Before I realize what he is doing Adam slides his arm under my legs and pulls me onto his lap.

"It's ok, Andie," he whispers in my ear.

I decide I can't take it any longer, worrying about Ian, feeling guilty. I throw my arms around Adam and bury my face in his neck. His arms wrap around my back sliding gently over my stitches. We stay like this for a long time. I try not to think about everything. I tell myself that he has been through so much too. We were thrown into this situation together and that must mean something. It has to mean something.

We stay together on the couch until the early morning light colors the sky. Then Adam is leaving to get ready for work and I head upstairs to wake Lina and get ready for the day.

--

The next few days pass by in a blur. I spend a day re-packing everything we brought to the townhouse. Ms. Black shows up each morning to work with Lina on her schooling. One day she shows up with two paper coffee cups in her hand, each with a familiar logo imprinted on them. She hands me one.

"I heard a rumor that this is your favorite."

I smell the cup. It is unmistakable, Starbucks coffee. None of these people know me very well, so I wonder who she has been speaking to.

"Sweet Jesus, how did you get this past the gates?"

"I know some secrets." She smiles at me. "And it's my favorite too."

Ms. Black helps me carry a few things downstairs for the move. I work up enough courage to ask what her first name is. She laughs and responds "Blithe. Now you know why I don't mind people calling me Ms. Black."

"Blithe Black," I repeat her name slowly, "I like it. That was my great grandmother's name, Blithe. It means happy you know?"

"Yes well, look where I am now. A happy person would not volunteer to be part of this."

"Wait, you volunteered?" I ask her.

"Yes. I was in Japan teaching at a private school for the children of U.S. Embassy personnel. Crane came to me, he made me an offer

I couldn't refuse, and here I am now."

Lina interrupts us, asking for a snack. I want to ask her more questions but now is not the time. "Well, Blithe, you work very well with Lina, and I just want to thank you for all you've taught her." I leave her with that and head to the kitchen to make Lina a snack.

Adam sends University Volker to help move everything to our new living quarters in the Chemistry Hall. One of the guards delivers a message that Adam couldn't help since he was busy organizing Volker assignments for the entire District. Now that Baillie is gone, Adam has taken over most of his responsibilities, at the suggestion of Crane. It's the first time a Volker has spoken to me. Usually they just stand nearby, watching. I look over the guard while he speaks. He's young, almost too young in my mind. Freckles stretch across the bridge of his nose. He bows slightly when he addresses me and when he is done. Then he returns to his post outside the townhouse.

On the last trip to move our things, Lina, Stevie and I ride with the guard who has been parked outside of the house the past few days. He escorts us to the fourth floor of the building. I notice security cameras outside the building, pointing into the laboratory area and the elevator. I have the uneasy feeling that this building has been enhanced only to more easily monitor us, under the guise of protection.

When the elevator doors open I am in awe. Beyond a set of large glass doors, the fourth level of the building has been transformed into a large open loft with hardwood floors, freshly painted white walls, granite countertops and top of the line appliances. The main living space is huge with floor to ceiling windows that face a different view from the atrium. There are floor to ceiling windows everywhere, giving a view of most of the campus and the lake. Lina runs excitedly in the open space opening all the doors. Some lead to closets, a pantry, a bathroom and bedrooms on each side of the living room. There are even glass doors leading to an open courtyard on the roof of the third floor.

"Mom, I found my room," Lina tells me excitedly. "And it's my favorite color, pink." She pulls my hand, leading me into the bedroom on the right, which is filled with shelves of books and toys. There is a large canopy bed and fuzzy plush carpet on the floor. The room is tastefully decorated with various shades of pink and white. Stevie runs into the room behind us and jumps onto Lina's new bed, barking a few times as though she's telling us she approves of the room too.

I leave Lina to play and unpack her things while I wander to the other bedroom. I am equally pleased with my bedroom. There is a large king size bed, a desk, the room is decorated with neutral earth tones and, again, large windows overlooking the forest to the west of the campus.

I turn around as I hear someone enter the room behind me.

"I take it you are pleased with the accommodations?" To my surprise Crane is standing in the bedroom behind me. Again in a black suit, this time a bright orange tie to match his hair.

"It's very nice. But it's too much. We don't need all this. We were perfectly fine at the townhouse." I walk towards the door trying to escape the room. I don't want to be alone in this bedroom with Crane. He steps in front of me, blocking my path.

"Ah, but you were not so safe there. Look what happened. You will find it much different here; there will be guards, alarms, cameras. Everything you need to feel out of harm's way." He smiles with a smug, satisfied look.

"Like I've said before, *Burton*, it feels like you are trying to keep me prisoner." I have never called him by his first name before, but I try and spit it out arrogantly with a hint of a soft tone, just like he does when he calls me Andromeda.

"On the contrary, as I know I've told you before, this is all for your safety." He pauses for a moment, staring at me. "I think one full day is enough for you to get settled. Prepare to get started in the laboratory and Catalina will start formal classes in the atrium." He drops the tone of his voice. "Must I remind you that the Volker have been assigned for our protection? You may want to reassess your relationships. After all you are a District Sovereign, not some feeble minded Resident from one of our factions." He gives me a stern look, as though I am a child who has done something wrong. Then Stevie is behind him, growling. "I will contact you shortly." And with that Crane turns on his heel and walks briskly out of the living quarters.

His warning about the Volker is unsettling. There is only one person he could be hinting at: Adam.

CHAPTER THIRTEEN

The next morning Lina and I wake early. I barely slept, due to a barrage of strange noises and bad dreams. Each time I closed my eyes Ian was there, accusing me. More than once I woke with tears fresh on my face and heaviness in my chest from the guilt of leaving Ian behind.

We get ready for the day and walk down to the atrium. Ms. Black is waiting for us.

"Catalina, welcome to your new classroom." She greets us both. "Congratulations on your first day in the lab." She turns around and takes a cup off the table behind her, placing it in my hand. "Enjoy."

I bring the cup to my nose and smell it. *Starbucks.*

"I don't know how you keep getting this, but you're going to have to stop before I come to expect it." I take a sip of the fragrant, hot coffee.

I look around and inspect the makeshift classroom. A chalkboard has been attached to the wall, the syllabus for the day is already written neatly on it. I kiss and hug Lina and point to the lab, showing her where I will be for the day.

I walk to the glass doors, standing in front of them, watching the lab staff inside. They're already busy running samples from all the residents. There is barely a noise when I open the door to enter, the rubber soles of my sandals quieting my footsteps. A short woman greets me as I enter. She is just a bit shorter than I am, barely reaching five feet, with almond eyes. Her hair is long and dark. She's dressed professionally with a white lab coat.

"Hello. My name is Kira, you must be Andromeda?" She holds her hand out.

"Please, call me Andie, when I hear Andromeda it feels like I am about to get in trouble." I give her a smile and shake her hand.

"Ok, Andie, as you can see your lab is already analyzing samples. We have begun separating the resident's genetic data from the samples that were taken, elongating the DNA sequences with PCR and running them on gels. It's all quite straightforward, as you know. I've read all of your papers. I have everyone repeating the methods you published. Soon we will have data for you to analyze. If you'd like, I can introduce you to the staff."

"That sounds good, Kira."

She walks me through the lab, which I find more impressive when I get a closer look at all the supplies lining the countertops. Expensive reagents, top of the line micropipettes and PCR tubes. Crane spent a lot of money, but it will be worth it. The best materials will help us turn out the best results. As long as I can remember what I have to do.

There are three other people working in the lab, two men and a woman, to whom Kira introduces me. They have strong Japanese accents and it's hard for me to make out what they're saying. I do a lot of smiling and nodding, trying to make it look like I am involved in the small conversations. Eventually I give up and tell Kira I want to get the computer on my desk organized for the data.

I sit down and adjust the office chair so I can reach the desktop comfortably. I search the desktop computer for the power button so I can turn it on. After a few minutes of searching I notice the computer screen in the middle is thicker that the other two. There are multiple USB ports lining the side of the monitor which must mean all of the computer's innards are housed on the back of the middle monitor. I push the power button and wait for everything to turn on.

I pretend to organize the computer, but mostly I move the icons around on the screens and try to get used to having three monitors.

I take a break to have lunch with Lina and Ms. Black. Then I return to my desk. I'm anxious, knowing that my work will ensure our safety with Crane. The human genome contains at least thirty thousand genes. Thankfully the government has identified many of those genes. But Crane wants me to dig deeper into the genome to look for biological pathways which haven't been highly researched.

Since I haven't been in a lab in over four years, I decide to review my old journal articles and prepare myself for the deluge of data I am about to receive. I search the computer for electronic copies and find an icon on the monitor screen in the shape of a book. When I click on it I see that Crane has made all the latest published research available. Of the few things I know about computers this also means that he has secured an internet access communications line to the outside world.

We can communicate to the outside world. I just have to figure out how.

CHAPTER FOURTEEN

After four nights of nightmares, of seeing Ian in my sleep, throwing his wedding band through the front window of our house, I decide I can't take it anymore. I have to see Ian with my own eyes. I have to see if I made the right decision by choosing Lina over him.

"I need you to watch Lina," I whisper to Ms. Black after lunch.

"Why?" She asks looking at me skeptically.

"I need to do something. It's important. I'll be quick. I know you'll keep her safe. *Please.*" I mouth to her.

"You had better hurry. School is over in less than two hours." She gives me a warning look. Then I am off.

Most people don't know that there is a tunnel in the basement of this building. I remember it from when I went to college here. It was reserved for those blustery cold days when walking across the icy wind blown campus was unbearable. I use the elevator to get to the basement level and walk down the main hallway. There are no security cameras here. I see the familiar old wooden door with a desk pushed in front of it. I push the desk out of the way and pull open the heavy door. I flick the light switch on the wall. Bright fluorescent lights illuminate a long windowless hallway that leads to the biology building. I run down the hall and yank the door open at the other end. Thankfully it's unlocked. There are two doors, one leading into the lower level of the biology building and one leading outside. Since I know they have been using the biology building for testing the residents and classes for the younger residents, I push hard on the door leading to the outdoors. The fresh air and sunlight wrap around me as I leave the cold underground tunnel. For the first time in a long time I have some tiny sense of freedom. But I know it won't last long, because I have to come back here for my daughter.

I run across the campus parking lot to the nearby street. My old house is not too far from here, maybe a thirty minute walk. I walk fast, keeping my head down. No one looks at me. Not even the Volker passing by in black SUVs, or any of the residents working outside, sweeping the streets and sidewalks.

By the time I make it to the bridge my heart is thumping hard in my chest. I'm halfway to my old house now and I know Crane will make me pay dearly for this if he finds out.

Today it's hot outside and a thick line of sweat trickles down the middle of my back. I walk faster, being just five or six blocks away now and the anticipation is growing, tingling in my arms and legs. It is all I can do not to break into a sprint. I keep walking, moving over to a side street where I will be less noticeable. It's not long before I can see the house. My house, with the plants still flowering in front of the porch. The flag is gone, but it's still my house. I pause for a moment before walking up onto the porch. The house looks empty. Even though it's only been a few weeks, it seems like forever since I was here last. I step up on the porch and reaching for the door, I inhale deeply and turn the door handle. It's unlocked.

The house is immaculate. It still has the familiar smell of lavender, the smell of home. But it looks bare with all of Lina's toys gone. All of our family pictures have been taken down from the walls. I head to the office, to the filing cabinet drawer where I keep all of my old files from the research lab I worked in. The drawer squeaks loudly when I pull it open. Thankfully all my old files are there along with the memory card I was looking for. I grab the small memory card that's attached to a black lanyard and place it over my neck. This has all the data I analyzed, my old files, calculations, and spreadsheets. This is my back up plan if I get caught.

"What are you doing in here?" asks a familiar voice.

When I turn around Ian is standing in the doorway. He looks thinner and his blonde hair is cut short making it look dark. I stop myself from running at him and throwing my arms around him. I remember all too well what happened last time I did.

"Who are you? What are you doing?" He asks, looking confused.

"It's me, Andie. Don't you remember me?"

Ian stares blankly at me. He has no idea who I am. "Am I supposed to know you?" he asks flatly.

"It's me, your wife. Don't you remember me?" I plead with him.

"I don't have a wife."

He is not accusing me, holding me accountable for my actions, for abandoning him and for not saving him too. This is not the Ian from my dream.

I hear the front door open and bang against the wall.

"Andie!" It's a voice I recognize immediately. *Adam.* I brush past the confused and slightly irritated Ian.

"Adam. What are you doing here? How did you know-"

"Stop," He interrupts me sternly. He's angry, like I've never seen him before. "Let's go."

"What is going on here? What do you two think you are doing in my house?"

Ian has followed me into the living room. "Who are you people?" he asks, his voice getting louder. He's starting to get annoyed.

Adam interrupts him holding the palm of his hand up in front of Ian's face. "Remain calm, Ian. This was a mistake. Remain calm, Ian. Remain calm."

Ian stops and cocks his head to the side. His expression changes slowly and he becomes more relaxed.

"Remain calm," Ian repeats to himself, pondering the phrase in his head.

Adam backs up and takes my hand, pulling me out of the house, closing the door behind him and bringing me to a waiting SUV.

"How did you know where I was, Adam?" I get the feeling Crane is keeping a closer watch on me than I originally thought.

"Let's just say I had a feeling." He throws the vehicle into gear and speeds off. "Do you know what Crane would have done if he had found out you went there?" I can tell Adam is angry with me. He drives fast through the town streets, ignoring every stop sign and traffic light.

"I don't care." I cross my arms over my chest. "I had to get some files."

Adam stares me down from the driver's seat, he doesn't slow the vehicle. "You're lying. You went to see Ian." My cheeks start to flush with embarrassment. After all Adam has done for me and I lie to him. Here I am, still afraid to trust him. "I'm sure Crane hasn't instructed you on how to deal with the residents yet? You can't just force yourself on them. Drop in and say hello. They have to be prepared, even the smallest glitch in their day can set them off. You have to make sure they stay calm, we can't risk an uprising."

"I'm sorry. I didn't know-" I start but Adam interrupts me.

"That's right you don't know. Crane has you secluded in *this* little bubble. He doesn't tell you things." I start to wonder if Adam is talking about more than just dealing with the residents. "I'm not Crane, but I also don't want to find your bloodied body on the side of the road, *again*." His voice lowers and the angered look on his face softens. "We've played that game already. I'm sure you remember quite clearly because I do."

We're back on campus now and Adam slows down. He parks behind the chemistry building, throwing the SUV into park before it has come to a complete stop. The force of the suddenly stopping vehicle throws me forward; Adam throws his arm in front of me, stopping me from hitting the dash.

"Sorry," he says, his arm lingering a little too long in front of me.

I unbuckle my seatbelt and get out.

As Adam escorts me into the Atrium, the Volker by the door looks shocked at my sudden appearance outside. Adam salutes the guard and walks towards the elevator with me.

"Show me how you got out, Andie."

I'm reluctant to show him, because I know my secret passage will most likely disappear. Then I will be truly trapped in this giant glass building. Still, I take him to the basement level and show him the tunnel.

"It's the secret tunnel everyone always talked about in college. Only a few students got to use it, so not many know where it actually is," I tell him.

Adam looks down the long hallway, impressed.

"Good to know." He flicks off the hallway light, leaving us with only the soft glow from the elevator light. "Andie." Adam's face is by my neck, his nose rubbing against the cartilage of my ear. We haven't been this physically close in a long time. We haven't had any time alone with my work in the lab, taking care of Lina and him running the Volker faction. "This could work out well for both of us. Have you told anyone else?" he whispers in my ear. The moist heat from his breath sends tingles down the back of my neck.

"No," I croak out. I take a moment to clear my throat. "I haven't told anyone but you."

"Good," he replies. I feel him step closer to me in the darkness. His hands brush my cheek as they move to my hair, his fingers entwining in my curls, tipping my head back. His mouth finds mine. His lips feel warm and firm. My arms move on their own, up his chest and around the back of his neck into his hair. He pushes his body up against mine until my back hits the cold cement wall behind us. "I've been waiting to get you alone for so long." He doesn't give me any time to respond before his lips are back on mine, kissing me harder, hungrier than the first kiss. He leaves a trail of damp kisses across my jaw line, to my ear, my neck. I can feel the heat flushing to my face, my heart fluttering, my ears ringing, my entire body feeling like it is on fire. He moves his hands down my shoulders, my sides, stopping at my waist, wrapping his long fingers around the sensitive skin just above the waist of my jeans, pulling me closer to him. Then his lips are back on mine. His warm hands stretch around my back, pulling me even closer to him.

Somehow, he tears his mouth from mine, both of us breathing heavily; he rests his forehead against mine. "Andie…" Listening to Adam say my name sends more tingles throughout my body. "It's time to go." Placing his hand on the side of my neck, he kisses me one last time, and I'm sure he can feel my rapid pulse in response to what he just did to me. I don't want to leave this place, this moment in time, but I know he's right.

He takes my hand, pulling me to the elevator. Once we are inside he resumes his professional Volker stance, with his hands behind his back. I know he is doing this because of the cameras monitoring us, but I want him near me, I want his hands back on my waist, and his lips back on mine.

As Adam escorts me to the lab we stop to see Lina and Ms. Black on our way through the atrium. He pulls a small flower out of his pocket for each of them. Lina squeals with excitement when he places it in her little hand.

"It's a little rose, I l-o-v-e roses," she exclaims, giving Adam a hug.

I watch them, Adam reaches down to hug her back, smiling widely.

He leaves me at the front door of the lab, and returns to whatever he was doing before I got myself into trouble. I return to my desk and the data I was working on. The lab workers mill about. I don't even think they noticed I was gone. I stare at the spreadsheet in front of me and try to clear my head, which is hard to do after what just happened in the dark hallway. I press my fingers to my lips, feeling something, something other than the remnants of Adam's heated kisses on my lips. It's not long before I can place it, because I had a similar feeling when I abandoned all those babies at the hospital: guilt and shame.

CHAPTER FIFTEEN

Something on my desk is ringing, an endless shrill ring. It sounds like a phone. The lab workers stop what they're doing, looking at me, waiting for me to answer it. But at first I can't find where it's coming from, until I finally notice a small black phone tucked into the corner of the desk.

When I answer it I hear Crane's voice on the other end. "There will be a Committee meeting in one hour. I will send an escort. I look forward to seeing you soon." Then I hear the click of the other line hanging up. He didn't give me a chance to talk or say goodbye. I wonder if it was a recording.

We haven't had a Committee meeting in over a week and I worry if Crane found out about my escape, if he will hand down some punishment in front of the other committee members to humiliate me. I save my work and stand up to find the lab manager, Kira. She's sitting at a computer in the corner, carefully entering Resident codes into a file so we can identify their data.

"Kira," I touch her shoulder, startling her. "Crane called a Committee meeting. I'll be back when it's over."

She smiles and nods her head at me. Sometimes I wonder why I bother telling her I'm leaving, everyone in the lab must know I'll be back; there's nowhere else for me to go.

I walk to the atrium where Ms. Black is working with Lina. Today there is another child with her, a little boy around the same age. He's been selected from the population as being gifted and from now on he will be schooled with Lina, together they will be prepared as the next generation of District Sovereign. I shudder at the thought of my daughter's future; it only intensifies my desire to find a way out of here.

Ms. Black stops what she's doing and waits for me to speak. "Crane has called a Committee meeting," I tell her.

"Lina, Cashel, lets clean up before we go," she tells the children.

Lina and the little boy stop writing. I help Blithe take them to the bathroom and collect a bag with snacks and a few toys. "How old is Cashel?" I ask Ms. Black while we are getting ready to go.

"He's seven."

"But Lina's only five. Should they really be working together?"

"Lina excels for her age group. You'll see. Just watch them." Ms. Black squeezes my elbow. "Don't worry, Andie, we won't let her hang out with the bad boys."

I force a smile through the realization that my child is growing up much too fast. Then it hits me. Her birthday is just a few months away, soon she will be six.

When we return to the atrium Adam is waiting for us. I control the urge to smile at him or touch him or show any hint that our relationship is anything more than professional, not with everyone here-and the cameras-watching.

"Are you our escort?" I ask when we get close.

"Of course, Crane only sends his best Volker." I let a small laugh escape. "Actually, I was nearby so I offered to collect you all since we are going to the same meeting." Adam now sits in Baillie's spot at the Committee meetings, as a voice for the Volker faction. "Would anyone like to walk today?" he asks.

I'm surprised when he asks. We haven't been allowed to walk more than a few hundred yards from the chemistry building.

"Yes! Yes! Let's walk," Lina speaks up.

Ms. Black and I both nod in agreement.

There's a sidewalk with a direct path to the now renamed District Headquarters building. We walk as a large group, Lina and the new boy stopping along the way to pick flowers, or to ask Ms. Black a question. I fall into line next to Adam, skipping a few steps to keep up with his long stride. Finally he slows a little.

"I forgot what it was like trying to walk next to you. Perhaps we should have driven."

"It's not my fault the world is filled with tall people," I respond.

He gives a light chuckle.

"What do you think this Committee meeting will be about?" he asks.

"Adam, didn't Crane tell you? The first rule of The Phoenix District Sovereign Committee meetings is you don't talk about Committee meetings." I wait for his response, but he doesn't say anything. "And the second rule of The Phoenix District Sovereign Committee meetings is you don't talk about Committee meetings." Still nothing. "Well, I thought it was funny," I reply to myself.

A thoughtful expression has crept up on Adam's face. "Andie, did it ever occur to you, if Crane doesn't want anyone talking about the meetings, it's because he wants to be there to control the course of the meetings? That he may be keeping something else from you? Sometimes rules are meant to be broken."

We complete the rest of the walk in silence, his words igniting an even larger firestorm of suspicion inside of me.

--

When we get to the Committee Meeting room it has been completely transformed. There's new plush carpet and heavy curtains hang on each end of the vast window. There are thin laptop computers at each of the seats around the large circular table. The room has been partitioned with a glass wall and door. On the other side of the glass the room is filled with toys, games, books, two computers, everything to keep a child entertained during a long Committee meeting.

Crane, Morris and Alexander are already sitting at the table. They rise, walking over to greet us as we enter the room.

"Ah, welcome," Crane begins, with his usual smug expression. "I hope you will enjoy the improvements to the room." He opens his arms wide, waiting for our response.

Today's tie color is red. I am not fond of the color red.

"It's very nice, Crane," I respond.

Ms. Black escorts the children to the play area. Alexander and Morris walk over and introduce themselves to Adam. They take the time to shake my hand and welcome me back, which I don't completely understand since I didn't go anywhere.

"Everyone, please take your seats and let us get started," Crane announces.

As I walk closer to the table I notice the seats are now assigned with plaques bearing our names. Alexander and Morris sit side by side, Adam is across the table from me, and my place is marked to the right of Crane's seat. Crane taps his hammer on the copper plate and the meeting begins. He instructs us on how to log into the laptops in front of us. From now on we will be taking notes and signing in agreement electronically. Crane informs us that we are working on a secure closed network to ensure the safekeeping of our work. "Let's start with updates on how each faction is progressing," Crane continues. "Morris, Alexander, let's start with you both."

Alexander and Morris nod simultaneously. They take turns talking about the factions that are keeping the District running. The Orderlies have done a spectacular job keeping the district clean, they have removed truckloads of litter and garbage from the town leaving it the cleanest it's ever been. The Navigators have produced adequate routes to provide transportation to all of the District residents with minimal fossil fuel consumption. The Currents have the hydroelectric plant on the river running at eighty percent and the nuclear power plant is running at thirty percent, which has been generating more than enough power to run the city. They continue for what seems like an hour or more. I start to lose interest until I hear Morris mention the farms beyond the wall.

Something I didn't know but eagerly learn by listening closely to Morris as he speaks, is that it seems the Cultivators are allowed to live outside the cement wall of the Phoenix District. Each day Residents are transported to the farms to help with the animals, maintain the crops, upkeep roads and disable the former main roads which were used to get into town.

"While the crops are already producing an excellent yield, it may not be enough to get us through the long winter. We may want to consider greenhouses or getting one of the local food processing plants operational so we don't have a food crisis come winter," Alexander says finishing his long discourse.

Crane is nodding his head in agreement as he responds, "We may need to start running the train again to collect supplies and bring them in. This brings us to our next topic. We need to assign a Runner for the District." Crane looks to Adam.

"I have a few recruits that may be viable options," Adam speaks up.

I have no idea what they are talking about. "What is a Runner?" I interrupt.

"Oh, Andromeda, I forgot you were not at our last meeting when we discussed the specifics of the District Runner," Crane smiles arrogantly at me.

I am surprised by his revelation, that there was a meeting held without me. "I thought meetings were only to commence if all District Sovereign were present?" I ask.

"Yes, but you were busy healing. I thought it best to let you mend. Don't fret. It was a very short meeting. I can fill you in right now." He clears his throat loudly. "We discussed the necessity for having a District Runner, as you know the rules of the District are that no one enters or exits the gate. Currently the rest of the world thinks this area is a desolate nuclear blast site. The Runner will be the only one allowed out and back in. They will collect supplies and organize shipments via the heavily guarded train which is located in the most northern area of the District, complete with a guarded entry and exit. The Runner will be heavily trained, a tracking device implanted under their skin so they can be monitored from here. They will also be responsible for transporting information to our Funding Entities."

"Okay," I reply. I feel stupid for not knowing that I missed a meeting. But Crane never said anything to me about. Adam must have been right. Crane has been letting us believe this entire time that the District Sovereign are responsible for making decisions for the Residents, for watching over them. But Crane is the one pulling the strings, organizing and planning. I know he's using us to manage the Residents, because he can't do it all on his own.

"So, Andromeda, how about you fill us in on your progress with your work?" Crane changes the subject, interrupting my thoughts. He can probably tell that I am seething.

"Every Resident's DNA sample has been analyzed with the microarray. And they're currently being assigned codes so their names won't be visible during analysis, to prevent any bias. Once the codes are fully assigned then I can begin my analysis. Currently, I'm backing up the raw data to a secure hard drive." I look to Crane when I am done. I know the only thing keeping me here, keeping me and Lina safe, is my ability to analyze that data and give Crane what he wants.

"Excellent Andromeda." His pleasure in my response helps me feel a tiny bit safer. "Everyone please sign their summary of today's meeting and then we can all get back to work, running the District."

We leave the room together but Crane stays behind working on his laptop. Breaking another rule, the Committee Meeting Room is to be locked at all times unless there is a meeting in session. Adam escorts us back to the Chemistry building.

--

"Mom, can Adam come over and make us spaghetti for dinner?" Lina is looking through the cupboards and the fridge for something to eat.

"Dinner's not for a few more hours, Lina," I call from the couch as I read a journal article on inherited behavior modification.

"But I'm hungry now."

"Lina, Adam has been very busy. I don't know if he has time to come over." He's been so busy I've barely seen him for days. But that doesn't stop me from reliving those few moments we had together in the dark basement of this building, when I showed him the secret tunnel.

"Please, Mom, please." Lina scrunches her face into a sad frown.

I could call him. The operator could connect me to where ever he is right now. But I've never tried it before. Finally I give in, "Okay, Lina. I'll try and call him."

"Yay!" Lina pumps her little fists in the air and runs in a circle.

I walk over to the phone on the wall and pick it up. There is a dull tone before it rings twice. "Phoenix District Operator, how may I direct your call?" The woman's voice on the other end is pleasant and polite.

"I need to speak with Adam Waters."

"I'm sorry that name is not in my directory. Is there someone else?"

That's strange, why would it not be in the directory. I think for a moment. "Do you have Colonel Waters, Volker Sovereign?"

"Yes, one moment." The phone rings twice, again, before it's answered.

"Hello." The voice is unmistakable.

"Adam?"

"Yes."

"It's Andie, I hope I'm not interrupting." I pause for a moment. "Lina wants you to come over and make spaghetti for dinner. If you can, she's been begging me."

"Sure. I'll be there later." He hangs up without saying goodbye. It feels odd, the conversation; his responses were short. He must have been busy with something I tell myself.

Lina and I busy ourselves with cleaning before Adam gets there. I look in my closet for something nicer to wear, but I am sorely disappointed. All I have are the few clothes from my old closet. I give up after a few moments and stick with the jeans and loose black top that I have on.

I'm helping Lina rearrange her stuffed animals when I hear the doors open from the elevator and someone shout my name. When I walk out into the living room I see Adam behind the glass door, carrying two bulging bags of groceries. I open the doors and take one of the bags from his hands. He sets the other bag down on the counter and pulls something out of his pocket. I watch him as he walks the perimeter of the rooms, near the power outlets and phone. He makes his way back to where I'm standing. "I was checking for listening devices." I look at the small, strange box in his hand. "It's a bug detector."

"Where did you get that?"

"I made it."

"How did you manage that?"

"I am a man of many talents, Andie." I eye him skeptically. "Anyway, lucky for you, Crane has allowed you some privacy, this place is clean."

"So we can say whatever we want?" I ask mockingly.

"Well, within reason." He smiles at me.

I hear Lina's little feet running across the room. "Adam! I thought you were never going to come." Her sweet voice takes on a grave tone. "I'm starving." She rubs her little belly dramatically.

"Well that's good. I brought all this food for you to eat. So, let's show your mom how to make the world's best spaghetti."

I watch as Adam helps Lina measure out spices and mix the sauce adding fresh spinach, onions and garlic. He pours out a box of dry spaghetti on a plate and has her break the long pieces in half before they go into a pot of boiling water. While Lina fills him in on the day of a five-year old, I set the table.

"Supplies are starting to get low at the store so I picked up a few things for you. I hope you don't mind." Adam sets a lid on the sauce and empties out the remaining grocery bag. He's brought us frozen vegetables, rice, pasta, milk, some canned fruit, and fresh bananas. Lina moves on to rearranging the silverware I set out.

"Thanks. How low is the stock?" I ask as I move towards him to put the groceries away.

"The shelves are still full, but I heard Morris and Alexander, they were at the store talking about how the last of the overstock had just been put out."

"But they said in the last meeting that we had enough food until winter."

"They must have miscalculated. I'm assuming Crane is going to start rationing out the food until the fall harvest has been collected. Even then, I'm not sure there will be enough."

"What should we do?"

"We need to get the Runner out of the District and get more supplies, soon." He gives me a concerned look. The timer on the counter rings. "Dinner's done."

We listen to Lina talk nonstop while we eat. She fills Adam in on her new classmate, Cashel, the boy who was chosen to be trained as one of the next District Sovereign with Lina. Ms. Black thinks there will be at least two more children of various ages joining them soon. Adam talks with Lina, asking her questions, telling her jokes. I watch them, completely absorbed in the easy way he interacts with her. He must notice because he stops a few times, making eye contact with me, smiling. I try not to let thoughts of Ian creep into my mind, the horrible dreams I've been having about him.

When the sun starts to set over the lake, I collect the plates and start cleaning up. And when I tell Lina it's time to get ready for bed she gives me an exaggerated pout-face. I get her bathed and dressed for bed, noticing as she puts on her pajamas that the legs end high above her ankles. She must have had a growth spurt recently, meaning the clothes I have from last winter are not going to fit her. The thought of having to find new clothes for her when supplies in the District are already low troubles me.

"Mom, I want to tell Adam goodnight," Lina pleads with me.

"Ok sweetie, be quick, you need your rest." I watch her run out to the living area and throw her arms around Adam's waist and tell him goodnight. I get her settled in the large canopy bed with Stevie sleeping at the foot of it. She pulls the small white owl out from underneath her pillow and cuddles it close to her face. I kiss her and tuck her in, her eyelids already heavy with sleep. She rolls over and closes her eyes.

"I love you, mommy," she tells me before falling asleep.

"I love you, my little Catalina."

Adam is waiting in the kitchen when I leave Lina's room.

"Is it okay for me to call you? You seemed distracted," I ask him.

"Crane was there. We were discussing the recruits who are being trained for the Runner position."

"How is that going?"

I watch his face closely as he talks. He tells me that there are two recruits, one is a former army ranger, and the other was training to be a local Sheriff. They were both struggling with memorizing-the now secret-routes in and out of the District. Then he tells me that he is taking them on a trial run, outside the cement wall to the chain link fence surrounding the District. "It's going to take a few days. I'll be gone."

"Why do you have to go?" I ask.

"Because I'm a Marine, this is what I've been doing for years, remember? This is going to be a dangerous job. The recruits have to be properly trained."

"You told them didn't you? What you did for the military? Do you think that was a good idea?" I feel like Crane is using him, just like he is using me. And I'm afraid of what he plans to do with us when we're done, or when the organization of the District fails, or if it prevails, under Crane's control.

"It was the best idea. You keep your friends close, but the Sovereign District Mediator closer." He walks towards me, invading my personal space, filling it up with his heat and electricity.

"Aren't you considered a District Sovereign now? We aren't allowed to leave, we decided in the committee meetings." I repeat the rule to him, "A District Sovereign is responsible for watching over the residents of the District. If you leave, how can you do that?" I don't want him to go beyond the cement wall. I don't want him to leave me and Lina here, alone with Crane.

"It doesn't matter. I'm the only one with intelligence training."

"You think Crane doesn't have some intelligence crony hidden away somewhere? He keeps bringing all these people from Japan to help out here."

"If he does, he hasn't told me."

"Are you coming back?" I'm afraid he will leave us and never return. I've already lost Ian and I can't bear the thought of losing Adam too.

He reaches out, pulling me closer to him, touching his forehead to mine. "Don't worry, Andie. I will always be back for you." He wraps his arms around my back. When he gets to the rough scars from the wolf attack he stops, pulling away abruptly. "Do you still have those stitches in?"

My face flushes with embarrassment. I pull away from his grasp. "I didn't have anyone to take them out," I tell him, walking away, tucking my hair behind my ear.

"Andie, they've been in for over three weeks-"

"I didn't want the wounds to pull open again," I interrupt him, defensively. "And besides you've been busy for weeks. I had to call you just to get you to visit. Who am I supposed to ask, Crane?" The thought of Crane touching me sends a chill down my back.

He sighs, "You know better than I do that they can't be left in. Go get your medical scissors. I'll take them out right now."

"Fine."

I head for the bathroom, searching the drawers for the medical kit with the small scissors. My fingers tremble as I search. I'm nervous, not that Adam is the one taking them out, I'm nervous it's going to hurt like hell because they've been in so long. I find the scissors and bring them to Adam.

He snips at the threads, the same way he did so many weeks ago, after the first round of stitches. The skin has grown around a few of the stitches and he has to pull hard to get them out. When he's done he runs his thumb over the three thick scars that slash across my lower side and back. I can barely feel it. The nerves under the skin have been too damaged, and the scar tissue too deep from being stitched together twice. I can, however, feel his fingertips pressing into the sensitive skin near my hip. I pull away from him and let the back of my shirt fall into place. After what happened in the basement, I'm not sure I could stop myself if it happened again, or the intense feelings of guilt afterwards.

I try and change the subject. "When are you leaving for this trial run?"

"Tomorrow."

"What? I thought you meant in a few days. You're leaving tomorrow? Were you even going to tell me?" I am suddenly furious with him and the fact that he waited until the last minute to tell me he was heading out into the forest beyond the cement wall.

"I was going to tell you-" He stands up from the dining room chair he was sitting in to take my stitches out.

"When?" I interrupt him.

"Andie, I just found out today. Crane ordered it." He steps towards me, his blue eyes pleading with me. "I told you, I need you to trust me." He reaches out, brushing his hand across my cheek. "I need to see what's out there, the train, how heavily guarded it is. I'm trying to figure out what Crane's plan is, so we can get out of here. But I need you to stay here, where you're safe, and wait for me to get back."

Oh how I want to trust him, part of me wants to let him be my knight-in-shining-armor, the one who can save us, who will help us escape. But I wonder how many private meetings he's had with Crane and what else he may be keeping from me. He keeps telling me to trust him. And I want to. But I have this nagging feeling that while Crane keeps me locked up in this glass building, there is so much more going on with the creation of the Phoenix District-things that aren't being discussed in the Committee meetings. Things they are keeping from me. So even if I don't fully trust Adam, I can't let him know. I need him to get us out of here.

I walk towards Adam and wrap my arms around his neck, standing on my toes to reach him. "I do trust you," I whisper in his ear, "I just don't want you to go."

He looks deep into my eyes and it's only a second before his mouth finds mine. *That worked a little too well.* His hand cups my jaw while the other presses me closer to him. And suddenly, it's like we're back in the dark hallway. My skin tingles under his touch. My head feels full and dizzy, my heart starts pounding faster. I move my hands to his chest, intent on pushing him back, but I stop, feeling the hard muscle under his shirt. And then, just what I was afraid of, I can't stop myself.

Adam lifts me in his arms in one swift movement, and carries me to the bedroom, setting me down near the large bed. I can feel the warm flush filling my cheeks, my heart racing. We're both adults, who are obviously attracted to each other, but I didn't intend for us to go this far, to wind up in the bedroom. The tension is thick and my heart races. I fumble with the buttons on Adam's shirt, nervous. I've never been alone with another man like this, only Ian, my now lost husband.

Adam covers my hands with his, stopping my feeble attempt with the buttons. He bends down, kissing me slowly. His lips move against mine, his tongue pressing into my mouth. I forget about the buttons and try not to let my knees buckle.

"It's okay," he whispers in my ear, kissing my jaw. He steps back and finishes unbuttoning his shirt. I try to keep my eyes on his face, his eyes, his dark hair, his square jaw. He stops for a moment, just before taking his shirt off, looking at me, offering me the option to stop this. Part of me wants to run from the room and stop myself before it goes too far, but the other part wants to be with him, to get out all the tension I feel every time he's near me. He pulls the shirt off his shoulders and holds it in his hand. I wish he would have prepared me, warned me, for what I was about to see. I knew he had a few tattoos. I've seen them peeking out from under his shirt sleeves. But I wasn't prepared to see this. I wasn't prepared for all the scars.

There's an entire barrage of them covering his upper body, his chest and abdomen, he turns around and I see they continue onto his back, across his shoulder blades. There are long slashes, small burn marks, large burn marks, and healed bullet pockmarks marring his body. There are deep purple marks with the tiny holes from a poor suture job across his ribs. They pull at his skin, skewing the natural outlines of where his muscle would be. He doesn't say anything, he just watches me, waiting for my reaction, his eyes hopeful.

"Oh my God, Adam, what happened to you?" I try to control my facial expressions, the shock that must be overly apparent on my face.

"My job," he replies, disappointment evident in his tone.

Adam starts putting his shirt on, covering up the scars, buttoning it up so I can't stare any longer. In only a few moments he is back to the handsome, dark haired man I've come to know. I stand still, unable to move, watching him. When the initial shock wears off, I feel terrible. He exposed what must have been a painful secret to me and I just stood there, unable to move like a jerk, a coward. He starts walking towards the door. And for a moment I'm filled with the sudden fear that he really is going to leave me. He is going to leave the loft and go for the trial run and never talk to me again and then I will truly be left alone under Crane's rule, with no escape.

Somehow I force my arms and legs to move and throw myself at him, just as he gets to the doorway of the bedroom. "Don't go. I'm sorry. I didn't know." I clasp my arms around his neck, crushing myself to him.

"There's no way you could have known. No one knows. You're the first person I've shown."

"Don't go, please." I pull him by his arm to the overstuffed couch. Both of us sink into its deep cushions. Adam reaches over and pulls me onto his lap. I rest my head on his chest, feeling the strong thud of his heart and I listen as he tells me the story of how he earned his scars.

He was on a mission in Iraq, there was a breach of security, and someone had released a list of all the agents that were currently working in the Middle East. Since Adam was their best man, he was sent in to recover the list and find out who sold it. He was heavily disguised, but it wasn't good enough, they knew who he was. He was captured, imprisoned and tortured for information regarding U.S. Intelligence. The leaders of the Middle Eastern countries traded him for months, each trying new techniques to get information out of him. Eventually they gave up, dumping his body outside of a U.S. Embassy in Turkey, as a warning against further infiltration. His deployment to Germany was a guise for his family so they wouldn't have to see his battered body. There he received medical attention for his wounds, a thorough debriefing of what he saw, who he saw, and to undergo post traumatic rehabilitation. Then he got word of the accident and that his entire family had died. Finally, two months later they gave him leave to return and mourn.

When he's done I don't know what to say. My heart aches for all the pain he's endured. We sit in silence. Eventually both of us fall asleep, wrapped around each other on the couch. It's the first night I have slept in the loft and not been woken up by nightmares.

We wake early enough to get Adam out of the loft before Lina is awake.

"Come back to me," I tell him before he turns to leave.

And then Adam is gone, and I have no idea when I will see him again.

CHAPTER SIXTEEN

We have been held in the Chemistry building for over a month now. All of our lives, changed dramatically. From this isolated building I don't get to see any of the town or speak with its residents. I only have the information from the past committee meetings, because I'm quite certain that Crane isn't disclosing all of the details.

Crane doesn't call any Committee meetings. Instead he shows up at the lab, always unannounced and unexpected. He watches the lab workers, talks with Kira; he tries to talk with me. I can't help but be standoffish with him. I know there are things he is not telling me. He chose us as District Sovereign. Subsequently, I feel like he should be telling us everything. Finally, after his third visit, I give in and show him some of the data I'm working on, mostly out of fear that he will take Lina from me again. Crane seems pleased with my progress and for that he relays a bit of information to me: The helpers from the Japanese District have been slowly dwindling out of our town since most of their duties are complete. The Phoenix District has now entered the phase where it's running smoothly on its own.

When Crane finally leaves, he stops in the atrium to watch Ms. Black as she teaches the children. Another child has joined the group. Another boy, this one older, is eight. Lina seems to get along well with them. Ms. Black takes them on guarded fieldtrips around the District. One day I went with them to the park by the docks. They were allowed to play with the other District children. This trip didn't seem as lonely as our last trip to the park, when all the mothers stood away from me, staring. This time I had Ms. Black to talk to. She tells

147

me that the boys were taken from their families; they live on campus with her now. They will be allowed to visit their families on the weekends. Their parents have been told that they are studying at a boarding school for advanced children. They don't know that their sons have been chosen as the next generation's District Sovereign. I feel sad for them, and grateful, that Lina is allowed to stay with me. Still, I wonder what Crane has told Ian about us, or if he even remembers us.

--

I work, patiently waiting for Adam to return from the trial run. The first day was the longest, dragging on, each minute feeling like an hour. I wanted to know what was happening, what he was seeing, what it looked like beyond the cement wall Crane is building around our town. Adam had told me he would only be gone a few days. Instead he is gone a full week.

Adam returns on the seventh day. After he debriefs with Crane, a Committee meeting is called. The heat of summer is starting to dissipate and we walk to the headquarters under Volker supervision. I control the urge to pick up Lina and run to the building to find Adam, so I can hear everything first-hand.

It's the first time I've arrived to the conference room before Crane. Morris and Alexander are there-they greet us kindly and we sit and wait. I watch the clock tick, slowly. Crane clears his throat loudly as he enters the room. Behind him follows Adam and an older man with gray sideburns, wearing a Volker uniform. I stare anxiously at Adam, but he makes no attempt to look in my direction.

"Welcome District Sovereign," Crane greets us all at once. "I would like to introduce our District Runner, Remington." Crane claps and gives us an expectant look.

We all take notice and clap our hands, greeting the man. I watch the man named Remington. He stands proudly with his arms behind his back. There's a bruise under his eye, a crack of blood in the corner of his mouth and a small bandage on his upper arm. Fresh blood has already saturated the thin pad, showing a dark stain against the plastic film that sticks to his arm.

"Remington has completed the necessary training for District Runner. As you know, he now also holds the title of District

Sovereign. He will be present at all Committee meetings starting today. Let's get started." Crane sits in his usual seat and our new member, Remington, sits next to Adam. During this meeting I notice that Crane asks specific questions of all of us. There are no moments of open communication where the entire Sovereign committee discusses the best options for the residents, as we did in the previous meetings. Crane asks about specifics: supplies, food, clothes, gasoline, and medical supplies. He asks Adam about equipment stock, guns, bullets, non-lethal methods, and uniforms. He asks me nothing.

Crane calls the meeting to an end. A page appears on our screens to sign in agreement. This time it is not a list of guidelines for managing the District. Instead it's a simple list of supplies for the Runner to retrieve. It includes food, yards of specifically colored fabrics, simple medical supplies and 300 gallons of gasoline. We all sign electronically and leave. Crane, Adam and Remington stay behind. I try my best to hide my disappointment for not getting to reunite with him.

I return to the lab. Ms. Black and the children resume class in the atrium. I sit in front of my computer, staring at the empty spreadsheet in front of me, thinking about Adam, what he saw, and why he was gone so long. Finally Ms. Black brings Lina into the lab and tells us both goodnight. I head to the loft with Lina, but not before I watch Ms. Black leave, holding the hands of Lina's classmates, talking and smiling with them.

Lina and I cook dinner and get ready for bed. After she is asleep I sit on the couch and try to read. Mostly I stare out the large window at the dark lake. My eyes drift to the phone on the wall. I want to call Adam but I know I can't. I have to wait for him to come to me. Eventually I fall asleep and the dreams start just as they usually do, with Ian standing in front of me, looking angry, yelling my name, throwing his wedding ring. Except this time I'm shaking, it starts in my shoulders, and then I feel something brush my cheek.

"Andie... Andie..." It doesn't stop. The dream continues, getting worse, but I can't wake myself up. I feel a sharp pinch on my upper arm and then another, strong enough to wake me. Adam sits next to me on the couch where I fell asleep. He's watching me as I look around and try to orient myself.

I rub my arm, noticing there is a slight red mark. "Did you pinch me?" I ask Adam. He's trying to contain a smile and doing a poor job at it.

"Sorry. But you wouldn't wake up. You just kept mumbling something about how awesome I am." I reach out and smack him on his arm. I can't wait any longer to change the subject.

"What did you see?" I ask.

He takes a deep breath in and leans back on the couch, away from me, rubbing his face with both hands. "Well, we started heading north, where the cement wall isn't completed yet. The recruits were out of shape, they needed a lot of reminding on basic survival skills. We got to the train station, there's one train and the Runner is the only person besides Crane who knows the code to run the train, and the code to open the fence on the outskirts of the District."

"Did you go beyond the fence?" I ask, eager to hear what has changed out in the real world.

Adam shakes his head no and continues. He gives me a detailed explanation of where they traveled to. How they had to build shelters at night and find their own food. All the main roads have been closed off. Trees have been pulled out into the road to prevent anyone from driving down them. The small single lane back roads, which pass through the forest, are still operational, mostly because the trees surrounding them provide heavy cover for any travel. Adam and the recruits saw at least three farms with fields of crops and cattle grazing. Crane wanted them to follow the entire length of the fence to ensure its intactness.

"You'll never guess this one Andie," Adam leans forward, placing his elbows on his knees. "The fence is electrified. We found that out the hard way. Three days into the trial run the younger recruit, Chad, decided he was going to try and get out, flee the District. We woke up in the morning and he was gone. When we were inspecting the fence we found his charred body a few hundred yards from where we were camped for the night." Adam looks back at me and I understand the seriousness of his words. If we plan to escape from the Phoenix District from under Crane's thumb, it will not be easy.

The electrified fence worries me, but it also brings another question to mind. "So now that Remington is trained and ready to go, what's to prevent him from just leaving and never coming back once he programs the train?"

Adam smiles slyly at me. "Crane fixed that good. The transmitter gives Crane the ability to monitor the Runner from inside the

District, it includes a black button. All Crane has to do is press the button and the Runner receives a lethal dose of potassium from the transmitter. The Runner drops where they are and ta-da-"

I finish his words for him, "instant heart attack." We sit in silence for a moment, absorbing.

Finally Adam breaks the silence. "Did you miss me while I was gone?"

"I think I missed you a little tiny bit." I hold my index finger and thumb less than an inch apart to show him. Then I change the tone of my voice, looking down to the floor, embarrassed after our last night together. "I didn't think you were coming back." He reaches for me, dragging me onto his lap. I wrap my arms around him and bury my face in his neck, breathing in his scent, thankful that he is safe.

CHAPTER SEVENTEEN

Life falls into a steady hum drum of sleeping, eating, and working. Once a week or so, Crane beckons us for a Committee meeting. Remington makes a successful trip as the Runner. It takes him almost a week, but the train shows up with the necessary supplies to sustain the residents for half the winter. Crane never discusses what information the Funding Entities received.

Cool fall air blows into town. Lina and I spend most of our evenings outside enjoying the nice weather, letting Stevie run on the open grass in front of our building while the Volker watch us. I continue to analyze the residents' genes and Adam continues to work as the Volker Director, there is an influx of residents who have been cleared to train for the Volker faction. Crane runs Adam ragged. He works late training the new recruits and assigning them to positions. I barely see him, except for at the Committee meetings, and even then he seems distant and distracted.

Now, it is late September and most of the lab workers have been sent back to Japan, their work here complete. Kira is the only one remaining; she merely visits the lab a few days a week. Crane has assigned her to help out in the school, teaching chemistry and biology. Most days I work in the lab alone, calling Kira only when I need something or have questions. Today I have been on a roll and I'm almost done separating the residents into familial groups when I hear the hushed whoosh of the lab door opening. I hope to see Adam stopping by to fill me in on some District secret, but when I turn around and stand up, I see Crane walking towards me.

"Ah, Andromeda," Crane raises his hands to the sky as he enters the room, as though he is praising his own existence. "I hope I'm not interrupting you." He smiles as he walks towards me.

"What do you want?" I ask, trying not to sound too rude, but I don't want him in the lab. It is bad enough he keeps me locked up here.

"I was nearby and decided to stop in for an update on your work. Kira tells me that you've been going at it nonstop." He takes one of the stools from a nearby workbench and sits on it, rolling it up to my desk. "Come, sit, show me what you've been working on." He pats the seat of my office chair.

I wait for a moment, eyeing him suspiciously. He never stops here alone, never without a Volker trailing behind him. He must be up to something. Against my better judgment I sit down next to him, breathing shallow, so I don't have to smell his sickeningly sweet musk. I explain the data on the computer screens. He's engrossed, asking only a few questions about the analysis, but mostly nodding his head in agreement. I know he has a strong science background from whatever he did before he took over our town. The conversation is easy and I don't have to repeat myself or go into depth with scientific explanations. When I'm done talking I notice that he's staring at me. I push my chair back and stand up, trying to distance myself. He makes me uncomfortable being so close.

"This is good Andromeda, very good." He stands, pushing the stool back to where it was. "I want you to know that the Funding Entities will be pleased with your work." Crane walks closer to me, much too close. I try to back up further but I'm stopped by the hard edge of the lab bench jabbing me in the back. The smell of his cologne wafts up to my nostrils. I swallow hard at the saliva backing up in my throat. "When you begin the genetic pairing of the Residents, you must include yourself." He stops for a moment, giving me time to process what he is telling me.

"What are you trying to say?" He has stopped inching towards me and stands silently, watching me. "Are you saying I will be expected to… to have a baby?" My heart sinks. I want to run, to flee the room, to get away from him. How can he expect this from me? He's already taken everything from me, he's ruined my family, and now he wants me to bring another child into this world.

"Yes, Andromeda, you must include all of our District Sovereign. It only makes sense to incorporate our best and brightest when planning the propagation of the District." He pauses and looks around the room. "Have I ever told you how much I..." We are alone. My heart starts drumming in my chest. "How much I respect you, your ideas, your intellect? You were the perfect choice for this. I can see it now. All the time I spent searching, it was you. This, you, it all makes me so happy."

He's right in front of my face, leaning towards me. I arch myself back over the bench, trying to put distance between us. Suddenly, he is pulling at my shoulders to bring me closer to him and pressing his pale pink lips to mine. I push against his soft chest trying to get him off of me. Trying to get away from him. My heartbeat is pounding in my ears, panicked.

"Stop! Crane..." I push him hard, with all the energy I have in me, "Stop!"

He stumbles back, looking me in the eyes. His face is no longer soft and arrogant, but sharp and angry. And then, just as I least expect it, he slaps me hard across the face. I can count on my hand the number of times I've been hit in the face on purpose in my entire life, and they've all occurred since I've come to this place. It stings, less than when Baillie hit me, but it still hurts.

"Soon, Andromeda, you will have to stop making me wait for you, denying me what is mine. I will not sit back and wait much longer. After all I have given you, and each time I gave you more, this lab, your loft, *your daughter.* You remember this day, especially when you're pairing the residents." He steps back, looking around the room again. "Lucky for you, no one was here to see this."

I stare in disbelief and shock as he pulls a tissue out of his pocket and holds it to my bottom lip, almost comfortingly. When he pulls it back I see there is blood. He sets the tissue down on the lab bench. "Perhaps Colonel Baillie was correct to use a bit of force to encourage you." He turns and walks quietly out of the room, just the way he came.

At first I'm not sure what to do, or who to tell. I can barely believe what just happened. The last thing I would have expected was that he would want me to have a baby, *with him*, that he expects us to be paired. I'm sure the one thing Crane doesn't know about me is that I can't have more children. Ian and I tried for years to give Lina a sibling. The doctors had no explanation for why I wasn't getting pregnant. Eventually I stopped hoping that each month it would happen and we just accepted that Lina would be our only child. We put all our energy into giving her the best life we could.

I run to the door and see Ms. Black still teaching the children. Lina sits at one of the desks, working. Crane is gone. I pull an ice pack out of the lab freezer and hold it to my face. Now I know why there was no Volker following him into the lab. They would have been responsible for protecting me if they saw what Crane did. He would be putting his control over the District in jeopardy. I can't let anyone know what he expects of me. I could never do it, not in a million years.

--

It takes almost a week for the split in my lip to heal. I tell Ms. Black and Lina that it cracked from the dry air in the building. But Adam eyes me suspiciously at the Committee meeting that week. I hide in the lab, analyzing data for weeks, almost happy that I don't see Adam so I don't have to explain to him what happened.

Soon the cool, fall weather has brought the changing of the leaves. They start to turn bright colors and fall off the trees. October is here and Lina's birthday is just a few days away. Each week I've searched the grocery store for a gift for her. For cake mix, frosting, anything I could do to make her day special. And now it's the day before and I have nothing for her. I feel like the worst mother, unable to provide my daughter with a birthday party or gift.

As I sit in front of my computer, sipping at a cup of coffee, trying to think of what I could do for her, the phone rings. When I answer there is a message from Crane. "Dearest District Sovereign, tomorrow we will celebrate the birth of a very special little girl, our very own Catalina will turn 6. Please be ready promptly at nine AM for the festivities." The message ends, making my blood boil. How dare Crane take it upon himself to plan a party for my child without consulting me? He knows nothing about her.

--

I wake Lina with the happiest birthday face I can muster. We get ready for the day and when she asks where we are going I tell her it is a surprise. I don't let her know that I have no clue what Crane has

155

planned.

A waiting Volker SUV brings us to the cement wall at the edge of town. A row of SUVs are waiting as our driver pulls up, most likely with the remaining Sovereign. I see Crane in his unmistakable black suit get out and pull a brick out of the wall, behind it there is a touchpad. He enters a code and a portion of the wall slides open. After we drive through I turn around and see the wall slide closed. We are now in the forest and farmlands, outside of town. We drive for about ten minutes before we come to a farm. The vehicles park near a large red barn and everyone gets out. All of the Sovereign are there; Crane, Morris, Alexander, Ms. Black and the two boys in Lina's class. Ahead of everyone I see Adam get out of the first SUV, which drove Crane. Crane heads off around the side of the barn. Adam turns and starts walking towards us.

"Adam!" Lina runs to him with her arms open. "You came to my birthday."

"Yes, Happy Birthday, Lina." He picks her up and hugs her. "Now how old are you, ten or eleven?"

Lina giggles. "I'm six silly."

He puts her down and we walk together, following the same direction as Crane.

"Hi," Adam tells me.

"Hi," is all I have time to respond to him because as we make the short walk around the side of the barn, I hear Lina squeal with excitement.

"Look, Mommy, look. Did you ever see anything so great?"

My reaction is a mixture of awe and frustration, Crane really outdid himself. There are picnic tables all assembled under a large white tent-too many picnic tables for just us-decorated with pink and purple tablecloths. Balloons and streamers dangle from the large tent supports and overhangs. It continues with pink plates, cups, napkins and silverware which are all set out.

"It's beautiful, Lina." I lean down to hug and kiss her. She runs off with Cashel and the older boy, Marcus. I follow them to a large inflated tent that they jump in, bouncing higher and higher. I turn at the sound of air brakes squealing. When I look back towards the barn I see there are two buses unloading streams of children. Crane must have pulled them out of their classes and brought them here to celebrate Lina's birthday-the first day of celebration in the District-my daughter's birthday.

The day is chaotic and I follow Lina closely. The children take turns jumping in the inflatable tent and then the farm animals are brought out. There's a petting zoo with goats and rabbits, pony rides, horse rides, cotton candy, and ice cream, everything a kid could want at their birthday party. A buffet table is set up with hot dogs, hamburgers, and the usual picnic fare. When everyone is finished eating, a large cake is brought out in the shape of the number six. It's frosted beautifully with pinks and purples to match the decorations and six large sparkler candles. Everyone sings *Happy Birthday* to Lina. She scrunches her face up as she thinks about her wish before she blows out all six candles with one large breath. We all clap and cheer for her.

When I look around the tent I see Adam off to the side watching us. I want to talk to him badly, but there are too many people here. We've barely spoken since he got back from the trial run, and that was almost two months ago. I'm not sure if he's been avoiding me intentionally or if he has actually been busy.

After we eat cake, we are escorted out to one of the fields and everyone is allowed to pick a pumpkin to bring home. The children run excitedly through the field, trying to choose the best one. After everyone has a pumpkin, the teachers pack the school children back onto the buses and get ready to leave, but not before each one stops to say goodbye to Lina on their way out. After they leave only the District Sovereign are left. Crane walks towards us, smiling.

"Happy Birthday, Catalina, I hope you have enjoyed your party." He holds his hand out for her to shake. She tries to hide behind me. I remember Crane's warning from the lab, and I have to do what I can to make him think he might actually have a chance at getting paired with me. I don't want to pull Lina into his twisted game, but right now our safety depends on it.

I bend down and whisper in her ear, "Lina, Mr. Crane is the one who organized this party for you. I think it would be nice if you could tell him thank you. Do you think you could do that for me?" She nods her head yes.

"Thank you, Mr. Crane." For the first time she shakes his hand. From the beaming smile on his face I can tell that she has made his day. "Mommy, I have to go potty," Lina whispers to me.

"I'm assuming there's a bathroom here?" He points towards the old farmhouse on the other side of the tent. I pick Lina up and carry her away from him as fast as I possibly can.

When I open the door we enter into a large kitchen where there are people cleaning dishes from the party. They stop and look at us when we enter the room.

"We are just looking for the bathroom. Could anyone point us in the right direction?"

There is an older woman by the sink. "It's right over here, ma'am." Lina and I follow her to a small hallway with old hardwood floors and milky white walls; she opens a door with an old crystal door handle, behind it there is a simple but clean bathroom.

"Thank you," I tell her smiling. She looks at me as though she is pondering a thought.

"We hope you were pleased with the party." She tells me.

I remember what Adam told me after I went to see Ian; that the residents can't be surprised, that we have to prepare them, calm them. But this woman is different, she doesn't have the monotone voice, the glassy sheen over her eyes; she seems fully awake and alert. There are footsteps in the hall behind her. The woman turns abruptly to leave, not waiting for my response. And as she makes her way back to the kitchen, I see Adam pass her in the hall.

"Go potty Lina. I'll wait out here for you." I usher her into the bathroom, but I keep the door cracked a tiny bit so I can see what she's doing.

Adam walks up to me without stopping. "You aren't supposed to go anywhere without a Volker guard." At first I think he's joking with me but when I look into his eyes I see that he is completely serious.

"Even to the bathroom, Adam? That's a little extreme." If he is going to pester me I decide I'm going to make it worth his while. "What's wrong with you? We haven't seen you in weeks. You don't even talk to me anymore."

"Crane is running me ragged, Andie. I barely have time to sleep." He rubs his face and runs his hand through his dark hair. "What happened to your lip?"

"What?"

"Your lip, a few weeks ago, it was split. What happened?"

I can't bring myself to tell him that Crane slapped me across the face. As a Volker he would be responsible for doing something about it. I'm sure none of them want to hand down a punishment to Crane.

And it's been so long.

"I ran into a door." As soon as it's out of my mouth I know it's a bad lie.

Adam eyes me suspiciously. "Has anyone ever told you that you are a particularly bad liar, Andie?" He walks closer, closing the space between us and reaches out, tucking a piece of loose hair behind my ear. The action sends a shiver down my spine. It's the first time he has been close enough to touch me, the first time he has been within five feet of me in months. I remember the way he pulled me to him when we were in the basement, when I showed him the tunnel. I want him to do it again, here, now.

I don't like to lie, I don't want to lie. "Crane did it." I blurt it out.

"What do you mean Crane did it?" he asks quietly.

"He split my lip. He slapped me." Adam eyes me, using whatever technique it is to tell if I'm lying to him.

"How could he slap you?"

"It happened in the lab one day. He stopped by to check on my work. And... and..." I don't want to tell him about the genetic pairing, that Crane wants me paired with him. I do my best to keep a straight face, to make it look like I'm telling the truth. "I told him something he didn't want to hear. And he slapped me across the face. There, are you happy I told you?" It was a bit easier, because I only told a half truth. But I don't think Adam is happy at all. He looks pissed, worse than when I ran home to see Ian months ago.

"How, wasn't there a Volker with him? We are sworn to protect you. That shouldn't have happened."

I shake my head. "No, he came into the lab alone, I was in there alone. No one else was there to see it."

He's clenching his jaw and his fists and I am afraid that I have angered him, much worse than ever before. The toilet flushes and Lina comes out of the bathroom. Adam doesn't say another word he just escorts us out of the farmhouse.

The party is over and we pack up for the day. We are driven back to the loft. Lina falls asleep on my lap during the ride. I hold her, barely able to believe that she is already six and this is the only birthday her father has ever missed. I hope that in her excitement over the party she didn't have time to realize this also.

I carry her up to the loft. When the elevator doors open I can see something in the living room through the glass doors. Stevie is waiting by the door, pacing, and there's a pile of something brightly colored on the floor. I hesitate before walking into the loft. As I get closer I see it's a pile of brightly wrapped presents in the pinks and purples of her party.

Lina wakes up as I set her on the couch noticing the pile of presents. "Mommy, are those for me?"

"I think so birthday girl." I can only assume that they are from Crane. Lina opens all the gifts excitedly. There are toys, coloring books, books for her to read, piles of clothes in three sizes, enough to last her a whole year. There's a mirror and brush set, a heavy winter coat, a snowsuit, fancy dresses and shoes. At the very bottom there is a perfectly square box with a large pink bow. Lina sits next to me as she opens it, slowly. Under the wrapping paper is a heavy wooden box with a gold clasp on the front. The box is carved with swirls and stars and stained a dark cherry color. At first I think the box is a gift but then Lina opens the clasp and lifts the lid.

"Wow!" I stare in disbelief at what's inside the box. Sitting on a pillow of pink satin is a sparkling tiara. The tiara is heavy and there are diamonds, rubies and some light pink colored gemstone that I can't identify, all set in the thick gold. I start to wonder if it could even be real. I pick it up and feel its weight. I place the tiara on her head. It fits perfectly and she looks like a real princess. I hand her the mirror that she unwrapped a few moments ago and watch as she admires herself.

"You look just like a princess, Catalina." I kiss her cheek, and then get up to clean up the boxes and paper. Lina helps take all the new toys to her room, wearing her new tiara and doing her best to impersonate a princess. When the living room is all cleaned up and all the new clothes hang in her closet, we get ready for bed. Lina selects a new book from her gifts and reads it to me. Then I pull the sheets up to tuck her in.

"Can I sleep in my crown?" She asks, her eyes heavy with exhaustion.

"Here, let's set it on your night stand for the morning, we don't want to break it."

"Mommy, I miss Daddy…" she starts to tell me, her voice low and sad.

"I know, sweetie. I miss Daddy too." Tears start to well up behind my eyes.

"I miss Uncle Sam too. They weren't at my party, Mom. They never miss my birthday."

I can't stop the tears, "I'm so sorry, Lina. They didn't mean to miss your party." I wipe at my face, trying not to upset her with my crying. But I never wanted this for her. I never wanted her to grow up without her father there every step of the way.

"I love you, Mommy." She reaches up and touches my face.

"I love you too, my little Catalina." I pull her covers up to her chin and sit on the floor next to Stevie until I hear the steady, slow breaths, which could only mean she is fast asleep.

CHAPTER EIGHTEEN

Days and weeks go by. Lina continues with her schooling. I continue my work. Now a Volker stands at the door to the lab. I still don't see Adam. One night Lina asks if he can come over to make spaghetti but when the operator tries to get a hold of him there is no answer. Lina and I both go to bed disappointed that night. And all I can think is that I must have made him incredibly angry at Lina's birthday party.

For the Thanksgiving holiday Crane sets up a feast at the high school. The District Sovereign are required to attend. Lina dresses in one of the fancy dresses she got for her birthday and wears her tiara. We're kept away from the Residents at a heavily guarded table. It makes me wonder what the point of getting us all together was. The Residents point and watch us, some wave and smile like they know who we are. But they have been instructed not to approach us.

Crane wears his usual satisfied, smug look during the entire dinner. Adam is seated at the other end of the long rectangular table, away from us. A few times when I look his way I catch him looking in our direction. We don't get a chance to speak and he leaves before we do. As we are walking out the door I scan the room. I see a thin blonde haired man sitting at a table with three other women. It looks like it could be Ian. I want to watch and see, but I don't want Lina to see him. I know that it will upset her beyond belief if she sees her father because with the medication Crane has him on, he has no clue who she is. I usher her out of the dining hall and we go home.

That night Crane sends a Christmas tree and decorations. Lina is excited for Christmas and we sing carols as we decorate the tree, it gives us something to focus on. It takes my mind off the constant dwelling on how I'm going to get us out of here. This was always my favorite time of the year, but now it brings me sadness. I have Lina but I still feel alone without Ian, and now without Adam. All I am left with is the nagging knowledge of Crane's expectations.

December brings freezing winds and piles of snow. There's almost five feet in the first week. Crane informs us that the crews have been working to keep the town cleared of snow and ice. A new faction has been designated to visit the Residents' homes and ensure that they have heat and that their pipes haven't frozen.

Since most of the town is Catholic, Crane decides to hold services at all of the local churches. He also throws a Christmas party for the Sovereign. We return to the high school dining hall. There's a large Christmas tree and someone has dressed up like Santa Claus. When I bring Lina to meet him I notice he has pale blue eyes. Since Adam has been missing the whole day I can guess that it has to be him dressed up in the red suit and fake beard. He does a good job; all the children giggle with excitement and whisper in his ear what they want for Christmas. Once again Crane delivers gifts to the loft for Lina. She opens them excitedly. When she gets to the last box she brings it to me.

"Mom, this has your name on it." She hands the gift to me. It's small and neatly wrapped. The tag hanging off the side bears my name. I open it slowly. Trying to control the trembling of my fingers, I know if Crane sent me a gift then he is going to want something in return. I pray silently that it's nothing extravagant or extreme, like Lina's birthday tiara. But when I open the top of the similarly carved wooden box I'm disappointed to see an exquisite gold locket fitted with diamonds and emeralds.

"Mom, it's beautiful," Lina exclaims as she reaches out to touch it.

"Yes it is." I watch her be mesmerized by the fancy jewelry. "Lina, I want to remind you that when we love someone, it matters more in how we treat them and what we say to them. Love isn't bought with fancy gifts." I don't want Crane's technique of gift giving to turn her. Ian and I always provided her with what she needed, but we never spoiled her with frivolous gifts the way Crane is doing now.

"I know, Mommy. It's like how I love you and you love me. And how Daddy loves us and we love him, even though he isn't with us anymore." I hug her tightly, afraid that she will see the tears in my eyes again, like on her birthday. She hugs me back and when I have control over my emotions I get up and bring the necklace to my bedroom, hiding it in the back depths of the closet where I don't have to look at it.

--

January brings more snow. The Committee decides to send the Runner out again for more supplies; rations are getting low, and people are running out of food. I don't tell anyone but I had been giving Lina half of my dinners every night because the grocery store was exceptionally low on many items. We decide on a listing of supplies. Crane thinks it's a good idea for another team to go out and check the security of the stone wall and the electrified fence. I look to Adam who is seated across the table from me. His jaw is clenched tight, he knows as well as I do that this means he will spend a full week or more out in the freezing winter. Crane smiles proudly after he tells us that he has procured snowmobiles for the team and heavy winter gear. This information doesn't help change the look on Adam's face.

--

By mid-January the pairings are almost complete. I go to Kira's computer and find the codes for the District Sovereign. I pull their genetic information and save it in a separate file. Alexander and Morris are too old to be paired. That only leaves Crane, Ms. Black, Adam, Remington and me-an uneven number-not enough women to make the pairing equal. I will be damned to pair myself with Crane and be responsible with pairing Adam with someone. I don't care what Crane wants, if we are trusted to make decisions for the Residents then we are capable of choosing our own pairs and I would rather be thrown out into the wilderness than pair myself with him.

Once all the samples are loaded I compile the data in a spreadsheet, organizing by easily distinguishable characteristics. My fingers fly across the keyboard as I systematize the samples first by similar physical characteristics, facial features, nose shape and height. Then I am able to organize them into families depending on how similar or dissimilar their physical characteristics are. From there I can assign groups that would allow the best genetic diversity, the least possibility of inbreeding, and pair them to other groups. When the samples are finally organized by families I pause, pushing my chair back from the desk so I can observe from a distance and think. It's when I stare at the large computer screen for a few minutes that I realize there are too many samples for the small town of Phoenix.

Our population never made it over ten thousand. But there are at least four times that many samples here. I stare at the groups until I can see their physical features in my head. Short fair skinned people with light hair and light eyes, typical North American Caucasian. Then there's a dark skinned group with black fine hair and strong aquiline noses, Classic Native American. Next, a tanned skin group with large wide eyes and mouths, it could be Latino. There's a grouping of black skinned people with curly hair and smooth skin, African heritage. Lastly, there are short yellow skinned people with almond shaped eyes and wispy black hair, Asian. These features may not be expressed strongly on all the people here but their genes don't lie. They carry the genetic framework from distinct cultures. The lab has a large map of the world on the wall, and I stare at it for a long time. Based on the genetic traits these samples carry, these look like groupings of people from the South, the Midwest, the Northwest, each corner of the United States. Then I realize what I'm looking at; we are not the only District.

My head fills with hundreds of questions. Did they too have the fake earthquakes? Was there the guise of nuclear contamination? Do they have the stone wall and electric fence? The train? A Runner? The factions? The Sovereign? Who is running them?

And if there are other Districts is there another person doing what I'm doing right now? Because if there is, Lina and I are no longer safe-we are expendable.

CHAPTER NINETEEN

Each month Crane sends Adam to check the integrity of the cement wall and the outer electrified fence. He monitors the Gateway, the most northern area of the electrified fence where the train exits and enters. Remington is sent out for more supplies. This time it takes him almost two weeks.

I keep my secret, my knowledge that there are more Districts. I send Crane watered-down updates of my work, telling him that I need more time, avoiding him.

Now that it is almost March, I'm afraid I can't put him off much longer.

I sit in the empty lab, alone at my desk. I should be completed with the pairings by the end of the night. I decide to take a break and check on Lina in the atrium. Ms. Black has the children painting the glass walls of the building for an art appreciation class. They are anticipating spring and Lina, Cashel and Marcus have created a rich flowering garden with the paint, almost covering the windows that span the front of the atrium. I watch Lina as she stands on a stool, painting a large sunflower on the glass. It's moments like these that I wish I had a camera, so I can document what she's doing, her projects and her growth, her childhood. Instead I watch her and I try to burn these images of her childhood into my brain.

I go upstairs to the loft and make myself a cup of coffee. Now that I'm so close to completing this project I know I will be up late putting the final touches on the pairings and double-checking my work, preparing a report for Crane, trying to hide the fact that I know about the other Districts.

The Volker guard who waits outside of the lab follows me, waiting outside the glass doors to the loft. I make coffee for the both of us. When we get back to the atrium Ms. Black is ending class and the children are cleaning up from the long day of learning. I walk off to the lab and save my work, sending it to the laptop in the loft-which Crane has so graciously provided me with-enabling me to work at night while Lina sleeps.

We head upstairs to our usual nightly routine of taking Stevie out, cooking dinner and getting ready for bed. After Stevie has run a few laps through the snow banks in the open area in front of our building, we head back upstairs, her long hair clumped with ice. We start on dinner and just as we sit down to eat the Volker guard from downstairs knocks on the door.

I motion for him to come in. They don't usually come up here at night. There was only one other time, when it was snowing so hard the day guards' replacement couldn't make it. The day guard stayed in the loft with us for dinner and slept in front of the door for the night.

"Sorry to disturb you but there is an emergency at the hospital," the Volker tells me as he enters the loft.

Crane was able to get the small local hospital up and running to treat injuries, illnesses and perform monthly physicals on the District Residents.

"What does that have to do with me?" I'm not sure why exactly I'm being bothered with this.

"Dr. Akiyama, from the hospital, is going to call in a moment and explain the details to you."

As soon as the words are out of his mouth the phone rings, and I walk over and answer it. "Andromeda? Can you hear me?" The doctor is on the other end of the line. I haven't seen Dr. Akiyama since last summer when he stitched my back, but his voice is easy to remember.

"Yes, Doctor." In the background I can hear the familiar beeps and alarms of a hospital monitor. "What can I do for you?"

"We have a situation at the hospital. It's an emergency. I need you to come down here."

"I have Lina here. I can't leave her." Lina watches me from the dinner table.

"I need you to find someone to watch her. This is urgent." I can hear it in his voice. "Please come quickly." I hear the clatter of metal and someone asking him a question, and he hangs up abruptly.

There's no one I would trust to watch Lina. Ms. Black has the boys and I'm sure this Volker is going to escort me to the hospital. There is one person whom I trust more than anyone else here, but he's been hard to locate for months. If they want my help at the hospital then Crane is going to have to give him up for the night. I pick the phone back up and when the operator answers I tell her exactly who I want to speak with.

"I need Colonel Waters, Volker Sovereign."

"I'm sorry. There is an order not to disturb him at this time."

"This is an emergency-" She starts to interrupt me. I hate to drop the emergency bomb, but Adam told me that if there was ever an emergency we are to state that we are a District Sovereign, our name and who we need to talk to. Since the Volker are our protectors, they are required to stop what they are doing and respond. I figure what better time than now to test out his instructions. "This is District Sovereign Andromeda Somers, I have an emergency and I need to speak with Colonel Waters."

"Yes ma'am," the operator responds, changing her tone, the phone rings twice and before he answers.

"Yes." His voice is heavy, tired, and I feel a little guilty that I might have just woken him up.

"Adam?"

"Yes. What do you need, Andie?"

"They need me at the hospital and I need someone to watch Lina."

"Can't Ms. Black watch her?" he asks.

"I'm not leaving her with anyone else. If you don't come then I'm not going to the hospital."

"I'll be there in a minute," he responds.

I hang up the phone and walk back to the table where Lina is sitting. "Lina," I tell her, "I have to go to the hospital, the Doctor needs my help with something. Adam is going to come over and watch you."

I was afraid that she might be upset but at my mentioning of Adam's name she raises her arms in the air and hollers out an excited, "Yay!"

Adam arrives within ten minutes. He's out of uniform and looks tired. I truly must have woken him. It's been so long since he has been here that I'm not sure how to approach him. I struggle with the desire to hug him and yell at him at the same time.

"Do you know what's going on at the hospital, Adam?" I ask.

"No. I haven't been told about anything. Your guard can fill me in after he escorts you there."

I tell him Lina's bedtime routine and I remind Lina to brush her teeth before bed as I hug and kiss her goodbye. "Thanks, Adam." I tell him as I'm walking towards the door. He meets me halfway and we walk to the door together and for the first time in months he places his hand on the small of my back, sending tingles up my spine, shooing me out the door.

"Don't worry, Andie. You can trust me. I'll take care of her."

I watch him through the glass door as the elevator closes and the guard and I descend to the lower level.

--

The hospital looks the same. There have been no changes to the external structure or the internal structure. When the Volker escorts me inside he brings me to the third floor, the level usually reserved for labor and delivery. Dr. Akiyama must have been warned I was in the building because when the door to the elevator opens he's standing in the hallway waiting for us.

"Thank God you're finally here." He pulls me by the arm down the hallway, the guard follows us.

"What's wrong?" I ask, still not sure why I'm here.

"Is is true you are certified in neonatal resuscitation?"

"Yes, we were required to at the hospital I worked at."

"And you were working in a neonatal ICU before you commenced your duties here?"

"Yes."

"Good, we have a situation and I need your help. I can't do this by myself anymore. None of the other nurses Crane has provided me with have your training." He stops outside a patient room and hands me a set of light green scrubs. "I need you to change and scrub in."

I stare at the scrubs in my hand. I haven't been a nurse in a long time. I left that occupation behind when I fled the city to find my family.

I use the bathroom in the hallway to change into the scrubs and I clean my arms up to my elbows at the medical sink outside the patient room. From inside the room I can hear monitors beeping and a woman moaning.

"Are you ready?" Dr Akiyama pops his head outside of the door and grabs my arm pulling me into the patient room. It has been almost eleven months since I have stepped foot inside of a laboring mother's room. But everything is the same as it always is: woman, belly, monitors.

A pregnant woman lies on the bed, a thick band around her pregnant belly monitoring the baby inside. I look at the monitor, watching the infant's heartbeat. With each contraction it slows, much too low and never quite gets back to its normal range. I look at the mother's distended abdomen, she's an average size woman but her pregnant belly is much too small to be full term. She's breathing fast and wincing through the contractions, her forehead caked in sweat-this has been going on for some time.

Dr Akiyama pulls me over to a warmer, similar to what we used in the NICU, a small open bed with its own heat source and an examination light. I haven't been to a delivery since before the day of the earthquake, when our lives were changed forever. I try to remember what I did in the four years that I worked in that hospital, going into the delivery room, what we looked for, what we monitored.

"How old is this baby?" I ask the doctor.

"Almost thirty-four weeks." I know this. It's seven weeks too early. It could be a perfectly viable baby or a train wreck that I have no way of saving here. "She's fully dilated and effaced. Now that you're here I'm going to have her push. I need you to be ready for this baby because I'm bringing it to you."

I pull a pair of gloves out of a box on the wall and turn on the warmer. There is a stethoscope and suction waiting. I look around the room and see a man standing by the pregnant woman's head. He's wearing a mask and scrubs. Usually that is the spot reserved for the father. But no one should be having babies right now. I haven't completed the genetic pairing.

I hear Dr. Akiyama counting for the mother, instructing her when to push and when to wait. I hear him say that the head is out. He tells the mother to stop pushing while he suctions out the mouth and nose. Then he tells her to push hard. There is the metallic snip of chord clamps and medical scissors. Then he is next to me, placing a small, pale baby on the warmer. It's a boy, a tiny little baby boy. I stare at it for a moment, unsure of what to do next, trying to remember.

"Andromeda!" The doctor yells at me.

And that's all it takes. After years of training and getting yelled at in the delivery room each time I did something wrong or not fast enough, I return to the methodical assessing nurse that I was almost a year ago. I take warm blankets and scrub the baby with them, wiping off the blood and birthing fluids, trying to get him to cry. The baby's toes and hands are still blue, but the center of his chest is pink and red. I wrap an oximeter probe around its hand and use the stethoscope to listen to its lungs and heart. His breath sounds are strong, but wet sounding. I take the suction tubing and use it to suck the fluid out of the infant's nose and down the back of its throat. I check the baby's pulses on his tiny wrists and ankles, feel the soft fontanels on the top of his head, he has feathery blonde hair matted to his head. I watch the newborn and the clock, waiting for the baby to "pink up," turning from a dusky blue hue to bright pink and to breath in a normal rhythm. I place a small hat on his head and wrap him in three blankets and turn up the temperature setting on the warmer. I change my gloves and give the baby a minute to warm up.

After a few minutes I continue. I touch the side of his mouth as though I was going to feed him. He turns his head in the direction of my finger. I feel inside his mouth, checking the roof for a cleft, making sure he sucks. I un-wrap him and feel his ears, his collarbone, extend his limbs out, count his fingers and toes. I turn him over and run my finger down his back, checking to make sure the vertebrae are in a straight line and that there are no openings in the meninges. I check his genitals and rectum to make sure everything is present and intact. Then I wrap the baby in a clean set of blankets. He's been out for almost ten minutes now. The blue tinge has left his mouth and hands. There's a pacifier on the warmer, when I place it in his mouth he sucks hungrily.

"Is my baby okay?" I hear the mother ask Dr. Akiyama.

I stare at the child, watching, another five minutes pass. I stare at him longer, waiting for the swelling to go down, for his facial features to settle from being pushed out of the birth canal. He is so small that it doesn't take long. I look under the hat at his blonde hair again, pale features, and at the baby's nose, which is already high and arched. Dr. Akiyama moves to my side.

"How is he?" The doctor pulls his mask down and changes his gloves, examining the baby.

"He's breathing on his own, has a strong suck, his oxygen saturations are within the normal range. For a preemie he's doing well." I continue to watch the baby closely. I can't help but feel this baby looks familiar, as though I might know his parents from somewhere.

"Good. How does he compare to what you've seen in the NICU?" He looks back at the parents and then back towards me.

"He's breathing on his own and as long as he keeps doing that, the only things you will have to worry about are maintaining his temperature and getting him to eat." The doctor walks back to the parents to fill them in on the baby's status. I watch as the mother smiles at the doctor. The father just sits there, presumably shocked, as all first time fathers are in the delivery room. Usually they don't know what to do with themselves; they pace, and then get faint, and then they are afraid to touch the baby. It's always the same.

Dr. Akiyama is back at my side. "Doctor, whose baby is this?" He looks at me skeptically. "Who are the parents, what are their names?" He looks back to the parents and then to me. I can tell he's hiding something from me. There's something he doesn't want me to know. "Who are they, Doctor?" My heart is starting to beat heavily in my chest. He doesn't want to tell me. I watch the parents. The mother smiles as she looks at the tiny baby bundled on the warmer. A nurse helps her change her gown and get comfortable in the bed. The mother reaches over to the father and takes his hand. He still looks like he's in shock, like he doesn't know what to do. All I can see are his brown eyes since the rest of his face is covered by the surgical mask. Then the mother reaches up, trying to get his attention, stroking his cheek, and pulls the mask down.

"Andie…" Dr Akiyama must be trying to warn me, the tone of his voice is much lower, but it's too late. My heart picks up the pace, thumping wildly in my chest, my hands are in tight fists at my sides. I knew the baby looked familiar but I wasn't prepared for this, to see who the father is. In the corner, at the head of the bed sits a proud new father, and it is Ian.

--

I leave the room. I collect my clothes from the hallway. The Volker who escorted me to the hospital is at the nurse's station talking on the phone. He must be talking to Adam, filling him in on why they needed me here. Dr. Akiyama follows me out of the room.

"Andie, I'm sorry. Andie, stop, please, I need your help. I need you to tell me what to do with this baby." He grabs my arm and I jerk it back from him.

All this time I have been alone, taken away from my husband, feeling guilty for leaving him, for barely having a relationship with Adam, and he's moved on already. He's replaced me. He's found someone who could give him another child.

I am furious and heartbroken. "You could have warned me! You could have done something," I tell at the Doctor. "Any one of these guards could have told you that father in there is my husband!"

"Andie, keep your voice down, please." He pleads with me, closing the door to the room where we just came from.

"They all know. Every single one of them knows who we are!" I point to the Volker in the hallway. The one who escorted me here puts down the phone and walks towards us. "You could have-" the tears are starting and I can't stop them. "You could have done something. I didn't need to see that. I don't need to see any of this," I fall to the floor, sobbing to myself. The men stand around me, unknowing of what to do with me. Someone hands me a box of tissues. I do my best trying to clean up my face, to catch my breath, before I stand up, I turn to Dr. Akiyama. "You need to keep the baby warm. He's too small to keep his own temperatures up." I wipe at my eyes again, trying to stop the tears that keep leaking out. "He needs to be kept clothed and bundled under the warmer, if his parents want to hold him, that's too bad. He comes out to eat every three hours; the mother needs to breastfeed him. If that doesn't work contact me and I can tell you a few other methods to get him to eat. I don't want to have to put an IV in him, but I can if it needs to be done. Monitor his temperature and his vital signs right before he eats. Other than that, the baby needs to sleep and grow."

The infant isn't critical and Dr. Akiyama should be able to manage his care. I collect my things from the floor and then leave without saying anything else.

The Volker drives me back to the loft. Since Adam is upstairs with Lina the guard stays at the front door to the building. When I get to the loft Adam is waiting by the door. His arms are crossed and he stares at the floor, focusing on something. My sadness has turned into white hot anger by the time I get to the door.

"Andie," Adam reaches for me as I walk through the door. I swerve to the side to avoid his grasp. I throw the clothes that I carried home on the floor, wishing they were made of glass so I could watch them shatter into a million pieces. Maybe breaking something would ease my anger right now.

"Is Lina asleep?" I ask Adam. I feel him grab the back of the scrub top but I pull myself forward quickly, ripping it out of his grasp.

"Yes, she's asleep. Andie, wait." He follows me as I walk to Lina's room to check on her. She's sleeping soundly and innocently in the large plush bed. Stevie lifts her head off the end of the bed where she lays and perks her ears at the sound of me entering the room. I close the door behind me, so I don't wake her. Adam is waiting for me when I leave the room. He reaches for me again, grabbing the scrub top.

I slap at his hand. "Don't touch me, Adam!" I glare at him and stomp towards the phone. I know who I'm going to yell at, who I am going to make pay for what I just saw. I pick up the phone and the operator answers.

"Burton Crane," I snarl into the receiver. For the first time the operator doesn't respond. The phone rings only once before Crane picks up.

"Hello?" he sounds surprised that he's getting a call this late.

"I need to see you. Now."

"Andromeda?" My name unfurls off his tongue slowly, like a sweet surprise.

"Yes, Crane. I need to see you now." I think I actually stamp my foot on the floor as I say it.

"Well then. I will be there momentarily." I slam the phone down hard, not giving him the chance to say goodbye.

Adam follows me down to the atrium as I wait for Crane. "Are you sure this is a good idea Andie?" He asks me in the elevator. "Don't you think you need a moment to cool down?"

"I've been cooling down all winter, Adam." I try not to yell at him, but my words echo loudly off the metal elevator walls. "I've been doing what Crane asks me, keeping my head down, putting up with you ignoring me. I'm done with it. I'm sick of Crane trying to run my life and Lina's life."

When the elevator doors open I stomp to the front door of the building and pace in a large circle waiting for Crane to show up. I catch a glimpse of myself in the mirrored glass. The scrubs hang loosely off me; I almost resemble the nurse I once was. Adam stands by the elevator. At first I think he might be hiding from me. But I realize he may be shielding himself from Crane's view, so he can watch.

Finally a car pulls up and Crane gets out. He takes his time walking into the building, adjusting his scarf and gloves, wiping off his heavy wool coat when stray snowflakes land on it. Finally the door opens and he comes inside.

"Ah Andromeda, what a pleasant surprise in the middle of the night." He holds his arms open and smiles at me. "To what do I owe this pleasure?"

I'm not sure if he hasn't seen the look of flaming anger on my face or if he just doesn't recognize it. I can't hold it in anymore. "Why are people having babies, Crane?"

"Well, whatever do you mean, Andromeda?"

"You know what I mean. I was just at the hospital." I pull the front of the scrub shirt out at him, pointing out the fact that I am wearing hospital scrubs. "Do you know what I just saw at the hospital?"

"I think I might have an idea about that."

"I haven't completed the genetic pairing, Crane. So let me ask you again, why are people having babies?"

"I'm sure you haven't noticed because you have been working so hard all winter long, but the population has taken quite the hit, Andromeda." Crane pauses dramatically. "At least one-quarter of the population has died already."

"What? Why haven't you told me this information?" My arms are tight with anger and I resume pacing as we speak. "Why haven't I been told?"

"I didn't want to upset you. Since you're so busy and all. See what it's doing to you now?" He points at me.

"Explain. Right now. This was never discussed in any of the Committee meetings. Do Alexander and Morris know?" He shakes his head no. "What about Remington, Ms. Black, Adam?" He shakes his head no again. "So you haven't told anyone?"

"Well, our good doctor has informed me of the many deaths. So, he knows."

"What are they dying from?"

"There's a combination of factors." He brings his hands in front of his chest, tapping his fingertips on each other. "This isn't the healthiest community in the country, as you know. And certain medications are not available to us: there are cardiac medications, diabetic medications, asthma medications. The list goes on and on. Either way, we can't risk the population getting too low. I had to make a decision to allow some of the women to get pregnant. But there have been, complications, just as you've seen tonight. The women keep delivering prematurely, their babies too early to be viable."

I run the facts over in my head for a moment and the answer seems almost too easy. "It's the medications, Crane. I can't believe you haven't realized this yet. You can't give those hormones to a woman and expect her to carry a fetus without any ill effects." He should know this, it doesn't make sense that he would let this go on.

"Yes well, Ian's child is the first to survive, thanks to you, that is." He cocks his head to the side and raises his eyebrows waiting for my response.

"That's great, Crane, I'm really glad I was there to experience the whole thing. I'm sure I can thank you personally for that."

"I should thank you, for helping bring the firstborn of the Phoenix District into this world. There should be a celebration."

"What is the point of the genetic pairing? I'm almost done with it. I was going to finish tonight before I was called to the hospital." I have finally stopped pacing and my voice has lowered.

"Ah! Excellent! Just in time." He's back to smiling now.

"And now that I have completed the pairings what will I do?"

"The population will grow, Andromeda. Children will grow up, babies will be born. You will be responsible for their pairings also. Your job will never be completed as long as the Phoenix District remains prosperous. This is excellent really, you are just in time."

"Just in time for what?" I eye him skeptically.

"Just in time to withdraw the medication and welcome the Residents fully alert into the Phoenix District." My stomach drops at his words. He continues. "I think we should continue this conversation at another time. Perhaps after you've had time to rest. Goodnight, Andromeda!" He bows oddly to me, and then walks out the door.

I watch his car leave before I stomp back to the elevator. Adam is waiting with the door open. He follows me back to the loft, quietly. I open Lina's door and check on her again. She and Stevie are still both fast asleep. When I turn around Adam is standing in the living room, waiting to see what I do.

Normally, after a less than stellar night at work, I would help myself to a few glasses of wine to numb the pain and disappointment. Crane has outlawed all alcohol for the Residents but he included a bottle in one of the many gifts he has given me. I walk to the kitchen and pull it out from the back of the cupboard where I stashed it behind the cooking pans.

"Do you want some of this?" I ask Adam harshly as I twist open the cap on the wine bottle.

When I turn around he is running his hand through his hair. "Sure. Why not."

I don't have any wine glasses so I pour some into two coffee mugs and take a long gulp of the wine. It is dry and strong. I hand Adam his mug as I walk towards the living room and sit down on the floor with my mug and the wine bottle. Adam follows, sitting on the couch across from me.

"What did you think of that conversation, Adam?" I take another long swallow of the wine, hoping the spirits will numb the events of the night that are still sharp in my mind.

"It's all a little much." He takes a sip from his mug.

"That's all you have to say?" I figure since I'm on a tirade calling everyone out; the doctor, the Volker, Crane, why stop at Adam? "After all this time, Adam, you haven't spoken to me in months. One minute you're saving us from wolves, you're pulling out my stitches, you're kissing me in the basement, asking me to trust you, and then you're gone. I think I even called you a few weeks ago and you didn't answer. I take it all very personally." I take another long drink from my mug, emptying it, and then refill it from the wine bottle.

"You don't understand, Andie." He sets his mug down and rubs his face. "Crane is running me ragged. He has me out surveying the wall, the fence, the gateway, assigning new recruits, training Remington. I barely have time to sleep."

"And all this time I've been wondering what I did wrong to put you on edge." My lips start to tingle from the wine. Seeing Ian tonight, seeing his newborn son, it was like a slap in the face-another one-from Crane. Ian is gone, forced to move on, following the path designated by us, the Sovereign. I have been alone with Lina and the threats from Crane, alone with the knowledge that he wants us paired. I am tired of taking orders. I stare at Adam as he leans forward to take a few sips from his mug. I decide it's time for him to know some of what I've been keeping from him.

"Do you remember at Lina's birthday party? When I told you Crane slapped me across the face and split my lip?" His eyes dart to mine. Good, I have his attention. "He was trying to kiss me, Adam." Now his eyes flick open a little wider.

"What do you mean he was trying to kiss you?" He twists his face into a scowl.

"Just what I said, he was trying to kiss me, and I pushed him away. That's why he slapped me-for *denying him*." I raise my fingers to quote the phrase in the air. "That was right after he told me that I would be expected to reproduce and that he expects us to be paired. Me and Crane, can't you just picture it in your head like a sick putrid little love story?" I take another long drink from my mug, trying to erase the image of Crane from my mind. "Does it make you want to vomit? Because I do, every time I replay it in my head."

Adam stops, frozen, watching me. "You're serious." He knows when I'm lying, and I'm guessing it didn't take long for him to realize this is not a lie. It's the cold, hard, disgusting truth.

"Unfortunately I am." I refill my mug, knowing well that I shouldn't, my lips are fully numb now.

"This is bullshit." Adam stands abruptly and paces the living room. "Why didn't you tell me this before?"

"You don't talk to me anymore. We've gone over this already, Adam." I wave my hand at him, dismissing the conversation.

"I can't protect you if you don't tell me these things. Crane keeps me too busy to watch you all the time like I did before."

I laugh a little, the wine exaggerating my responses. "You used to watch me?"

He just stares at me, rubbing his jaw, fidgeting.

I kick off my shoes and socks, rubbing my feet into the plush living room carpet. Adam continues his pacing. Now I know I've truly made him mad. I watch his jaw tense, his fists clench. I drain the mug. He runs his hands through his hair and I watch as the muscles in his arms push through the thin cotton of his shirt as it rises, just to the top of his jeans without showing even a wink of skin.

I can feel the heat in my cheeks from the flush of embarrassment. I'm not sure if it is because the last man I looked at in this manner I was married to or because I just can't stop watching him, talking to him, trying to make him angry. I stand up and walk over to Adam, waiting for him to stop pacing in front of me.

"What?" He asks as I stand in front of him.

"I'm tired of this, Adam. I'm tired of Crane controlling me. I'm tired of living in fear of him. I'm tired of you being gone all the time. I'm tired of being trapped up here, alone." I reach out and grab the front of his shirt, crumpling it in my fist and pulling him towards me.

"Andie, stop." He puts his hand over mine; it's warm and heavy, just like I remember. "You're drunk already. It's only been like five minutes."

"What can I say? I'm a cheap date. Most men like that in a woman." I pull myself closer to him, invading his space. "Did you hear me Adam? I'm done with you ignoring me all the time." I stand on my toes and wrap my arms around his neck. "I need you," I breathe the words into his ear, trying my best to imitate what he did to me in the dark hallway so many months ago.

He grabs my upper arms trying to stop me, holding me still. I can see the muscle in his jaw tighten. I kiss him, hard at first, and his response is immediate. His hands are in my hair, against the small of my back, pulling me closer to him, pressing my body to his, tipping my head back as his lips kiss me back. He tastes sweet, more so than the wine, and it's intoxicating. Each time he pulls his lips from mine I ache for them to return. The wine is having its full effect, clouding my mind, lowering my inhibitions. I clench his shirt in my hands, to pull him back towards the bedroom, but he stops me, holding my face between his warm hands.

"Are you sure you want to do this, Andie?" His eyes search mine, using whatever method it is to see if I'm telling the truth. Last time we were in the bedroom together I was too stunned by his scars to do anything. And then he was gone.

He stands rigid in front of me, waiting for my response.

"Yes."

This time I do not fumble nervously with the buttons of his shirt. I know what lies under it, I'm no longer afraid of the scars marring his body. Adam watches me as I reach out and run my hand over them, feeling the long slashes across his ribs, the burn marks pocking his upper chest, the three bullet wounds near his shoulder which have turned his skin into a jagged landscape.

I'm afraid the effects of the wine will consume me soon; it is already making me wobbly. I fumble with my own clothes, the stiff scrubs, not out of nervousness but because my fingertips are swollen and clumsy with intoxication and I can barely keep my balance. Somehow, my body knows this is not Ian, and my heart races with the anticipation of the unknown. Adam steps towards me, assisting, and before I know it he has our clothes off, discarded on the floor. He reaches for me, pressing his lips to mine and my bare body to his. We stand, kissing, with nothing between us but the thin gold band on my left ring finger. Adam reaches down, slowly dragging his hand across my side, pulling me into his arms and carrying me to the side of the bed. The wine sloshes in my stomach as he sets me down. And when he bends down to kiss me again I feel the wine burning up the back of my esophagus. I try to ignore it and focus on the task at hand, the burning deep inside me and the desire for him to continue.

Suddenly my mouth starts to feel heavy, filling with thick saliva. I pull away, closing my eyes and taking deep breaths. Now, I realize that it has been much too long since the last time I consumed alcohol and that downing almost the entire bottle in just a few minutes was not a good idea. But I want so badly to continue, I want to carry on exploring each other and extinguishing the tension that has been hovering around us for so long. Now that I know for certain Ian has moved on without me. When I open my eyes Adam is pulling me back to him, bending down to kiss me again. Saliva gushes into my mouth, making my tongue heavy, churning my stomach. I reach out, placing my hand on his chest.

"What's wrong?" Adam whispers, his voice thick, heavy with desire.

I can't respond, I know what will happen if I open my mouth. I quickly turn away from him, running naked to the small master bathroom, slamming the door behind me and locking it, vomiting the bottle of wine into the toilet.

--

I hear Adam knocking on the door but I can't open it or respond between the retching of my stomach. The last thing I need is him in here, offering to hold my hair back. When it feels like my insides may have settled, I sit on the floor of the bathroom feeling ridiculous. Here I am naked and vomiting. No better than a drunk college girl. Adam knocks on the door again, but now, I am too embarrassed to respond. I brush my teeth and take a quick shower. Thankful that there are towels in the bathroom since my clothes remain on the floor in the bedroom.

When I'm done, I stand wrapped in a towel, with my hand on the door handle, trying to work up the courage to face Adam again, without puking. I take a few deep breaths and open the door. Adam sits on the end of the bed, fully dressed, my discarded clothes now neatly folded in a pile next to him. He watches me, saying nothing about my alcohol intolerance. I walk to the dresser and pull out undergarments and sleeping clothes, and then I return to the bathroom to get dressed.

Adam is still sitting in the same place when I walk out of the bathroom, dressed in my pajamas. I walk towards him, slowly, nervously. "I'm sorry," I tell him as I stare at the floor, embarrassed.

He laughs a little. "I've never had a cheap date do that before," he responds, pulling me into his arms. I hold my hand over my mouth and try to quiet my stomach from the movement. "Another time then." He pulls me down onto the bed, and we lay together, curled round each other, with my head on his chest and his lips pressing against my forehead. I feel ill from the wine and my failed seduction. And I'm sure the uneasy feeling in my stomach includes the reaction from seeing Ian and realizing our marriage is over and things can never go back to the way they were. After a few short minutes my tears saturate Adam's shirt.

Afterwards, when I'm done sobbing, Adam pulls the heavy blanket at the foot of the bed over us both and reaches out to tuck a few stray hairs behind my ear, kissing me.

"You can't let Crane find out, Andie." He tells me softly.

"Find out what?"

"About us."

"Why?"

"Don't you see? He planned this so thoroughly, taking over our town, protecting you, making you Sovereign, the luxuries he affords for you, you being present at the delivery of Ian's baby. He planned it, he had to. A person like Crane, he doesn't plan to lose. If he wants you, he needs to think he is going to get you. He can't find out about us, no one can."

"Does this mean you're going to disappear and ignore me for another seven months?" I ask him half joking, but mostly serious. "Because I'm not sure I could handle that right now."

"I've told you before. I'll always come back for you."

"Good." I reach up and pull him down to kiss me.

CHAPTER TWENTY

"Mom, wake up. Stevie has to pee." Lina is shaking my shoulder and Stevie is pacing the room, whining, waiting for someone to let her outside. I wake panicked, afraid of what she will see in the room. But Adam must have cleaned up before he left. The scrubs I wore home last night are folded neatly next to me.

"Okay, Lina, just give me a moment."

When I bring Lina to the atrium, Ms. Black says nothing of Ian's baby being born. Crane must be keeping it a secret. I've discovered lately that he is excellent at keeping secrets. The Volker guards greet me at the entrance to the lab making no mention of my outburst at the hospital. I try not to think about last night, about Ian's baby, my accusations towards Crane, Adam.

I delve deep into the data analysis, burying myself, ignoring the world around me.

By lunch time my analysis is complete.

All of the current District Residents have been assigned their genetic pair. Female residents over the age of 35 have been removed and males over the age of 45 have also been removed, since their reproductive organs are highly prone to genetic errors. Thankfully, Crane allowed me to leave a few current families intact, even though he ruined mine.

I call Kira to the lab so she can match the Resident codes with their actual names. The children of the District have been assigned their own genetic pair but they will not be told of their match until they are of age.

I call Crane and tell him that I have completed the task, slamming the phone down before he has time to respond to me. I tell neither of them that I have pulled the Sovereign names from the analysis, and they sit in a separate file, unpaired. I save the completed file on a removable drive and set it on Kira's desk. Then I go to the atrium and sit on the tall curved stairwell that leads to the empty second floor of the building and watch the children and Ms. Black.

A Volker guard walks up next to me. He's the same one from yesterday who brought me to the hospital and then brought me back to the loft, a completely changed person.

"I heard you're done with the pairings." This is new with the Volker, usually they don't talk to me; they just stand quietly, watching, protecting. This one must be testing his boundaries.

"News travels fast I guess."

"Do you know who I've been paired with?" I look at the guard, he looks hopeful, possibly even a little excited.

"How do you know about the pairings?" I wasn't aware that anyone outside of the Committee meetings knew of my task, or what I was responsible for. The knowledge that I am directly responsible for deciding who will spend the rest of their lives together gnaws on my conscience. Especially because somewhere in that list was Ian's code.

"Only some of us know," he responds sheepishly.

"I don't know the names. They've been assigned by codes. Kira will be here soon to fill in the actual names."

The Volker walks back towards the laboratory door and waits.

It's only a few minutes before Kira walks in the front door letting a cold rush of air into the large atrium. She brushes the powdery snowflakes off her parka and stomps on the carpet to get the snow off her shoes. I wave to her and she walks to the stairwell where I'm sitting.

"The file is on your desk."

"Great, it shouldn't take me long. Did you tell Crane?" She takes her gloves and scarf off, stuffing them into the canvas bag slung across her chest.

"Yeah I told him." I don't tell her that I slammed the phone down in his ear.

She leaves me at the stairwell, almost running towards the lab, and I wait.

A static energy hangs in the air of the atrium. Kira should be done soon, placing the names with the resident codes. The front door swings open again, letting another rush of cold winter air rush across the atrium. This time it's Adam. He heads straight for the lab. I make no effort to call him over to me, especially after his warning last night; no one can know about us. He's in the lab for a few minutes before he walks out, searching the corners of the atrium and walking over to the stairwell where I'm sitting.

"You're done with the pairings?" Adam asks, also seeming a little anxious.

"Yes. How do you know?"

"Crane is calling a Committee meeting. I've been sent to collect you."

"I don't want to go to the meeting, Adam."

"Why?"

"Because I'm going to have to explain to Crane why I removed all the District Sovereign names from that list," I tell him.

I'm sure Crane will be furious with me. He warned me, he's been sending me gifts, giving me my space, he didn't even yell at me for confronting him in the middle of the night. I know what he expects, but he's not going to get it.

"Don't worry. The building will be filled with Volker. You'll be fine."

"Are you sure?" He offers his hand to help me get up from the stairs. "How do I know he doesn't have your entire faction in his pocket, Adam? That he could snap his fingers and you would all turn your backs? Crane organized this District. He was successful with the one in Japan. I don't doubt there are a lot of people that would look the other way if he wanted to punish me."

"Yes, Andie, he did, but the Funding Entities have ensured that the Volker do not answer to Crane, the Volker will always be your loophole of protection."

"How can you be so sure?"

"How can you still not trust me?"

I take Adam's hand and he pulls me to stand next to him. We walk across the atrium to collect the children and Ms. Black.

--

"I would like to begin this meeting with a round of applause." Crane claps his hands together, high in front of his face, and we do as we are asked. "As some of you may know, last night we had our first birth within the walls of the Phoenix District. This is a joyous day. All that we have been working towards together is finally coming to fruition." The rest of the Sovereign smile and clap with Crane, everyone except for me. I watch as Adam even plays along. "Now that Andromeda has completed the genetic pairing of the residents the next topic on our agenda is waking up the town." Crane pauses, waiting for objections. "I would like to suggest the same format we followed in Japan, which worked quite well. The medication will be withdrawn in a slow manner, a titration, where each resident will receive less and less over a period of time. Once the medication has cleared their systems they will be confused and disoriented, but for a short period of time. Once we explain to them what has happened they will resume their lives as they have been since the blast."

"How long will it take?" I ask.

"Approximately a year," he adds without pausing, almost dismissing me. "We will start with the laboring factions first, the Orderlies and Navigators, and those who are mostly uneducated. Then we move onto the other factions; the Currents, teachers and medical staff. We found in Japan that the educated residents were able to assimilate much easier when they saw the rest of the District cooperating."

This means one thing to me. Over the next year Ian will wake up, and since he is one of the nuclear engineers at the plant, he will be one of the last residents. I wonder if he might remember us, knowing that everything which has happened would surely break his heart.

The meeting continues with updates from the Sovereign. Another list of supplies is prepared for Remington. More food, clothes, medical supplies for the impending baby boom Crane is expecting and seeds to get the crops started in the spring.

I watch Crane as he speaks, trying to control my facial expressions, trying to make it look like I am simply listening to him run this meeting, because I don't want him to know what I am truly thinking: I need to get us out of here, soon.

CHAPTER TWENTY-ONE

It's night. Lina is fast asleep and I should be too. But I can't sleep. Not after today's committee meeting. I sit in a dining room chair in front of the large windows facing the lake. The moonlight is glowing off the snowflakes, giving them the effect of tiny lights falling from the sky. The heavy grumble of a snow plow passes by the building. There is a knock at the door. When I turn around I see a Volker guard standing there. As I get closer I notice that it is Adam. I open the door and let him in. He looks out of place in the head to toe gray outfit.

"What are you doing here in uniform?" I ask.

"I had a late meeting with Crane." Something is wrong.

"Come in, what's wrong?"

I take his arm, pulling him towards the kitchen and as I do the cuff from his rolled sleeve rises above his elbow. He tries to pull his arm back but it's too late, I've already seen it. The blood soaked bandage on the soft inner tissue of his forearm. Just like the one Remington had after he passed his training and was designated the Runner, Adam has been injected with a transmitter.

"Adam? Why do you have a transmitter?" I try to control the panic in my voice, the realization that Crane is once again about to take someone away from me.

"I didn't have a choice, Andie."

"What do you mean you didn't have a choice?"

"Crane keeps complaining that Remington is too slow. He takes too long. The last time he went out he was gone almost two weeks. Some supplies have been missing and Crane has seen him deviating from his travel pattern. I'm being sent to follow him."

"And what does he want you to do if you find Remington breaking the rules?" Adam looks out the window, at the falling snow. "Adam?" He won't look at me. He stares off in the distance, towards the lake. "Adam?"

"Kill him."

"And would you?" I'm sure he has before, killed a person. It goes with the territory of being a Marine. For some reason, this realization doesn't bother me one bit.

"I'm not going to give Crane anything to hold over my head and control me. But I do need to find out what Remington has been doing out there for so long." He pauses for a moment, looking back in my eyes. "But now, I have Crane's full trust. I'll have the codes for the Gateway and the train. It should make things a lot easier for us, for you and Lina, to get you both out of here."

"That's not going to help you, Adam, when Crane pushes his little heart attack button."

He sighs heavily and reaches out, drawing me to him. "I know," he responds solemnly, wrapping his arms around me, pressing the length of our bodies together. "I leave in the morning."

Adam stays the night but unlike last night we sit on the couch, wrapped around each other, talking. I rub my finger over the bandage on his arm feeling the hard lump from the small transmitter under his skin. I lay my head on his chest breathing in his scent, trying to memorize it. During the long stretches of silence, when I'm unable to stop my mind from running, I think about Ian waking up in a year only to find his life changed, his wife and daughter two years older, and untouchable to him, forced to move on. That is, if he remembers us at all.

I have come to the realization that Crane will use whoever he can against me, to make me cooperate and continue the pairings. This is already evident with the way he dangled Lina over my head until I agreed to work with him and the birth of Ian's child. The only way that I can keep Ian safe from Crane's grasp, and off of his radar, is to move on. Ian may not remember us, but as long as I hold him close to me, his life will always be in danger.

Now, there's Adam. Our protector-the only one I can trust right now-and for some reason I'm drawn to him, more so than I should be, more so than any wife of another man should be. And Crane is sending Adam on a mission, with the ability to take his life with just the push of a button.

During the wee hours of the morning Adam gets up to leave. We stand in Lina's doorway and watch her sleep for a few moments, her face peaceful, innocent, not deserving of everything that has happened.

"I don't want you to go again," I whisper to him as we stand there. "I don't want to be left here with Crane looming over me."

"Now that you're done with the pairings you can prepare. Crane said you are free to do as you please until the next generation is ready to be paired. I need you to collect supplies and prepare Lina." He kisses my forehead, pulling away after a few minutes to look into my eyes.

And now he is gone, the first of us able to get outside the gates of the Phoenix District.

CHAPTER TWENTY-TWO

When it's time, I wake Lina and get her ready for class. I bring Stevie with me and we sit on the curved stairway to watch Ms. Black instruct the children in writing, reading and mathematics. I run my hand over Stevie's long shaggy black hair. The process of getting out of the District consumes me. I have to take Lina, I can't leave Stevie and then there's Ian. He has no idea who we are right now and dragging him along with us would be futile. Walking back to Phoenix was hard enough, taking four days, with just me and Adam. Sneaking out with a six year old and a dog will be much harder, almost impossible. And if Crane finds us I'm sure he will put an end to our lives, all of us. Hopefully, while I'm collecting supplies, Adam is formulating some type of a plan, because we can't get out of here without him.

While Lina is in class I busy myself with cleaning the lab and the loft. I make a pile of clothes on the floor of the closet, things we might need on a spring trek through the woods.

Two days after Adam left to follow Remington, I was called to the hospital to check on Ian's baby. This time they were smart enough to get his parents out of the room. While I was there I was able to collect some supplies; a scalpel, sutures, bandages, irrigation solution, antibiotic ointment and sterile gloves.

It's been four days since Adam left and Crane has called me to a meeting. As the Volker guard escorts me to Crane's office I tell him, "Do not to leave my side." I don't trust Crane and I definitely don't want to be left alone with him, especially after what happened last time.

"Yes ma'am," the Volker replies, nodding to me.

As soon as the door to Crane's office opens it is obvious that he is not happy.

"Andromeda, come in. Volker, you wait outside." He dismisses the guard with the wave of his hand.

"No, I want him here." Crane stops and glares at me.

"Have it your way then." He swings the door closed and walks to his desk to sit. "It appears, Andromeda, that you have forgotten a key piece to the pairings." He raises his eyebrows expectantly.

"I'm not sure what you're talking about." It's another bad lie. I know exactly what he is talking about. I pulled the Sovereign from the list. I've been expecting this meeting.

"Dear Andromeda, I thought I made the details of our agreement clear. You were to pair up the residents *and* the Sovereign." He taps his fingers on the smooth wooden desk expectantly.

"I won't do it."

"Why not?" Crane rises from his desk chair and starts walking towards me. Now I'm thankful that I thought to keep the Volker with me. Especially if he tries anything like he did last fall.

"I refuse to pair myself, Crane. Besides, I'm already married." I try my best poker face. I have already decided to set Ian free, to protect him by moving on. I just have to make sure Crane sees that. "What am I suppose to tell Ian when he is woken up in a year?"

"I told you to forget him, Andromeda, you need to move on. Was being present at the delivery of his child not enough for you? He won't remember you. I've already seen to that."

"What did you do to him?"

"Nothing that you could do anything about, consider him lost to you. It's best you move on, you and Lina both."

Knowing that Lina will not have her father pains at me. He won't be there to see her lose her first tooth, get her first haircut, see her turn sixteen, get married, he's going to miss it all. I look away from Crane, mostly because I can feel the tears welling up in my eyes. "I'm not ready."

"You need to find it within yourself to get ready, Andromeda. The District is waiting on you."

"You can't expect this of me." I can feel my chin start to tremble;

I push my lips together and take a deep breath in. "What am I suppose to tell Lina? I can't do this. I'm not ready."

"Move on," he sneers at me, thoroughly agitated.

"Goodbye, Crane." I turn and leave without being dismissed. Another tick on the growing list of insubordination Crane is no doubt compiling against me. I'm sure none of the other Sovereign show Crane the same blatant disrespect as I do, one of these days it's going to get me in a load of trouble.

"You may want to reconsider who you chose to trust, Andromeda," Crane calls to me as I slam the door to his office.

Thankfully the Volker follows me and escorts me back to the chemistry building. I don't review the Sovereign data; instead, I review Crane's genetic data, searching for anything that I could use against him.

--

Adam is gone almost four weeks. Just as I am about to conclude that he must be dead and may never return to us, Crane calls a Committee meeting. After we are all seated, Crane and Adam enter the room. Adam must have just gotten back. He's covered in dried mud, with a scruffy beard, most of his knuckles are caked in dried blood and there is a dark bruise under his left eye. As I wait for Crane to start the meeting I notice Remington is nowhere in sight.

"I regret to inform the members of the Committee that our newest member will no longer be present," Crane tells us. "As expected, he was found to be involved in some peculiar activity which resulted in his termination." Crane gives us all a grave look. I know it is not one of concern for Remington, but a threat, that if any of us should try anything similar we will meet the same fate.

Crane doesn't go into detail of the activity Remington was involved in. Instead he continues the meeting with a review of the first group of residents who have started the medication titration. I watch Alexander and Morris give meticulous descriptions of how the residents are coping, they talk excitedly and animatedly. I wonder what Crane has against them, what keeps them here, participating in this overhaul of our town?

Crane commences the meeting by asking for a list of supplies which anyone may need. Morris tells us that the past two trips

Remington was on, only half of the food stock that was ordered was delivered and the District already needs more. I look to Adam, who, for the first time ever in a Committee meeting, is staring directly at me. No one has to say it. If we are short on food, Crane is going to send the Runner out to get more, and since Remington is out of the picture Adam is the only one to go.

--

It is late. I stare across the long living space, out the window at the misty rain. I wait anxiously for Adam, sitting on the floor next to the door. I jump to my feet when I hear his footsteps. Pulling open the door, I throw myself at him, my arms around his neck, squeezing him tightly to me.

"You were gone too long. I was afraid something happened."

"There was a situation." He releases me and pushes me back by my shoulders. "We need to talk." I follow him to the couch.

"What happened to Remington?" I can't stop thinking about Crane saying he was terminated.

"He has been reassigned. Crane can't afford to lose any more residents. He's been medicated, assigned to work with the convicts."

"What happened out there, Adam?"

"Andie, you will never believe it," he tells me, shaking his head in disbelief.

"What?" I ask.

"The world is continuing on as though the town of Phoenix never existed."

Adam launches into a detailed account of what he saw. There are barricades on all the roads and highways, blocking any traffic from getting within ten miles of the electric fence that encompasses The District. The National Guard has set up secured blockades to prevent traffic from entering the county. The large city where I used to work has lost over half of its population, the populace has moved away, afraid of the radiation they were told was haunting Phoenix County.

Remington had to travel to Pennsylvania and the Carolinas to collect the necessary supplies. He was unaware for most of the trip that Adam had hidden on the train, hiding in the rear cars, watching his every move. The Runner is under strict orders to collect the supplies, rendezvous with the Funding Entities' and return. Instead,

Remington was spending time in taverns where the train stopped, soliciting women. On the last stop Adam witnessed him telling a woman in the bar the secrets of the Phoenix District, that we were all there and still alive. Adam picked a fight with him before he could say much. That's how he got the black eye, the bloody knuckles. Remington was drunk but aware enough to recognize Adam, a fellow Volker and his superior. Adam dragged Remington back to the Phoenix District and reported to Crane.

"Now what?" I ask Adam, hopeful that he has a plan.

"Crane is sending me out in two days. You need to be ready to leave."

"So soon," I'm surprised and hopeful to finally get out of here, to get Lina to safety. "I can't believe we are going to get out of here."

"Andie," Adam's voice turns dire. "I can't get too far away."

"What? Why?" My stomach sinks at his words, I thought he was going to leave with us, escape and never look back, I thought we were going to do this together.

"The transmitter." He holds his forearm out at me. There is a small red mark where the transmitter was injected into his upper arm.

I almost forgot. "I can take it out," I tell him. I have the medical supplies I collected after he left.

He stares disbelieving at me. "How would you take it out?"

"I have supplies, from the hospital." I go to the closet and get the things I stole from the hospital. Adam follows me to the table as I lay them out. "I just don't have any anesthetic. They had that under lock and key." I stare at the supplies, confident; the only thing making me nervous is the suturing. I have never stitched a wound before, but I have watched many times and even practiced with a tomato once.

"So you would cut this thing out of me. And I'd feel it all?" His eyes shift from the gleaming scalpel to my eyes.

"Unfortunately." Adam stares for a few moments then he takes off his thin khaki jacket throwing it on the floor, and starts rolling his sleeve up to his shoulder.

"Do it."

"It's going to hurt," I warn him.

"I'm sure it's nothing that I haven't felt before." He looks at me expectantly. He doesn't have to elaborate; I've seen his scars, and I know that he was the receiver of something very painful.

I scrub his arm with soap for three minutes and then I wash my hands and arms for the same amount of time. Thankfully the scalpel came packaged with a sterile drape, which I use to cover his arm. I hesitate, just before pressing the sharp scalpel to his skin. I look at his face afraid for the pain he is about to feel. His face is calm, hopeful; he looks to his arm, waiting for me to cut the transmitter out.

I press down and the sharp scalpel cuts into his arm smoothly, like it's made of soft butter. A thick rivet of blood starts flowing around the scalpel and down his arm. The transmitter was injected within the top layers of subcutaneous tissue and I don't have to press down far before I feel it. There isn't much scar tissue collected around the transmitter and once I get the skin open I easily pull the small metallic object out of his arm with a pair of tweezers, dropping it into a nearby bowl. I irrigate the area and then do my best at stitching the small wound. It takes only five stitches. I coat it with antibiotic ointment and cover it with fresh gauze. Only when I am done do I realize that Adam never made a sound the entire time I was cutting into his arm and stitching it up.

When I am done we both stare at the almost flat, oblong transmitter in the bowl. "What do we do with it?" I ask Adam.

"I have to keep it near me, so Crane thinks it's still in. It's just so small I'm afraid I'll lose it." We stare at it a little longer. I notice that there is a tiny red light blinking.

"I have an idea," I tell Adam. I get up and go to the bedroom closet, digging in the back for the extravagantly carved wooden box Crane gave me for Christmas. I bring it back to the table where Adam sits, waiting.

"What's that?"

"A gift I never wanted." I open up the wooden box, and there it remains, just as the day I opened it; the jewel encrusted locket Crane gave me. I pinch open the clasp and the locket opens to a hollow center. Using the tweezers, I place the transmitter in the middle of the locket and then carefully pinch the clasp closed.

"Now what?" Adam watches me closely.

"Give me your arm." I wrap the long chain around his upper arm and adjust the locket so it falls against the sensitive skin of his inner arm. I pull his sleeve down covering the locket and his wound. "If you notice any drainage from the transmitter we can only assume it is the potassium and Crane is done with you, you are dead to him." I watch Adam's light blue eyes, waiting for his next move.

"This is an expensive piece of jewelry Andie." Adam eyes the small bulge where the locket rests under his sleeve.

"Enjoy it. I hope you don't mind that I re-gifted." I stand up and start cleaning, throwing away the bloody drape and washing the scalpel and tweezers in the sink. I find a small towel to wrap the medical supplies in, so I can take it with us when we leave.

Adam watches me from the chair. When I go to the bedroom closet to place the medical supplies in my travel pile he follows me. "Andie, what about Ian?" He asks me.

"What about him?"

"If we're going to leave, do you want me to get him out too?"

I can't believe he is asking me this now, after all we've been through, he waits until we are about to leave to ask about my husband. "Crane did something to him while you were gone. He confronted me for not pairing up the Sovereign and when I brought up Ian he informed me that Ian won't remember us. I'm not sure how he did it, but he made it clear that Ian is not the same. He doesn't know us and he won't remember us."

"Andie, I don't want you to regret this."

"I regret that I can't save Ian." I close the closet door and face Adam. "But he's gone now. Crane took him and the only way I can keep him safe is to move on." I stare at the floor, ashamed.

And then Adam is walking towards me, pulling me into his arms, pressing his warm lips to mine. Too easily I reach up, wrapping my arms around his neck, running my fingers through his dark hair. A deep groan escapes his throat when my fingertips brush the sensitive skin on the back of his neck.

"Andie," he whispers in my ear. "The whole time I was gone, I couldn't stop thinking about you." Then his lips are back on mine, his long fingers entwined in my hair, tipping my head back. But that's all. He doesn't press on, and neither do I. Both of us are too consumed, boiling with the anticipation of escape.

Before Adam leaves in the early morning he wakes me up, brushing his thumb across my cheekbone. "Be ready, Andie. We leave tomorrow night. I'll come for you and Lina."

--

Today is escape day.

While Lina is in class I get an escort to take me to the grocery store. I find that Alexander and Morris were right when they said that we were low on supplies. There is only two or three of each item on the shelves; however, the cereal and grains are completely out. I stock up on small items that are easy for travel; raisins, nuts, peanut butter, a few bottles of water and pretzels. I wander the store, searching for anything else I could bring with us. At the end of the sparsely stocked bread isle I find a section with school supplies. The pencils and papers are fully stocked, which is understandable since the District has taken over the schools, supplying each child with the necessary items needed for school. Parents are no longer responsible for buying them. Hanging on a hook are three large backpacks. Exactly what I need. The colors could be a little better though. I look up and down the long grocery isle. My Volker guard stands at the end of the aisle, talking with another Volker. I take two of the backpacks; one is light pink the other brown. I roll them up and hide them in the bottom of my grocery bag.

I return to the chemistry building just as Ms. Black is finishing class. I bring Lina upstairs with me and cook a quick dinner. I tell Lina we are going on a trip to see Uncle Sam, her uncle, my brother. She seems genuinely excited since she hasn't seen him in almost a year. I'm not sure how else to explain what we are doing, since we will be sneaking out of the District in the middle of the night, trekking through the woods since travel by car is no longer viable. The main highways have been mostly destroyed to prevent easy access to the District.

We clean up and shower like we would any other night. But this time we dress in dark clothes. Dressing Lina for the night is hard since most of her clothing is brightly colored in pinks and purples. I dig in her pile of clothes and find a pair of jeans and leather boots. As I dig further I find a dark brown turtleneck and an oversized coat that is colored light brown. When she is all dressed I step back and take a look. She would be barely recognizable in the dark clothes if it weren't for her thick mane of blonde curls cascading down her back. I do my best at French braiding her hair, the curls kink her hair, causing large uneven bulges in the braid.

Next I dress myself. Finding dark colors is easy since my closet is filled with mostly black and brown colored clothing. I decide on a pair of heavy jeans, a black shirt and black jacket. In the pile of gifts from Crane are two scarves, one is a mixture of purple hues, the other browns. I pull them both out to bring with us. Lina claps with excitement when I show her the pink backpack I picked up at the store. When I tell her to pick out two toys to bring with us, she chooses her trusty stuffed owl and, of all things, the fancy gold tiara Crane sent her for her birthday last year.

The closer to nightfall it gets the faster my heart starts racing. My fingers tremble as I pack the food, the water, a bag of kibble for Stevie, and extra clothes in my backpack. I find my work bag with the reflective blanket still stuffed in the bottom from my trek home with Adam over a year ago. I hide the backpacks in my room and wait for Adam to show up.

As we wait Lina sleeps on the couch with Stevie curled up next to her. I know I should get some rest but instead I pace the loft. The sun has been down for hours and it's already close to midnight. I still haven't heard anything from Adam. I'm starting to think that maybe I should just leave on my own. I've lived in this county my whole life and I know most of the back roads and trails. The hard part would be getting past the electrified fence on the other side of Oswego Falls. I don't have the codes, but I'm sure I could find some way through.

Finally, there's a knock on the door. Stevie runs past me to answer it. I can see Adam behind the heavy glass, dressed in black cargo pants, a fitted black jacket and a black knit cap. The dark clothing is a stark contrast against his blue eyes, which seem to be glowing. I open the door to let him in. He's relaxed and smiles at me. I am far too tense to smile at him.

"Are you ready?" I nod yes to him. "Get your things."

I grab the backpacks from the bedroom and wake Lina up. I take the purple scarf and wrap it around the top of her head and loosely around her neck, to keep her warm and help camouflage her. I do the same for myself with the brown scarf. The pink backpack came with a waist clip and I have it adjusted to fit on Stevie's back. Within a few minutes we are ready to go.

"Ready," I whisper to Adam. I pick Lina up from the couch; she wraps her arms and legs around me, laying her head on my shoulder. "Lina, we have to be very quiet now. You can sleep on my shoulder if you want." She nods sleepily at me as we follow Adam into the hallway.

He brings us to an empty stairwell down the hall from the

elevator. One of the few places where there are no cameras. I follow Adam down the five flights of stairs to the basement level. We head for the underground tunnel which I have used to escape before. Instead of leaving through the door that exits directly to the outside, Adam brings us through the Biology building, leading us through the basement and up a flight of stairs. The building is dark and empty. Our footsteps leave soft echoes on the linoleum floor. Stevie follows closely without needing to be told. Once we reach the main floor Adam walks us across the length of it until we reach a side door on the opposite side of the building. Adam stops for a moment, pulling a key out of his pocket and unlocking the metal security door. Once we are all through he pushes the door closed and re-locks it. Across the parking lot is a black SUV, one of the Volker vehicles. I reach out and grab Adams arm, to warn him.

"It's our car," he whispers to me. "Come on."

He leads me by my free hand as we walk towards the waiting SUV. Adam opens the back door. I snap and point at Stevie, she jumps up onto the passenger bench. Adam supports my elbow as I slide in with Lina on my lap, then he gets behind the wheel. He sits and waits for a moment, looking around the parking lot and buildings. I look at the glowing digital clock on the dashboard; it's just after one in the morning. My heart is beating fast with anticipation. Lina sleeps soundly on my shoulder. Adam starts the vehicle and drives slowly out of the parking lot, heading out onto the main streets. He accelerates, driving fast. The town feels eerily empty as we pass all the dark houses, which are filled with residents who are fast asleep, resting up for the next day's hustle of keeping the District running.

"Where are we headed?" I ask.

"We have to go north to the train station. Crane is expecting it to leave by morning."

"You usually run in the middle of the night?"

"Always at night, never during the day. The road stops in about twenty miles and then it's another four on foot to the train station. The station and the Gateway are guarded but they're expecting me and I will be able to sneak you into the last car without anyone noticing."

After Adam's explanation there is nothing left to talk about. I sit back, holding Lina close to me as she sleeps. I watch the dark forest and empty buildings as the SUV speeds down the highway. After less than thirty minutes Adam pulls off the road, parking at an empty rest stop. He gets out and opens the door for us. Stevie jumps out and paces the dirt parking lot. Adam supports my arm as I scoot out of the vehicle carrying Lina. The early spring air is cool and damp. I am grateful that it's not raining.

"This way." Adam walks towards the woods, stopping to hold back a heavy branch of brush. I hesitate, staring at the woods. The last time Lina and I were out we were attacked by a hungry pack of wolves. Adam must sense my hesitation. "It's ok. I take this trail all the time at night. Worst case scenario, I have a gun if we need it."

I trust him. "Okay," I whisper.

"And stop whispering, no one is out here to hear us."

As I walk under the brush I can see that Adam is right. He hands me a flashlight and walks ahead of us, illuminating a dark but cleared trail. Stevie runs ahead of us, sniffing each tree. I shine the light towards the pink pack on her back every few minutes to make sure she hasn't gotten too far ahead of us. Thankfully the ground is even and free of debris, but Lina is fast asleep, and carrying her forty pounds of dead weight starts to slow me down. I fall further and further behind Adam and Stevie, carrying her and the fast paced walking has me almost out of breath. Finally Adam stops and walks back to me.

"Do you want me to take her?" He asks as I reach him, out of breath.

"Yeah, I'm sorry, she's too heavy." Adam lifts Lina out of my arms.

"Adam's going to carry you, Lina," I tell her as he shifts her weight.

"Hi, Adam," Lina mumbles as she wraps her arms around his neck and lays her head on his shoulder.

"Hi, Lina." Adam rubs her back and starts walking ahead of me. I watch him walk quickly on the trail, his back tall and straight, even under the weight of Lina. I realize, if I had left without him I probably would have never made it, I would never have been able to transport Lina to safety by myself. Stevie circles back in the woods and reappears walking next to me. I reach down and pat her head.

We walk for what seems like hours on the dark trail. Adam doesn't seem to tire at all carrying Lina and keeps up the same pace.

"What happens after we get past the gates?" I ask him.

"Then I have to get you two to safety. Don't you have a brother who lives near the city?"

"Sam, yeah."

"Hopefully we can stash you there until I'm done."

"What do you mean until you're done?"

"I have to finish the job, Andie." Suddenly I think Adam isn't talking about his job as the Runner.

"What do you mean, Adam? I thought we were getting out of here together. I don't want to go on without you. What if Crane finds us?"

Adam stops and turns to look at me. I can barely see his face in the dark woods. But a few slivers of moonlight drift down between the leaves, illuminating his bright eyes in the darkness.

"I have to go back, Andie."

"What are you talking about?"

He lets out a heavy sigh. "It's no coincidence I walked back to Phoenix with you, that you found me lying in the road. I parachuted out of a helicopter. I was sent to find you and escort you back to Phoenix."

I step back, the shock obvious on my face. All this time, everyone warning me who I should trust, I thought Adam was the only person whom I could trust. But this whole time, he was the one who brought me here, who brought me into this hell.

"I trusted you." I reach for Lina. "Give me back my daughter."

"Andie, wait." He pushes my hands away. "This is about more than you and me and Crane. I was sent in here on a mission, I can't leave until it's complete."

"Shut up!" I snap back at him. "I don't know why I ever trusted you in the first place." I reach for Lina again but he grabs my arm, holding it tight, pulling me to him so I can see in his eyes.

"I didn't even know if I would find you, I didn't know this is what they had planned. I didn't plan on, on-"

I interrupt him. "What Adam? You didn't plan on what?"

"On falling for you." He lets go of my arm, and moves his hand behind my neck. The movement is so quick I barely realize what he's done, he's pulling my face towards his, pressing his lips to mine. On any other day, any other day before this one, I would fall into him and return the kiss. But right now, I want nothing more than to slap him across the face for all he's put me through, for not telling me the truth. I yank my head away from him.

"Don't you ever touch me again! Now, get us out of here, Adam."

The rest of the walk is in silence. I no longer follow Adam with the hope that we are going to escape together. Now, I follow him with the sole expectation of getting my daughter out of this godforsaken place.

CHAPTER TWENTY-THREE

The gray moonlight fills the sky and filters through the leaves. The branches have been trimmed back creating a soft glowing tunnel. Lina is still sound asleep on Adam's shoulder. The light is getting brighter and I can see that we are nearing the end of the tunnel. Adam slows, creeping towards the exit. I do the same and reach down to hold Stevie's collar, preventing her from bounding out into the clearing. I can see the shadow of the large black train in front of us. Adam pulls back a thick branch that covers the exit. He waits, looking up and down the length of the train. Then he looks back to me, for the first time in hours.

"Let's go, quickly." He holds the branch as Stevie and I walk past him. The train is seven cars long. Adam brings us to the sixth car and pushes open the heavy metal door.

"Stevie up." I pat the floor of the train car and she backs up, running and leaping into it. I place my hands on the floor of the train car and jump, struggling to pull my lower body into the car. I feel Adam push up on my feet to help.

"Don't touch me!" I snap back at him. Once I get myself inside I turn around to get Lina. Adam passes her to me then reaches up to pass me his flashlight. I take it from him, refusing to look at his face. He grabs my forearm.

"Andie, I need you to trust me, now more than ever." He waits, holding my arm until I look at him. But I can't bring myself to look in his eyes, he's hurt me far more than I think Crane ever could have.

"You should have thought of that before." I yank my arm away from him so hard I almost fall over.

"I'm sorry, Andie." With that he slides the heavy door to the train closed.

I catch one last glimpse into his eyes just before the door closes.

I lean back against the hard metal wall of the train car. It smells old, musty, there is a heavy layer of dirt covering the floor. Stevie wanders through the large cargo area. I flick the flashlight on and look around. It is empty and almost pitch black with the flashlight off. Somehow, Lina continues to sleep.

Now we wait. I fume over Adam's lies to me, barely noticing that there's a tiny tingle of joy over being free of the District, finally, and getting to see Sam after over a year without him in our lives. Suddenly, I am hit with a wave of nausea, similar to what I would experience after a night of work in the NICU. I lean my head back against the wall and close my eyes, hoping that maybe if I can get a little bit of sleep it will help pass the time.

The dull heavy sound of the train horn wakes me and the train car jerks hard into motion, sending me falling onto my side and hitting my head against the metal wall. The train starts moving slowly.

"Mom?" Lina wakes up.

I sit up and pull her onto my lap. "It's ok, Lina. It's just the train."

"What happened to the seats?" She looks around the car with the flashlight.

"It's not that kind of a train. Just sit with me until it gets moving. I don't want you to fall."

From a small crack between the metal walls, I watch the trees pass in the moonlight as the train moves. Adam said the train travels for about five miles before it reaches the Gateway then he has to get out and punch in the code to get the electric fence to open. At this rate it feels like it will take forever to get through the five miles.

Lina lies against me and I un-wrap the scarf from her head and mine, placing them in my backpack. "We aren't coming back are we, Mom?" she asks. I should have known she would sense that the trip wasn't right, sneaking out at night, walking through the woods, and now the train.

"No, honey. I hope not."

We sit in silence and listen to the train, the way it creaks and groans. When it stops I look out the crack. I can see the electric fence stretching through the forest. It must be twenty feet high with a thick curling of barbed wire on top of it. "Look, Lina, we can see out through this crack." I point to the thin strip of pale light on the wall. Lina adjusts herself so she can see out of it.

"Mom, why are there people outside?" She asks.

"What?" My heart starts fluttering.

"Look." She points in front of the car. But I don't need to look. I can hear men arguing, and the voices are familiar. Before I have time to stand up and run to the other side of the car with Lina, the heavy door concealing us opens.

There stands a group of men, mostly Volker. As my eyes adjust to the bright light, I see Crane looking very out of place in his suit and Adam, standing behind the crowd, his arms crossed over his chest, angry.

Crane speaks first. "Andromeda? How very odd it is to find you here." He smiles his signature smug smile. "We have Catalina also, and even the dog." Stevie growls at him from the open door. "Come now, Andromeda, get yourself out of there so these fine men can escort you home."

My gut drops, my heart races, I'm sweating. We had been wanting to escape for weeks, months even. And then Crane waltzes in destroying our hopes of escape. Adam watches me intently. I do my best to climb out of the train car and turn to reach up for Lina. Once she is in my arms I don't set her down. She buries her face in my neck, scared.

"You see, Adam. I told you that you were hauling precious cargo." Crane looks expectantly between me and Adam. He must have known or sensed something between us. This must be why Adam had been ignoring me for so long, trying to lead Crane away from our relationship, so he wouldn't sense that we were plotting behind his back. I know that I have to at least try and preserve Crane's trust in Adam. Because even though I am angry with him, he kept his word. And he is the only one who can save us from whatever punishment Crane has planned.

"I followed him," I tell Crane, my voice shaky. "He didn't know, he had nothing to do with this." It's the best lie I've ever told, it even sounds believable coming out of my mouth.

Crane raises his eyebrows. "You followed Adam through the woods, at night, with a child and a dog? I find that hard to believe, Andromeda."

"It's true. I've been watching him for months. Keeping track of when he leaves, what truck he drives. We snuck out, at dark, hid in the trunk, waited under a blanket and the trail was easy to follow." I do my best to keep my face calm and relaxed so Crane will believe me.

"Well, this is some interesting news. All this time, I never suspected you would try this, that you could plan it. I never took you for a stowaway. Are you so unhappy with our service here, Andromeda, even after all you have been provided with, the status you've been assigned?"

"I miss my life, before this." That was easy to tell him, because it was the absolute truth.

"Well, I am sorry for you. District rules supersede here. You will be brought back to your living quarters." He turns stoically to Adam. "My apologies Colonel Waters, you may continue on with your duties. Godspeed." Crane waves his hand in circular motion, signaling the Volker to collect us.

We are ushered to a small road near the fence where there is a waiting line of black SUVs. I carry Lina and Stevie follows us closely. The Volker break up, some of them walking back towards the train and the gateway, a few others get into waiting SUVs and driving off. One guard remains; he opens the back door of a vehicle. I tell Stevie to get in and place Lina beside her and buckle her in. I close the door and walk around to the other side of the SUV with the Volker; he opens the rear door and waits for me to get in. There is a loud, static crackle from the radio inside the truck. He opens the front door, reaching for the radio. And that's all it takes, one small distraction.

Suddenly someone is pulling me by the arm, backwards, away from the SUV where Lina and Stevie are. I hear Stevie barking and Lina yelling my name.

"Help, help!" I yell just before a hand clamps over my mouth.

The Volker looks up from where he is stretched across the driver's seat trying to answer the radio. He slams the door shut, locking Lina and Stevie inside and yells for the other Volker who should be nearby. He doesn't run for me, for whoever is dragging me, to stop them. I'm thankful that he doesn't leave Lina's side, that he stays to protect her.

I hear the hustle of people running through the woods from where we came, footsteps, shouting. But it's too late. I turn to see who is pulling me, only to find it's the last person I want to be stuck in a vehicle with. *Crane.* I struggle, but somehow he's stronger, much stronger than the last time he tried to manhandle me months ago in the lab. I am unable to push him away.

"In the car, Andromeda!" He yells fiercely at me.

"What are you trying to do, Crane?" I struggle with him, trying to push him away from me, slapping at him, but all it takes is one hard shove from him and my head hits the side of the SUV, hard.

I can feel the warm trickle of blood down the side of my face and just before I crumple to the ground he shoves me hard, again, pushing me into the back of the SUV. I fall onto the bench seat, my vision blurry, my head fuzzy. Crane slams the door, then climbs into the driver's seat and starts the car. He doesn't give it time to warm up before he accelerates fast. I hear the tires kick up rocks and hit the vehicle that Lina and Stevie are in as we pass them. I sit up and turn to see a row of Volker standing, watching as Crane drives away. Some of them have their pistols aimed, ready to shoot. But no one fires. No one wants to risk hitting me with a bullet.

Crane speeds down the dirt road kicking up dust and rocks in his wake. He skids onto a paved road, hitting the incline hard, causing my head to hit the roof of the SUV. I reach up, touching the top of my head, trying to hold pressure on the sharp stinging sensation. It's when I slide my hand down the side of my face, feeling something wet and sticky that I remember Crane bashed my head into the side of the vehicle. I pull my hand away and stare at my palm caked in thick, dark blood. And I'm not sure if it's the blood, the two hits to the head, the lack of sleep, maybe it's everything combined which is just enough to make me pass out.

CHAPTER TWENTY~FOUR

Somehow, I am back on the train. This time Lina is sitting next to me on a plush bench and Stevie sleeps at our feet. We watch out the window as we pass by the trees and houses. Lina excitedly points out deer and birds and horses that we pass. Her hair is flowing, a mane of curls, so blonde they are almost white. I reach up and run my hand over her hair, pulling her to me and hugging her. "I love you, little Catalina," I whisper in her ear. She smiles up at me. I haven't seen her so happy in so long. I look around the train and it's empty, except for us. Then I remember we left the District, we are on our way out. We are finally free.

But something is wrong. My vision isn't as clear, the edges are cloudy, the sun too bright. The train jolts to a stop and I hit my face on the seat in front of us. When I look back to Lina she is no longer there sitting next to me. I hear her voice, yelling, screaming, calling me. But I can't see her anywhere except when I look out the window; I see a man dragging her away. He is tall, slender with blonde hair. I know who he is before he even turns around. It's Ian, dragging Lina away from me. I try to stand, to run after them, to stop him, but my hands and feet won't move. They're heavy like they are stuck to something. The train jerks into motion again, hard, causing me to smash my face onto the seat in front of me. My vision fades away quickly and everything goes black.

--

This time when I wake I am in a dark room with damp cement walls, my cheek pressing against a musty, pale linoleum floor. There are no windows, just a single bare bulb hanging from the ceiling and a door with a small square window. Dread fills me, this is not a dream. This is real. This is Crane's doing. The Volker would have deposited me back at the loft to resume my duties. They would not be involved in whatever Crane has planned. I try to push myself up off the ground but my arms are secured together in front of me with a plastic zip tie. The door opens and in walks Crane carrying a chair. He closes the door behind him and sets the chair down, sitting in it. He sits there, watching me, like I'm nothing more than a caged animal.

"Where's Lina?"

"You needn't worry about your child any longer. We had an agreement, you broke it, you've lost her, for good this time."

"No!" I scream at him, at the thought of losing her. His words should crush me, but instead they infuriate me. "What do you want from me?" I ask him, annoyed.

"I'm just observing, Andromeda. Trying to figure out where I went wrong with you." He taps his index finger on his chin and continues to stare at me.

I struggle to sit myself up. Somehow I manage by raising my leg and pushing off the hard floor with my elbow. I adjust myself, sitting cross-legged, letting my tied arms lie in front of me, my fists resting on the floor.

"We are not compatible, Crane." He sits there, tapping his chin, waiting. "We cannot be paired."

"What makes you think that?"

"First of all, I can't have any more children and you are genetically incompetent."

"Really?"

"Did you think I wouldn't find it, that you could bury it in your piles of data? It was almost too easy to find it, Crane. You carry a bad gene. You know this though, spinal muscular atrophy. Any child you bring into this world with your DNA will most likely suffer a horrible, incurable death. But I'm sure I don't need to explain this to you. You seem well educated and knowledgeable. You know this already."

"You know, Andromeda, we could have worked around both of these issues. I've found ways to work around them before."

"It doesn't matter, Crane. I want nothing to do with you."

"Yes, I have begun to realize this; your blatant disrespect for me, even after all I've given you, is quite obvious. You were different before. I never saw this in you; the deceit, the defiance, the poor attitude. Perhaps it was simply muted by the hopes I had for us."

"What did you think was going to happen when you ruined my family, when you ruined my life? Did you think I would run to you, willingly, with open arms? With all your power and knowledge? This is your fatal flaw, Crane. This is why your little experiment here will never work. You can't control people's emotions. You can't force someone to want you; no one can manipulate the human heart that way, especially you."

"Yes. I suppose you are correct, Andromeda. Still, I was hoping you'd be different. I was hoping you would see what we are trying to do here. The Funding Entities will be saddened to learn about what you've become. And it pains me to know we can never replace you." He continues tapping his chin. I listen to his words, trying to understand what he's saying to me, and the only thing I can conclude is that he's going to kill me. He raises his index finger in the air, pausing for a moment. "Yes, well, I cannot replace you, but I can make sure you never try to leave again. I was hoping it wouldn't come to this, Andromeda, but it seems you need clarification on the rules of the District. Of all people, I was certain you would understand this the most, well, with all that you have to lose."

He stands and walks towards me, there's something shiny in his hand, silver and pointed. I flinch as he points it towards me, expecting him to cut me with it or stab me, but he just cuts the zip tie that was holding my hands together.

"Just to make it fair," he says.

I scramble to my feet, not knowing what to expect next. The sudden movement causes me to sway, and my head to feel heavy. Crane picks up his chair and walks out of the room closing the door behind him.

I wait for a moment, looking around the room. I can hear the sound of deep voices outside the door and I walk over to listen. I'm not tall enough to see out the small window and there is nothing to stand on in here. Someone wiggles the lock, I back up to the middle of the room. The door opens and in walks a large man, a dark man. It takes only a few moments for me to recognize him, which is easy, because last time I saw him he was dangling my body over a bridge.

"Baillie," I whisper. This causes a loud burst of his familiar laughter to erupt from deep within his chest. "I thought you were dead. The Volker shot you. I saw you lying in a pool of blood." He keeps laughing and for a moment I think I must be dreaming. I look around the room, trying to find an escape, a weapon, anything. I rub my eyes hard, trying to wake myself up, but when I open them he's still in the room with me.

"It's amazing what modern medicine can do these days, isn't it?" He erupts in laughter again. I'm not sure if he's laughing from his statement, which really wasn't funny, or from my bewildered response to him entering the room. "Crane tells me I was reassigned to the convict faction. He only just withdrew my medications to deal with you." His heavy southern accent is the same. He talks slowly dragging out the conversation. But I want him to stop, to stop talking and leave. "According to him, if I do a good job, he will reinstate me."

"Oh God no," I hope he doesn't hear me talk under my breath, but still he erupts in laughter.

"Enough with the talking. I've been waiting to do this since I first met you." Baillie cracks the knuckles on both of his hands. Crane should have left my arms bound, because there is no way in hell that this could ever be a fair fight.

I am not a fighter, but I will not just stand here and make it easy for him. Baillie is at least double my size, a monster, but I am short and quick-I hope. He lunges at me and I kick him in the shin as hard as I can, then I sprint to the other side of the room. Baillie just laughs, lunging at me again. This time I aim for his groin but I miss hitting the inside of his thigh, provoking another bout of laughter from him. I try the same method of sprinting away from him but his long arm shoots out hitting me in the face. I drop backwards falling to the ground. I try to roll, but it took me too long to recover, Baillie is looming over me in no time. I look to the door to see Crane watching from the small window, and for the first time ever, I think he might actually look sad. His image is just enough to distract me from trying to get away from Baillie, from trying to brace myself, and I'm not sure if he is truly so strong or if it's the anticipation of the pain that makes Baillie's second hit feel like a Mac truck is running into my face.

He doesn't stop punching. I brace my arms in front of my face but it does nothing to stop him. I don't give them the satisfaction of tears or pleading. I take Baillie's pounding like a man, quietly. Not that my lungs ever have a chance to refill with fresh air, that I could get a second to say something. Instead, I hold my breath. I'm sure I hear my nose break, my ribs crack and just before I'm ready to pass out the door opens.

"Enough!" Crane yells to Baillie. He must be satisfied, the show must be over.

They leave me alone on the floor, blood pouring out of my nose, barely able to inhale from the pain in my ribs. The metallic smell from all the blood is too much, it clogs in the back of my throat and I spit out a few clots onto the pale floor. I watch them ooze across the linoleum, creating sticky gleaming paths, bouncing off each other as they drift to a divot in the flooring. It's not long after the globs of blood stop moving that I close my eyes.

Too soon I hear the door creak open. Using my arms I pull my body across the room to the farthest corner and try to curl into a ball, hoping I can make myself small enough that he won't see me in the dark corner. But he stands, waiting, with his arms crossed across his chest. *Please leave please leave please leave.*

But he doesn't. He stomps to my corner and reaches for my foot. I try and kick him away but it doesn't work. He waits until the right moment, snapping out with viper reflexes, grabbing both my feet as I kick. He pulls me across the floor, back to the middle of the room and waits, crossing his arms and staring at me. I don't know what he wants. I can only assume that he's giving me a chance to defend myself, which is a joke. I push myself up on my knees, bending over on my elbows so I can get a few deep breaths in. I push my feet under myself then slowly, steadying myself, I stand.

There is nothing to hold onto once I am up, and it's not long before the room starts spinning around me. I close my eyes, hoping that when I open them Baillie will be gone and I will be back somewhere safe with my family. But when I open them Baillie remains. He reaches forward and pushes my right shoulder with his index finger. I wobble backwards, barely able to steady myself. He reaches out to push on my left shoulder, and this time I slap his hand away. I realize that I should have just stood there, not reacting to his taunts, because he kicks his long leg out, sweeping my feet out from under me. I fall hard on the ground, no longer containing the reflexes to catch myself, to soften the blow of the fall. With one swift stride he pulls me up by the collar of my shirt and throws me back against the musty cement wall. My body slides down to the floor and it's only an instant before he is pulling me up to my feet again by my collar. This time I lean my head forward and bite him on his arm, as hard as I can, trying to pierce his dark flesh with my teeth. My feeble attempt to fight back brings a deep rumble of laughter from Baillie's chest and more pain.

Baillie continues with his work. It seems like every hour he enters the room, but it must be once or twice a day. The rest of the time I am unconscious from the pain, from the inability to breathe, from the realization that I may die without ever getting to say goodbye to Lina or Ian or Adam. I want to scream or cry, I'm not sure which, but I won't give Crane or Baillie the satisfaction. The only thing that gives me the spark to drag my carcass off the floor each time the door opens, is the hope that I might be able to get out and find my daughter. But it's so hard, Baillie is so strong and unrelenting. Just once it crosses my mind, that this is how Adam must have felt in the Middle East; ready to give up, ready to say something that will force them to kill you and end the pain.

On what I think could be the fourth day, I make no attempt to move when the door opens. I tell myself that if I feign death then he might stop and leave me alone. I have nothing left, Crane has only allowed me a few bottles of water, but no food. My heart rate is much too high, not from fear but from the lack of blood running through my body. I've lost too much, the pale floor now streaked with varying shades of red and brown.

Baillie stands over me tapping a baseball bat in his palm. I watch him from the slit of my swollen eye, through the thick crusting of blood across my lashes. I'm not sure if it is tears or blood I feel trickling down the side of my face. But I am almost certain that there is not enough moisture left in my body to produce either. Baillie kicks my feet a few times, then my arms, taunting me. But it's no use. I see him lift the bat high in the air. I close my eyes; I have no way to brace myself for the impact. My body is a jellied mess of bruises, oozing and bleeding wounds. I'm sure there is more than one broken bone. I haven't been able to move my left arm for at least two days and there are sharp pains that shoot through my chest during the few shallow breaths I can take.

I wait, unmoving. I try to open my eyes, looking into his, hoping there might be some compassion, but his eyes are crazed, they don't see me.

Goodbye Lina, I love you, I tell myself.

I had hoped I might be able to find my way out of this hell, but I know I most certainly will not. I will not survive the baseball bat in Baillie's hands. Just as I expect him to hit me, as I expect to feel the bat squish into my tissues, busting them apart like a rotten melon, I hear the faint sound of the door opening and a voice- not Crane's voice-this time it's someone older with the hint of an accent. I crack my eye open again to see a short Asian man enter the room carrying a pistol. He aims it at Baillie yelling something to him. Baillie gives a scoffing laugh and then starts to bring his arms down directing the bat at my limp body that lies on the floor. The gun fires and a small trickle of blood dribbles out of a wound in the middle of Baillie's forehead, just before he flops over onto the ground.

For a moment, during the few seconds of consciousness that I can muster, I think that I just saw Morris shoot Baillie dead.

CHAPTER TWENTY-FIVE

Men in gray uniform flood the room; Volker. One bends down to scoop my body off the ground. I make no attempt to move or struggle. It feels as though I have no bones left, just floppy cartilage holding my vital organs together. The Volker carries me out of the building and to a waiting car. He sits with me on his lap and I wonder if it's Adam, but when I try and breathe in between the sharp pains in my ribs, it's not his familiar scent that I smell.

I drift in and out of consciousness. I feel the pain of the Volker laying me down, a bright light being shined into my eyes. I'm not sure if my pupils react, or if they could even see my eyes at all, since they are mostly swollen shut and crusted with blood. Someone tries to move my broken arm and it takes all the strength I have to muster a groan, warning them that the bone is snapped in half just not yet poking through the thin layer of skin on my bruised arm.

This time, when the doctor cuts my clothes off, I don't care who is in the room. I make no attempt to cover myself or have him ask people to leave. I almost hope that he will let me waste away and die, because death would most certainly feel much better than the pain I am feeling right now.

There is a pinch in my arm from an IV being placed. A woman's voice whispers that she is sorry as she pushes the needle deeper into my arm. I want to laugh at her. I can barely feel it, everything else overriding her tiny pinch. There is pressure from medical tape and the cool rush of fluid pouring into my vein. Just as I'm thinking they will never give me pain medication I feel the warm tingle of morphine enter my vein, but it's only enough to dull the pain, and I can feel everything the doctor is doing.

He starts cleaning wounds, stitching, palpating. If I could talk, I would tell him to order an x-ray already, but he must see the bruises on my ribs because not long after that I hear the clicks and hums of a portable x-ray machine. The warmth from the morphine is starting to dissipate just as I feel someone touch my broken arm. I want to tell them I need more, but my jaw won't work. I can't make the sound come out. And I know what's coming; they must have seen the break in the x-ray. I have no muscle tone left to brace myself for the pulling and straightening that comes with setting the break, getting it ready for casting. The pain is sharp and strong, almost worse than when Baillie snapped it with the punch of his heavy fist. Thankfully it's just enough to send me back into unconsciousness.

--

I wake more than once from the pain, not knowing what day it is or what time it is. I push the button in my hand to release more pain medication, my limbs feeling heavy and sore. The room is empty except for the rhythmic beeping of the cardiac monitor. If anyone enters the room I wouldn't know or care right now. But there is a nagging feeling in the back of my mind, it hovers over me as a heavy cloud when I wake to push the button, there is something or someone that I am missing.

--

There is a sharp pain in my left arm and it wakes me, slowly at first. I pat the bed looking for the button, for more pain medication, but I can't find it. The pain gets stronger and I reach over to hold my broken arm to my chest, trying to relieve the pain but instead of soft skin my hand meets a hard heavily textured cast. I open my eyes, able to see through both of them for the first time in days. I think *days* is the right word. There is no crusted blood to look through. Someone must have washed it off. I squint at the bright light coming in the window. It takes a few minutes for my eyes to adjust and inspect the room, a typical hospital room. White walls, white floor, a small bathroom near the door and sink with large mirror facing the bed.

For some reason someone thought it would be a good idea to place a teal and peach border of wallpaper across the middle of each wall. I stare at the border and count the feathered pattern across the wall in front of me. When I get to the corner of the wall, I am done counting and there is an odd number of colored blobs on the wallpaper. This discovery infuriates me and I want to get up and tear the wallpaper off the wall-maybe it's a reaction from the morphine.

My legs are restless from days of inactivity. I throw the knitted white blanket off me, only to be greeted with dark bruises covering my pale legs. I scoot to the end of the bed and roll my legs so they dangle off the edge of the bed, monitor leads tug on my skin. I pull them off and throw them on the floor. The sensations from the bruises to my legs and ribs mask the pain I was just feeling from my broken arm. I stare at the cast on my left arm. It extends from my fingers halfway to my shoulder. I take a few deep breaths and push myself to stand. I hobble over to the large mirror that's attached to the wall over the sink. At first I am shocked by the person looking back at me; there's a thick camouflage of bruises covering my face, my eyes, nose, and jaw. There's the gleam from medical glue on my eyebrow and lip, and a new bump on my nose from where Baillie broke it.

As I stand looking at myself in the mirror, the door to the room opens. I half expect to see Baillie waltz in, but thankfully it is just a Volker guard. He swings the door wide and looks around the room before he notices me standing at the sink. He nods, then closes the door. I stand at the sink for a while, then I pace the room, trying to get the blood flowing in my legs. It's not long before I'm exhausted and return to the hospital bed. Just as I get myself covered there's a knock at the door and not a moment after it opens and Morris is escorted into the room.

"Andromeda, you are awake. We've been waiting." Morris walks to the bedside. Usually he greets me kindly in the committee meetings, shaking my hand with a smile that wrinkles all the way to his eyes. This time he greets me with a warm hug and sits close to me on the edge of the hospital bed. I stare at him for a moment, shocked from his emotional greeting, and from remembering that he is responsible for saving my life.

"Thank you, Morris," I whisper to him. He reaches out and squeezes my hand, just the way my grandfather would do when I was a child.

"How do you feel?"

I shrug. Anyone who looked at me right now could see that I don't feel well. "Where's Lina?" I look behind him, hoping that she will walk into the room.

"She has been staying with Ms. Black and the boys. We wanted to bring her here; we thought she might be able to help you." He pauses, clearing his throat. "We thought she might be able to help you wake up."

"Why? How long has it been?"

Morris eyes me apprehensively. "Almost a week," he tells me.

I'm shocked by his revelation. I thought maybe a few days had passed since Morris' rescue, but not a full week.

"So why didn't you bring her?" He looks down at our hands and smiles, wrinkling his cheeks all the way to his eyes. He pauses for a while, and I wonder if he's trying to figure out what to say to me.

"Because of your screams," He pauses again, letting it soak in. "Even with the sedation, the hospital staff had to move the other patients off the floor. Do you remember dreaming, Andromeda?"

I shake my head no. I remember nothing, just the pain and the numbing morphine.

"It's ok. You're safe." He pats my hand. I've heard another person concerned for my safety say something similar. *Crane.*

"Is Baillie dead this time?"

"Yes. I assure you."

"And Crane?"

"Andromeda," he pauses again trying to assemble the words, "Crane has been dealt with."

"But how did you find me? How did you know where he had taken me?"

"I was assigned to keep a close eye on Crane. The Funding Entities didn't quite trust him. But they never expected this. That he would do something like this to you. I never expected it either. He's a brilliant man, Andromeda, but something changed in him when we set foot in Phoenix. The Funding Entities were so impressed with the Japanese District that they didn't want to risk pulling him out of the organization before the Phoenix District was complete. They're giving him a second chance. They can't risk this going wrong. They can't risk failure. We have no choice, his involvement is imperative."

"What are you trying to say, Morris?"

"We can't get rid of Crane just yet. We can only try and control him."

This time I pause, letting the realization soak in that Crane will be free to continue as he did before, he will barely face any punishment for almost killing me.

"And what happens to me?" I ask. I hope that he will let us go. Send us to a new life beyond the gates, back to the real world. But I know the rules of the District. Crane made sure to beat them into me.

"You will be relocated."

"Where?"

"Beyond the cement wall to the Pasture, a farm in the northern county where only a few will know of your exact location. It will be heavily guarded, as before, and well hidden."

"And Lina?"

"She will go with you. We will be relocating the entire Sovereign children's training program to the farm. The Funding Entities don't want Crane near the children. They don't want his negative influences impacting their training."

"Ian?" I ask, hopeful.

"I am sorry. But we need him at the nuclear power plant. We can't replace him and his current state remains."

I want to ask about Adam. But I don't want Morris to know our relationship may be stronger than just Sovereign committee members. "What about the Committee meetings? Will they continue?"

"Yes." My stomach drops. I will have to see Crane again. "We will do our best to make sure your participation is only by video conference." I close my eyes and sigh in relief. "Andromeda?" Morris waits for me to open my eyes. His brown eyes penetrate mine. "You do not realize how important you are, to all of us. This is much bigger than you realize."

I get the sense he is referring to something more than just the District.

CHAPTER TWENTY-SIX

Morris informs me we will be leaving in the morning. I spend the rest of the evening tossing and turning, unable to get comfortable. Morris' words keep ringing in my ears. Then there is the anticipation of reuniting with Lina in the morning, and getting beyond the cement wall away from Crane, where we will only have the electric fence to worry about.

A nurse brings me a bowl of rice and some pain tablets. I stare at the rice and realize that the reserves of the District must be low if this is all they can give me. I eat the rice and take the medication. Before long I am fast asleep.

If I dream I don't remember it and no one wakes me up to relieve me of them. I wake alone just before the sun rises. There is a folded pile of clothes on the chair next to the bed. I get up and try my best to stretch my sore damaged muscles. My next feat is the shower. I hang my cast outside the shower curtain and try to wash myself with my one hand. It's almost impossible but I leave the shower feeling refreshed. I stare in the mirror. The bruising has lessened to a dull yellow hue. I do my best to dry myself and get dressed. Whoever brought the clothes got them from the loft. I recognize the familiar undergarments, black khaki pants and white blouse. They even brought my favorite leather sandals. But when I pull on my clothes they are at least a size too big. I pull the shirt up and look at my bruised abdomen. For the first time ever I can see a rib bone sticking out at me. I let the shirt fall back into place and run my fingers through my hair, trying to de-tangle it. It has remained uncut for over a year, and my once short hair has now grown down past my shoulder blades. Since I have no hair ties I pull one of the cardiac leads off the floor and rip the ends off it, then use it to twist my hair up in a loose bun.

Just as I finish there is a knock and the door opens.

"Mommy!" Lina bounds into the room, throwing her arms around me. I want to pick her up, but it's impossible with the cast. Instead I sit on the end of the bed and pull her to me. I hold her for a long time, afraid to let go, afraid that I may never see her again.

The Volker motions for us to go. He escorts us outside of the hospital where there is a caravan of black SUVs waiting. He opens the door to one of the middle vehicles for us to get in. Stevie jumps out, she sniffs and licks at me and then jumps back in, waiting for us to follow her.

The caravan pulls away and heads north on Main Street. I watch out the window at the Residents. Some are working in the yards, sweeping streets, fixing streetlamps, gardening. Everyone is busy working in their assigned faction. Some smile and wave to each other, only one person stops to watch the caravan drive by. Some of them should be off their medications by now and learning how to live in a new society. A group of school children stand at the corner, waiting for their school bus. They wear dark blue uniforms and play games with their hands, chattering at each other. As we drive I realize that Phoenix has turned back into the town I remember as a child, where it was safe to venture out alone, neighbors were neighborly, parents didn't have to worry about their children's safety, the homes were neat, and people took pride in their work.

I wonder if maybe the Phoenix District isn't such a bad place to be confined to. Maybe it would even be safer here than in the outside world, if it weren't for Crane.

Once the caravan passes the bridge separating the District, it splits up. Our driver pulls onto a side street, making odd turns, sometimes driving in a complete circle. Every few moments I catch another black SUV on a nearby side street, doing similar maneuvers. As the driver continues we get closer to the edge of town, but instead of heading to the north roads he pulls to the eastern roads.

"What are you doing?" I ask the Volker curiously.

"Evasive maneuvers ma'am. Morris wants to make sure we aren't followed. There will be similar spectacles at all the exits."

"This is silly," Lina giggles as she rolls around on the bench seat, responding to the sharp turns taken by the Volker.

Once the cement wall slides open, two vehicles come up beside us, our driver speeds up and they play a game of cat and mouse, swerving between each other, slowing down, speeding up. Then one vehicle stops and drives back to town. This crazy dance we just witnessed was a ploy to distract and confuse anyone who may be following us.

The Volker takes a long, convoluted route along back roads, dirt roads, roads covered in fallen trees, and the fifteen minute drive to the northern part of the District has turned into a forty-five minute drive. Finally we drive up to a heavily wooded area and the Volker starts pulling off the road. It looks like he's going to drive directly into the trees but then I see a small pebbled driveway, barely the width of the vehicle. Tree branches scrape across the side of the SUV, reaching high into the sky, shading the driveway. As I watch ahead of us, I see that we are coming up behind another black SUV. We follow the other vehicle until it slows and stops and we can hear the dry scraping of stone and the squeal of heavy metal. We start moving again. Looking out the window I see we are driving past a large stone wall covered in dense brush.

Just as I was hoping we would get outside the District walls, I find that we have just been moved to live within another set of them.

We drive past more thick forest before entering a bright clearing.

"Look, Mom." Lina points out the window.

There are large pastures with cows, horses, alpacas and goats on one side of the driveway. We look out the other window and see large fields with freshly planted seedlings. Three large dogs run beside the SUV's, their heads reaching as high as the vehicle's windows. Chickens and geese swerve out of the road as the rubber tires of the SUV crunch down the stone driveway. Finally we come to a cluster of buildings and the SUVs stop. A Volker opens our door and waits for us to get out. We topple out in awe, looking at the spectacle before us.

"Welcome to the Pasture," the Volker greets us with a light Australian accent, shaking our hands. "My name is Elvis. I'll be staying here with you all."

On a normal day, almost two years ago, I would have joked with this man about his name. I would have made references to Elvis not really being dead. But today, after all I've been through, I can't even muster the energy to smirk when he tells us his name.

Behind him I see the three large dogs, the size of horses, walking up to inspect us. It's a breed I've never seen before. They look like mythological creatures, much larger than Great Dane's, with thick long hair rolled into dreadlocks. I grab Stevie's collar as she jumps out of the SUV, afraid that they might attack her.

"It's ok. They're familiar with your dog's scent-yours too, actually, everyone who has just arrived." I apprehensively release Stevie to see her bound at the dogs. They sniff each other in circles and bark playfully. Stevie runs back to us with the large dogs following her. "Meet the Guardians." Elvis holds his hand out and all three of the dogs sit as he pats their massive heads. "There's more all over the farm, we have about twenty of them right now. Think of them as your protectors."

I watch the large animals as they sit, looking not at us, but around us, behind us, inspecting the yard, the pastures, the fields. It's no wonder they are called guardians.

--

The buildings are a mixture of barns, garages and houses, all built in a circle with open grass in the middle littered with yard toys, picnic tables and a small inflatable pool. The buildings look old, but functional, with large sturdy front porches, complete with rocking chairs.

"What is this place?" I ask Elvis.

"It's always been here. Hidden in the forest. We were able to salvage most of the buildings with minimal work. You know how that old carpentry is, it could survive hundreds of years."

Elvis walks us to one of the houses. They are all white, with the simple construction of era's ago, and when we step up onto the porch, the old wood doesn't even creak under the pressure of our footsteps. We follow him inside and I am surprised that the interior is simple and clean with hardwood floors and milky white walls. We wander around, inspecting the kitchen and bedrooms, the living room. It's when we get to the office space I stop in disappointment. Of all that I was trying to escape in the District, it is clear my work will not be finished any time soon. Sitting in the middle of the office is my large wooden desk and computer from the lab.

CHAPTER TWENTY-SEVEN

Again, our lives have changed. The grounds of the Pasture are beautiful, an outpouring of nature at its finest, and for the first time in over a year, Lina and I are able to explore as we please. Ms. Black sets up a classroom in one of the small houses. Elvis helps her break down a wall, creating a large open space for the children to learn. We salvage tables and chairs from the barns and sheds then sand them down and repaint them.

Sometimes it's hard for me to do much with the cast on my arm. When the work gets too hard for my broken arm and ribs to handle, I leave to explore the grounds or rearrange our new house. Once again workers from the District packed up our things and moved them. But this time they only sent the necessities; simple clothes, a few personal items. Thankfully they brought Lina's beloved stuffed owl.

The Funding Entities, whoever they are, have stripped us of any luxuries. They want the children to grow and learn in a simplified manner without fancy clothes or expensive toys. They hope that it will help the children focus on human interaction and develop a new understanding of life where we are self-sufficient, and the little things are what matter most. To Lina this will mean no fancy birthday parties and rooms filled with presents on the holidays. But I think she will adjust fine. Especially after walking into one of the houses and finding it filled floor to ceiling with books and hearing Lina exclaim that it was "the best house ever."

Elvis is the sole Volker on the property. He seems at ease here, already tanned and rugged, a true outdoorsman running the farm, working with the Guardians and Stevie. More than once he has brought a deer or other game back in the afternoon, then cleaned it and cooked it for dinner. On nice evenings we collect around the picnic tables, eating dinner together as one big happy family.

Well, everyone else is happy. I do my best to smile and interact, trying not to let them see what Crane did to me. I cover up the bruises and cuts with makeup, scarves, long sleeves and pants-most of the time I'm boiling in the sun. Thankfully the woods and fields I walk during the day are much cooler from the nearby lake breeze.

Now I have nothing left to do but wait. Wait for my wounds to heal, for Ian to wake up, for Adam to return from outside the gates and find us. I hope he will find us. And then we wait for the next generation to be born.

One day, while Lina is in class, I walk through the open field behind the circle of houses and I get the sense that I am being followed. There is the soft hush of footsteps on the dried field grass, stopping each time I stop. The first time I turn around I see nothing, just the empty field and houses off in the distance. The second time I turn, I make sure to continue walking, and as I walk backwards I see the large Guardians following me silently; stopping when I stop, hiding in conspicuous spots, behind a small bush, crouching in the tall grass. There are even more at the forest edge, stopping behind trees, but their eyes are always watching. They follow me to the tall water tower at the far edge of the property. I stop at the bottom and look up. There's a ladder and an enclosed walking platform circling the highest part of the water tower. I reach out and grasp the warm, metal ladder, shaking it a few times. It doesn't give, it doesn't even wiggle. I want to climb it badly, to see how far I can see, to see if the view reaches beyond the fence or further. I lift my broken arm and try to wrap my fingers around one of the rungs but a sharp pain shoots up the broken arm, forcing me to let go immediately. Bringing my arm back to my chest, I squeeze my shoulder hoping that the pain will stop.

A few of the Guardians walk closer to me, closer than they have ever been. I could reach out and touch them, but their large size still frightens me. I look at their eyes to see what they are looking at. Instead of looking behind me or to the sides as they usually do, they all look up, straight into the sky. I follow their gaze but all I see is the light blue afternoon sky-there is not even a cloud present. One of the Guardians bark, which I have never heard before. It's loud and deep, reminding me more of a lion roar than a dog barking. More of the dogs start exiting the woods. Then there's another bark off in the distance, where the houses are. Some come to where I am standing near the ladder and the others gallop back to the circle of houses, where Ms. Black and the children are. I look around the property and back to the sky but see nothing.

Then, ever so faintly I hear a deep rumble far off in the distance. At first I think it is thunder, that there is a storm coming. But it gets louder and faster, reminding me of a jet passing overhead. There are more of the same sounds, but at different distances, further away and some closer, like a hundred jet engines are flying over us and around us. But as I watch the sky I see nothing.

Suddenly the sky is no longer rumbling, but the ground is. First it's mild, and I think I'm experiencing a bout of dizziness, but the ground shakes harder and deeper. And I know what I am feeling, because it wasn't that long ago when I experienced the same sensation in another life, in my old life, at the hospital.

Earthquakes.

But now I know that these are not earthquakes. I know what they truly are, I've seen their damage. They broke my town, my family, my body. Those are missiles flying through the sky.

EPILOGUE
ADAM

The train whistle is loud, monotonous, lasting entirely too long. I hate that it's programmed to go off every twenty minutes. It keeps waking me up, interrupting my thoughts. Not only is the noise preposterous, but the single bench is uncomfortable. It's unpadded, raw metal, too hard to sit on let alone sleep on. There's absolutely nothing to do in the dark metallic cabin of this train. I almost wish it was a coal engine so I could pass the time shoveling coal into the burners. Instead I sit here, staring out the window.

There isn't much else to do on these long rides south to collect supplies and rendezvous with the Funding Entities. It's no wonder Remington turned to booze and women when he was out running for the District. And night is even worse. Mostly I wind up laying on the uncomfortable bench or the floor, thinking, tossing and turning. The metal chain wrapped around my bicep doesn't help matters, most of the time it itches and cuts into the skin. I keep touching the locket, afraid that I might feel the potassium dose dripping out of it, which would truly be the end of my mission, because if Crane wanted me dead, getting back through those gates would be one of the hardest tasks of my life.

He must be using pure electrical energy straight from the nuclear power plant to electrify the fence. I didn't tell Andie, but that recruit's body was so charred it was almost nonexistent. At first we thought it was a burned tree. I've never seen anything like it in my life. It hums louder than any electric fence I've ever heard, so loud that there isn't an animal or a bug within a mile of it and the plants actually look like they are stretching away, trying to grow back into the forest.

The train brings me through downstate New York, to Pennsylvania and beyond, all the way to North Carolina, so I can collect our supplies. So far it has been stocked with rice and oats, canned foods, fresh vegetables, everything on the District list I was given before leaving. All I have left to do is leave the packet for delivery to the Funding Entities. This time the designated drop zone is a post office in Raleigh, North Carolina, which is perfect because my government contact can meet me there. Crane provided me with a map and a thick pre-sealed package, addressed to a mailbox in Sweden. I've tried to open the packages, but they're expertly sealed, with some kind of a metallic lining and wires in the glue which seals the flap. I have no idea what's inside and nothing left to go on besides their weight, thickness and address for delivery.

I stand and watch the stars in the dark night sky, knowing I have to get back fast. I can't believe Crane found them, hiding on the train. I thought for sure I was a dead man. But Andie saved me from Crane's wrath. I just worry about what he did to her and Lina.

I keep trying to bring my thoughts somewhere else, to focus on the job at hand, but I can't. I can't deny the fact that I've screwed up royally. Broken the basic rules of training, what was pounded into my head from day one. You don't get involved. You don't have relations, especially not with married women, especially not with the one Crane wants for himself. And you don't cross Crane, ever.

Barely anyone in the U.S. knows him but he's globally renowned as one of the world's richest men, making his trillions in genetic research, and getting involved in controversial experiments. First it started with stem cells and his research progressed from animals to humans. He kept his work away from U.N. sanctions by purchasing his own island, constructing his own buildings for the experiments, employing his own people, swearing them to secrecy. He made the transition from researching to cure illnesses to much darker topics, and this is why the strongest countries left him alone, because they fear him. He has a lot of dirt on a lot of powerful people.

Celebrities and royalty started soliciting him to select how they wanted their children to look and behave. It made him billions of dollars richer. He was the world's best kept secret. And once he had them all in his pocket; kings, queens, presidents, dictators, even our own president, they cleared the way for him to go further. He started in Japan and now here in the U.S., in Phoenix of all places, my hometown. Genetic engineering. Selective population control. Selective breeding. He tells them he is working towards a better society. For mankind. To preserve our earth which we know is already in ruins from the burning of fossil fuels, mining, and overpopulation.

The President of the United States came to me asking for help. He wants to know who is helping Crane, the "Funding Entities." And it's not that President Berkley seems worried about what Crane is doing, he just wants to know who else is involved. They came to me after the Middle East. They thought I was the perfect choice, being that my entire family was wiped out in that car accident. And then there's my training and the expertise in intelligence.

What I wasn't prepared for was Andie. She doesn't know how bad Crane actually is. She has no clue what he has done, or what he is capable of. He could have anyone in the entire world but for some reason he is drawn to her, probably for the same reasons I am and that her husband is. But she is in danger. I brought her into this situation and now I have to help her get out of it. I can't let her know how dangerous Crane really is or what is really going on. She's too stubborn. She would be the one to confront him, demanding answers and blowing my cover. She's an irresistible mixture of brains, tenacity, and awkwardness, and it's driving me crazy. I can't stop thinking about her. And I'm not sure how it happened because she's not my type at all, but there's just something about her. She makes it so hard to focus whenever we are in the same room. She clouds my mind, makes things fuzzy, she always has. Even on that first day, when she confronted those gang members and bartered for our lives with a box of baby formula, all without even knowing who I was.

When Crane made me Sovereign I didn't know if I could continue the mission. Being in the committee room with her across the table from me, I could barely function. Just watching her, with those penetrating green eyes, I thought for sure I would lose it. Each time I told myself to stop, to stay away, I know we both did, for months, all through the holiday season. Then I found myself getting closer. When she came to me that night, after Ian's baby was delivered, I couldn't resist her, I couldn't ignore her one second longer. Now, after telling her that this was all planned, that my mission was to find her and bring her back, to walk her straight into her own living hell, I'm pretty sure I may have lost her for good and I know the only reason she didn't slap me and run off on her own was because I was holding Lina. I know there's only one thing I can do to win her back, to make her forgive me. I have to find her brother, Sam, and bring him back to her. I can't let Crane take any more from her.

According to my contacts in the CIA, things are about to get bad. The U.S. government is on red alert, preparing for an attack of some kind. Most think it is terrorists planning an attack similar to 9/11, others think it's that political group, the Reformation, which has been quickly gaining members and planning to overthrow the election at the end of the year.

But I have the unsettling feeling that it has something to do with Crane. He's planning something from within the safety of his freshly built walls, in his new utopia, the Phoenix District.

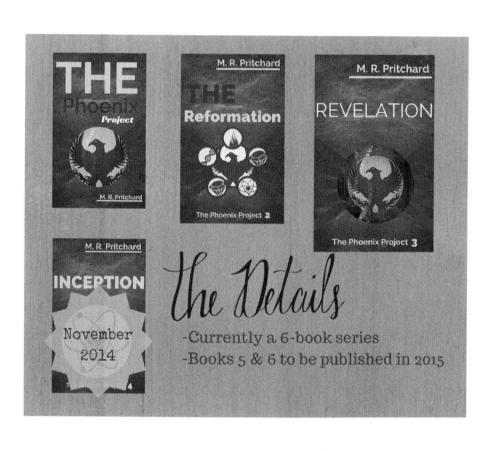

the Details

- Currently a 6-book series
- Books 5 & 6 to be published in 2015

ABOUT THE AUTHOR

M. R. Pritchard is a lifelong inhabitant of upstate NY. When she is not writing she is a NICU Nurse, wife, mother, gardener, aquarist, book hoarder and science geek. She holds degrees in Biochemistry and Nursing.

★ Connect with me ★

 amazon.com/author/mrpritchard

http://mrpritchard.com/

secretlifeofatownie.blogspot.com

facebook.com/MRPritchard

pinterest.com/mp30/boards/

@M_R_Pritchard

Acknowledgements

Many thanks to my editor, my reviewer, my beta reader, my graphic designer, the one who I bounce ideas off of, my husband, the father of my daughter, who puts up with my craziness, the one who has supported me every step of the way, and who sometimes cleans the snow off my car. Jorden, I love you, babe.

There is no way I would have ever found the courage to complete this book, and continue on with more, if it weren't for my encouraging family, friends, and fans. I thank you all from the center of my heart ♥

To my beta-readers: Heather, Jessica, Nora, Sandy, and Cynthia, you girls rock! Thanks for believing in me and listening to my blabber.

Lastly, there are not enough thanks I could give to Kristy Ellsworth. Thank you so much for all of your hard work and dedication on this project and all of the rest.

many thanks

Author Note:

Thank you for reading THE PHOENIX PROJECT, I hope you enjoyed it! Since there is no better way to share the love of a book than by word of mouth, please take the time to leave a review on Amazon.com or Goodreads.com or tell a friend about THE PHOENIX PROJECT Series.

M. R. PRITCHARD

Made in the USA
Middletown, DE
04 October 2016